THE NIBIRU CHRONICLES

PART 1
NIBIRU RISING

THE CONTROVERSIAL NEW TRILOGY FROM:
THE ANONYMOUS AUTHOR_OFFICIAL

The Nibiru Chronicles
Part 1
Nibiru Rising
Copyright © 2021 by The Anonymous Author_Official.

Every word from here out is a work of fiction. Names, characters, businesses, organizations, places, events and incidents either are the product of the author's imagination or are used fictitiously. Any use of actual persons, living or dead, events, or locales is entirely ficticious and from the imagination of the author. None of this is real.

For information contact :
Anonymous Publishing House
L23 - 111 Eagle Street
Sydney (Australia)
NSW
2000

theanonymouspublishinghouse@gmail.com
theanonymousauthorofficial@gmail.com

Book and Cover design by Anonymous Publishing House
ISBN: 978-0-6457208-5-3

Second Edition: March 22 - 2022
10 9 8 7 6 5 4 3 2 1

Acknowledgements:

There are a lot of people that helped bring this novel together and without each of you it might never have made it this far.

As an Anonymous Author it is hard to mention specific people but to the editor that picked apart the carcass that was the first draft, I give you special thanks for your patience and the positive way you tried to impart your changes.

To my many parents that have loved and nurtured me, but special thanks to my mother who always insisted I was capable of anything. We were each other's rock during the early years and even when so far away your strength keeps me typing and believing in my words.

To my Son who was there as always to provide his open mind for me to throw ideas into, often getting mixed around and coming out better,

To my Daughter who spent many hours working with me to get this ready for print, without her some parts still wouldn't have made sense.

To my partner, my love, keeping me going on those long nights typing away. Bringing me sustenance and encouragement. You are 50% of this baby. Thank you for you.

To my agent, sorry for insisting this one gets out, let's roll the dice, your words not mine. :-)

To the team at 7 Hills Tours in Rome, special thanks for the night time expedition and hot coffee, and sorry for not coming clean about the Church's role in the book, I just didn't think you would want to show me around if you knew what I had planned.

And finally, to all the conspiracy theorists out there that helped this all come together. Each of the thousands of videos and articles you wrote, directed, and shared, created the rich tapestry that helped birth this epic "truth" you are about to learn.

And remember, just because it sounds crazy, doesn't mean it is.

That's all, now to get on with the show. AAO

*"This is not, however, the detection or discovery of a new planet. It's too early to say with certainty there's a so-called **Planet X**. What we're seeing is an early prediction based on modelling from limited observations. It's the start of a process that could lead to an exciting result."*
Jim Green – Director NASA's Planetary Science Division

*"These distant objects are like breadcrumbs leading us to **Planet X**. The more of them we can find, the better we can understand the outer Solar System and the possible planet that we think is shaping their orbits—a discovery that would redefine our knowledge of the Solar System's evolution,"*
Scott Shepherd – Carnegie Institute of Science

"Musk has collaborated with NASA and the government in gathering intelligence on a brown dwarf star with seven companion planets that intersect the inner solar system every 3,6000 years, give or take.
Un-named Government source – Daily Mail UK

Introduction

As world events continue to unfold, more and more will witness the ugliness and the predominance of bullying behaviour. The rulers of the stronger nations are forcing their will upon the weaker and will become more demanding and unreasonable. Nation states are using an enormously oppressive power, much like that of masters over slaves.

History is repeating itself – again. There was once a super race of aliens known to the ancient people of the Earth as the Anunnaki. For many reasons, the Anunnaki have been reduced in power today. This race of beings thrives on conquest and enslavement of those who are under them. They believe their time on Earth will once again come.

Prologue

Atlantis

30,000 BC

E lliot closed his eyes, the blinding flash enveloped him, threatening to burn into his retina as his hair danced in the breeze that followed. He was merely a slave, therefore was not afforded the luxury of the dark goggles worn by the Nephilim and his Superiors.

The sickening opulence of the transportation hall was in stark contrast to the squalid conditions he and the other slaves had endured. Golden pillars stood like thick redwoods, stretching up to support a ceiling cloaked in black, dotted with solid, polished, cut diamonds; some as large as Elliot's head. The diamonds were laid out like stars in the night sky and paid for with the lives of those that mined them.

Bright orbs of white light hung at the end of thick golden chains, illuminating everything beneath them whilst leaving the upper reaches in darkness. The polished marble floor had brilliant white veins of black lightning running through it. Up above, in the middle of the room, placed directly under the small round hole in the blackness of the ceiling, a flawless, golden ball hung in a beam of directed sunlight. It hovered about a foot from the ground, rotating at a walking pace, emitting a soft hum that echoed off the walls around it.

Elliot's white tunic was immaculate as he held heavy thick robes in his lithe muscular arms. He turned and handed the thick maroon clothing to the Alaha that approached him. The Alaha were the most beautiful of the Anunnaki's creations. Originating as Elliot did, from the humanoid creatures on earth, before creationism. Their genetic structure had been designed, to make them the pleasure bringers of the time and thus, aesthetically, they were of the highest calibre. Each was adorned with thick blonde hair, bright blue eyes, and big full lips. Their tanned thin bodies and large breasts were barely hidden by the white dresses made to be worn by their masters. Elliot assessed this Alaha, she was obviously one of the lucky ones; despite a small scar on her neck, she appeared unscathed.

As she walked away, the door to the hall clicked and swung open, sunlight spilled in and the silhouette of, yet another Nephilim strode through. The bottom of its robe crept along the floor, as the slap of its feet could just be heard over its snuffled, laboured breathing. Its robe covered every inch of its skin, all the way up to the hood and only the dead yellow eyes that seemed to glow were visible. It stopped in front of Elliot. He looked down at the floor, he knew better than to look a Nephilim in the face. Its breath smelt of rotten meat and when it untied and opened its robe the smell of fresh Alaha drifted up into Elliot's nose.

Naked and with its robes around its green, three toed feet the Nephilim looked down at Elliot. It was about 7 feet in height; had green, almost translucent skin, over lean, well-defined muscles. With each beat of its heart, you could see the blood moving around its body. The sound of its nasal breathing played in Elliot's ears. His heart was racing, why was this Master still standing there? It grabbed Elliot's chin. It's long green fingers tipped with yellow nails and fresh blood under them, squeezed and lifted Elliot's gaze up to his. It's lizard-like snout smiled, revealing row upon row of small, sharp triangular teeth. It moved Elliot's head from one side to the other, inspecting him, even smelling him at one point. He looked into Elliot's eyes, and then used his long finger to open his mouth, inspecting his teeth.

"Such a shame," it said almost sadly. "Some of our best work."

It shook its head, stepped out of the robes on the floor and walked towards the golden globe. Elliot watched as it walked away. Its skin began to darken, and the small spikes along the spine turned from green to yellow. He was picking up the robes as the sound of the humming stopped. The Golden orb was stationary now, and the Nephilim put his palm flat on the surface. The solid gold texture turned into a liquid in its presence.

Starting at the hand, the golden orb lost all colour and went fully transparent, like a wave in a lake, spreading across the surface, turning it into a large floating bubble. The Nephilim stepped inside, through the surface like a ghost stepping through a pane of glass, crossed his legs and floated up, perfectly to the middle of the sphere, weightless. Then the bubbles surface filled again, gold enveloping it, it turned from a liquid into a solid once more. Gone, the Nephilim was inside the solid golden orb and it began to spin again.

Elliot bent down and picked up the robe, that was the 15th Nephilim today, this was unheard of. That meant only 1 Nephilim was currently in residence in Atlantis. He stood and closed his eyes. Above him, each of the diamonds began to glow, getting brighter and brighter. The orb was spinning faster and faster. Still only just above the surface. Then when all the diamonds had reached a blinding proportion, they simultaneously shot thick, solid, brilliant beams of pure white light at the globe. Hungrily the golden orb absorbed every drop, reflecting nothing. The humming was getting louder and higher in pitch, until. Fully charged, it shot its own beam of light straight up into the hole in the roof. It lasted only an instant but happened with such ferocity that it created a concussion wave that ran through the hall.

The dazzling beams of light stopped instantly, and the globe began to slow its spin. An Alaha appeared, took the robe from Elliot and walked away. This one wasn't so lucky, the scratches down her back and on the inside of her thighs were deep, and fresh; this sickened him.

This was the way in Atlantis. You dare not disobey the Nephilim, they were the creators, and they came down from the heavens and brought life to the planet. In disobeying them, certain death was almost secured.

Elliot's role as the chamber keeper provided him with a better life than most of the other Atlantian slaves. Those sent to the mines were lucky to survive a full winter, and at least Elliot was able to live within the suburbs surrounding the cathedral. However, he spent most of his time in the slums, playing dice and drinking the yeasty brew that filled his belly and slurred his speech. Conversation would often turn to the Nephilim and the Anunnaki.

Unlike the Nephilim, the Anunnaki were evolving and using genetic techniques to look more human than ever, there were also plenty of humans desperate for the approval of the Masters. So, conversations were always edited, just on the off chance one might be overheard. People disappeared constantly, either to the arena, to the mines or to the Palace. Some, it was rumoured, were sent up into the heavens, for the pleasure of those above. It wasn't just a rumour; Elliot had observed their entrance to the globe and saw them vanish.

The door burst open. The final Nephilim stood hunched over, holding his stomach with one hand and supporting himself on the door frame with the other. His hood was up, and his robe over his shoulders, but it was untied, and hung either side of its body. Dark red, almost black blood ran down his legs and dripped from his hand as he tried to stem the flow. Elliot stood frozen.

"Come boy, help me," it beckoned, waving its supporting arm and staggering forward.

Elliot rushed over and nestled himself under the armpit of the Nephilim and took its weight across his shoulders. He looped its arm over him and helped it into the chamber. Together they shuffled towards the golden orb which had resumed its position and gentle rotation.

The Nephilim coughed, spraying blood all over the marble floor and then, fell to its knees. Despite its resistance, Elliott tried to lift it.

"It's pointless boy, 1300 years and it ends like this," it spat a big mouthful of blood from its snout.

Its breathing was reduced to short, sharp intakes, interrupting its speech. It rested on its knees, one hand covering the wound and the other supporting its weight. It spat again, without looking up, it spoke to Elliot.

"You need to get out of here boy," more breaths mingled with the hum of the room.

"It's going to bury Atlantis." Another pause. More breaths, yet slower.

It spat again, and looked up at Elliot, the eyes didn't glow. "It won't be stopped," slower still.

"Go…" its final word came out as one long slow breath. With that, it lifted forward, its head resting on the ground; still on its knees, draped completely in its ceremonial robes. Elliot didn't need to be told twice; this was the final piece of the puzzle he had been trying to piece together all day. And suddenly, it all made sense. Never had he seen so many Nephilim teleporting in one day. They were fleeing Atlantis!

He pulled open the chamber doors and squinted, covering his eyes as he dashed out into the warm glow of the sun. There wasn't a cloud in the sky, nor a breeze in the air, the day was still and perfect. His first thought was for his sister, a slave at Anunnaki Marcella's villa, working in the kitchens. Then, his father, he'd been taken to the arena only about 10 days earlier. There was a chance he was still alive, and the arena was closer.

He jumped down the hundreds of jewel-encrusted steps, three at a time, thinking as he went. Coliseum first, find his father; then, go after his sister. The white limestone steps, walls, and statues reflected the sun into his face. A reflection from a green jewel blinded him for a second, causing him to miss a step. He fell, cracking his shin, elbow, and the side of his head on the unforgiving steps. He rolled clumsily, time after time, eventually coming to a rest at the bottom. He shook his head to compose himself, got up, and noticed something on the horizon, that made the hair on the back of his neck stand up.

Rolling towards Atlantis, like a wave directed to sand, was a bank of thick, black clouds. They were moving noticeably through the sky, dragging behind them a tail of flashing lightning strikes that scorched up off the ground.

'Ok, no time to sit around.'

He jumped to his feet and began to run. He crossed the arched bridge, over the lush valley at the foot of the hill that the chamber was perched atop of and made his way into the city. White dusty roads hemmed in by ornate architecture on both sides formed the maze that was Atlantis. Gold shone from the tops and frames of almost every limestone and marble building. The Nephilim's obsession for gold was evident in almost every structure in the Chamber Hill shadow.

There were statues on almost every street corner, some were solid gold, others were marble, and most were depicting either an

Anunnaki or Nephilim figure. The Nephilim, being the robed Royalty of the Anunnaki ruling classes. Elliot could hear the scorched sky moving closer, and deep rumbling thunder echoing from a distance. People everywhere were looking up towards the sky, fear, and bewilderment in their faces.

Standing like a guardian over the city was the immense Coliseum. It still shone in the sun, yet behind it, was the dark backdrop of the impending storm, and a giant fist of balled up energy. It resembled two heavyweight boxers about to go head-to-head. The dark mass of destructive cloud, encroaching on the solid unmovable mass, built as a playground for their gods.

The information he had was that his father was being held with a whole horde of societies' waste, scheduled for purification through pain, somewhere in the northern detention cells. He had no idea how to get him out, though knew he had to try.

It was when he got within sight of the Coliseum's Northern entrance that the first drops of rain began to fall, yet this wasn't normal rain. The people around him began to react to each drop in dramatic fashion, and the buildings and roads around him smoked gently at the touch of each drop. Elliot held out his hand to catch one. Within seconds, one landed causing his skin to bubble. He wiped it on his tunic and ran full speed towards the gigantic shelter in front of him.

The sky announced its intentions with a rumble of thunder that shook the very foundations of Atlantis; Elliot swayed and stumbled as the ground stirred beneath him, shaking the whole city like an earthquake. He ducked under one of the gigantic arch ways that cut into the Coliseums external wall, looking around him as the rain intensified, and bits of rock loosened then fell, exploding off the ground.

All of Atlantis was a cacophony of activity by now, most fearing that the Gods were angered, had scattered and hid. They knew from experience the painful consequences of the Nephilim wrath.

The rain was falling heavily, scarring those caught in its path, and melting its way through buildings, roads, and fauna. The Coliseum was no different, those outside scrambling to escape the rain, those inside struggling to get outside to see what was happening. Elliot used this confusion to make his way unnoticed to the holding bay, where he hoped his father was. As he went deeper into the Coliseum's dungeon-like foundations, the artificial light from the glowing orbs along the walls went dark.

Thankfully, dotted along this hallway were small circular, barred windows that let a little light in as he continued. He steadied himself against the wall as the earth shook again under the efforts of the thunder above. A small bald man hustled past him, muttering to himself, dust and small bits of stone fell from the ceiling and walls around him. Burnt into his thoughts was the sight of the lightning that was coming, he had no time and needed to get out quickly, and yet he was walking deeper and deeper into the city's biggest potential tomb.

By the time the next thunder clap had subsided, Elliot could hear strained, voices shouting for help, for mercy, for release. It was very quiet but grew louder as he jumped down four steps and into a much wider hallway.

Bingo. Thick wooden doors with fists pounding from the inside tucked neatly into the walls on either side of him announced the detention cells. However, there were no guards, no one to ask how to open the doors or to give him a key. He began to fear that the lack of any discernible plan was about to cost him, he had no more chance to open these doors than the prisoners did.

He ran up to the first door and began banging.

"Eadrich Aapo," he shouted

The banging from inside was accompanied by cries of,
"Let us out."
"What's happening?"

"Eadrich Aapo!" he repeated. "Do you know where he is?"

He shouted, straining his ear, trying to cut through the shouts, listening for his father's voice. Nothing, except barks of anguish. He moved on, to the opposite door and tried again.

Bang Bang
"Eadrich Aapo! Is there a Eadrich Aapo in there?"

This time, only one voice responded. "Open this door and I'll tell you where he is." A deep human voice boomed through from the other side.

"How?" Elliot shouted with his ear pointed to the door. He closed his eyes, straining for an answer above the shaking of the walls and ground.

"Keep going to the end of the hall and pull down on each wooden handle." The voice was again deep and profound, and under the circumstances, it was calm.

He didn't need telling twice, his leather sandals echoed off the wall as he ran. Cold stone walls, and thick doors lined his route. The prisoners were making a racket, and Elliot was sure he heard a baby's cries.

Then, there they were, jutting out of the wall, three wooden handles. He wasted no time and lifted all three in turn, celebrating internally as he was hearing heavy mechanisms clicking and turning.

Out of nowhere, he was hit with a force reserved for cracking rocks.

The entire left side of Elliot's body folded under the vigorous blow of the Ducaz soldier next to him. It drove its fist into Elliot's ribs, cracking a few and knocking him against the solid rock wall. The next punch was aimed at the side of his head. Elliot turned just in time to see it coming, the 7-foot muscular hulk of Ducaz looked like an alligator standing on its tail, just a little more leaner and humanoid. There was a torch on the wall behind it, giving it a demonic glow as it swung at his head. Its smile disappeared as it smashed into the solid stone wall, cracking the brick and his hand in the process.

Elliot ducked underneath and saw the anger in the Ducaz's eyes when it realized he had missed. Despite this, Elliot didn't hesitate to spring up from his legs and explode with a vicious elbow under the snout of the beast. The Ducaz's head snapped back, forcing it to stagger a couple of steps away. As quick as a flash, Elliot grabbed a torch from the wall and like a batter stepping up for the Yankee's, swung it at Ducaz's left knee. It buckled under the weight of the thick gold-plated bat, causing the Ducaz soldier to fall to the same height as Elliot. All in one movement, Elliot followed through and swung to destroy the top of this thing's skull.

However, the torch slapped into the Ducaz's palm, and his long fingers wrapped around it with alarming ease. Climbing to its feet, it shot out its other arm and clamped its hand around the shocked Elliot's throat. Then lifted him clean off his feet, dangling him at arm's length, half a meter in the air.

"Give in little human, the Gods favour me." The Ducaz loved being thought of as soldiers of the Gods; they, however, knew the truth about the Anunnaki and Nephilim.

The Ducaz smiled at Elliot's feeble attempts to punch at its arm, to try and free himself. It squeezed a little tighter and the deep long rumble of thunder, was loud in Elliot's ears as he began to pass out. Blackness crept into his peripheral and closed in from both sides.

Elliot dropped to the floor. He landed heavily and opened his eyes to see legs and feet all around him. The growl of thunder was all he could hear. As vibrations ran through the ground, Elliot saw the newly freed prisoners swarm over the Ducaz guard and take him down. They ripped into it with a ferocity and glee that they would have expected in return.

Elliot felt himself being pulled to his feet. At the top he found himself embraced by the familiar arms of his father. He held him at arm's length, inspecting his boy, jubilant and critical all at once.

"What the hell are you doing down here boy?" he shouted over the thunder and the feverous shouting of the escapees.

He had lank white hair that was thinning on the top, and a sharp nose. Wisdom and confidence spilled from his eyes, and his skin was smeared with mud and sweat.

"The Nephilim have left; they are burying Atlantis. We have to get out of here!"

"You sure El?" he asked

"100% dad, we haven't got long." He briefly detailed his encounter with the Nephilim and by now most of the prisoners were listening to this exchange. They were a mix of men, women and children; all those that had not been prepared to worship the Gods blindly or had simply made a joke that didn't please an informant. All looked worried but also exhilarated by their freedom, and a muttering expression of disbelief and dismissal spread among them.

Elliot turned to address them all.

"In less than one hour, Atlantis will be gone," he said, looking around at the faces, dancing in torchlight...

"I'm the chamber keeper and have seen all the Nephilim leave Atlantis in the last 6 hours. There are none left in residence. They have fled and are now purging the lands that they'll leave behind." Elliott turned to look at his father.

"We must escape Atlantis, and we must do it now! Outside, the rain will eat away at everything, and the storm will leave nothing behind. C'mon." He gestured and turned to run back up, towards the hall, back where he had come from; yet the big voice from before stopped him.

"Hold on, we can make it to the central chamber, here in the coliseum." Elliot didn't know how he missed him, while he was talking earlier. Standing closest to the dead Ducaz, stood a monster of a man, easily 8-foot tall and almost as wide. His eyes almost glowed with a white light against his dark brown skin, and shadows danced across his powerful, muscular frame. He smiled revealing dazzling white teeth that beamed like his eyes.

"Do they have a teleportation chamber, here in the coliseum?" Elliot asked.

The gargantuan man nodded. Elliot looked at his dad.

"Samara?" He asked, referring to his daughter and Elliot's sister.

Elliot's eyes welled, as his mind raced, looking for a way to reach his sister. Another violet shock from the sky knocked him off balance, and into a wall.

"There's no time," he sadly concluded

His father looked at him and took a deep breath.

"Ok, lead the way!"

Outside, the horror of the destruction of Atlantis, was in full force. Violent thunder was shaking the ground, and roaring through the air, assaulting the Atlanteans ears, adding audio darkness to their horror. The Curtain of rain was firmly cloaked over the city; in fact, it covered about a fifth of the Earth's surface as the Cosmic forces above threw the planet into complete disarray.

The sulphuric rain, fuelled by unprecedented volcanic activity across the planet, was corroding the beautiful white architecture. Yet, more disturbingly, it was eating away the skin of those trapped without shelter. The city smouldered, as the limestone reacted with the water, and like a slow burning fire, it was getting smaller and smaller.

One by one, buildings that once afforded protection from the rain, began to give up and fall. Some, collapsing in on themselves in dramatic fashion; others, piece by piece. Hundreds of thousands of years' worth of erosion, peeling away at civilisation's pinnacle in just a matter of minutes.

Like a candle shrinking under the flame, the Colosseum began to wane and shrink away from the heavens. Rain drove into it from every angle, and settled around its foundations, weakening it further. Rubble and fallen statues littered the roads and walkways around it, with each round of thunder further stripping its architecture to the bone.

Everything in Atlantis was soaking away, being washed into non-existence, and there was not a single thing anyone could do to stop it. Women sat, wrapped around their children, trapped inside their failing tombs. Some were singing songs, trying to project strength, despite the terrifying truth dissolving its way through their roof. Others got down to their knees and prayed to the gods to spare them. If only the latter had known the truth.

Elliot and the group of prisoners were deep inside the Colosseum, and as such, were not aware of the carnage the rain had brought with it, yet the thunder resonated through each of their bones and shook the floor enough to knock the unsuspecting off their feet.

As a group, they followed the dark skinned giant. He explained to Elliot he was brought to the coliseum from a distant planet, a few months ago. They had been so impressed in his achievements in the arena, that they had teleported him to an intergalactic contest called The Presidian, which took place on Jupiter's Lo moon. He had defeated a warrior, Arachnid from Sirus 4, as well as a giant bull like creature from Malonia prior to ripping apart the Anunnaki's champion, Ducaz. He was supposed to be fighting in the arena, though had been left in the cells for what felt like months.

The teleportation chamber was under the arena floor, which meant heading deeper into the Colosseum's warren of passages, cell blocks, and weapons stores. A final turn in the torch, lit passages as they came to an innocuous, wooden door. It resembled every other entrance, to every small cell they had passed.

"You sure this is it?" Elliot shouted, above the latest rumble of thunder.

Simeon looked down at Elliot with a smile and a shake of the head. He then lifted his massive foot off the floor, leaned back, and kicked through the 4-inch solid teak entrance, as if it was made of matchsticks.

Inside, looked very familiar to Elliot: the same black ceiling, dotted with diamonds, light orbs on golden chains, and even the same marble flooring. Yet, this room was not as tall as Elliot's chamber, nor did it have the golden globe in the centre. At the other end of the room, like a pulpit in a church was the control centre. This was a multi-teleportation room, capable of teleporting its subjects, less than a light year into space. Unfortunately, they would need the handprint of an Anunnaki to get it started.

Elliot turned to two of the freed prisoners.

"You two, we're going to need that Ducaz, by the prison cells."

Dust was falling, as the harsh sound waves from the heavens continued to shake every part of their world. They turned and ran.

No arguments. Elliot led the rest of them into the chamber. Shadows swarmed around the room as the light orbs swayed on their chains. Above the growling, Elliot could barely be heard.

"Everyone, find a crystal and stand directly below it." Elliot shouted to the room, as headed towards the control panels.

From up on the pulpit, he watched his father fussing around, hurrying people under the crystals. There was a young mother with her baby, tightly pulled to her chest. Three or four lone youngsters, huddled together for comfort and, what looked like a cross section of society from the soldiers to the Alaha women. They were all counting on Elliot to get this right.

He looked do down at the control panel, Anunnakian symbols blinked up at him. Though, he had never learnt the Anunnaki text or language, he had seen many Multi Being Teleportation's - MBT's, in his time at the main chamber, and so, hoped he would be able to work the system. The glass screen came to life as he stood over it, only showing, the outline of a three fingered hand. Ok, he would have to wait for the Ducaz.

Elliot could barely hear himself above the now present, constant rumbling.

"When the lights begin, you must make sure it is touching at least some part of you. Though, you must not look up directly into the light as, it will scorch your eyes," he warned.

Outside, the lightning was exploding its way from the outer suburbs through to the city centre, and heading towards the Palaces, Museums, Royal baths, and the Coliseum. Three hundred million volts of nature's most intense energy struck Atlantis time after time until, their strikes seemed as common as the rain itself. With the rain, the fate of Atlantis was already sealed, the lightning just helped to make it a more terrifying conclusion for those left. Suddenly, any shelter that was left was being blown apart, buildings collapsed completely, and bridges were detonated by multiple strikes. Children screamed, mothers wept, fathers hid, nothing and no one was spared.

The prisoners dragged the Ducaz, feet first, through the destroyed door and into the chamber. Elliot directed the two men to bring it up to the control panel. They pulled it up to the pulpit and, with Elliot's help, managed to stand it upright, long enough to get its palm print on the screen. The second it came to life, the two men and Elliot abandoned the Ducaz, causing it to drop clumsily to the floor. Elliot then directed the two men to get under a diamond, above the loudest roar of thunder yet. The room resonated to the point of cracking like glass as it shook long and hard. One of the golden orbs yanked free of its bindings, smashing onto the floor, spilling a glowing liquid that ran like water: the second globe immediately followed. Elliot tried to shut out the noise and focus on the control panel.

It was a flat 19-inch, touch screen plasma. On it, were a selection of Anunnakian symbols each floating in its own, coloured, three-dimensional, transparent ball. A shape like an elephant's head, spun in a green ball at the top of the screen, Elliot touched it.

The page then swept away to the right, and another zipped in from the left, depicting a visually stunning simulation of the Solar System. It was three dimensional and showed Jupiter in the foreground, with the other planets disappearing into the distance. Small flecks of stars glistened all over the screen and in the centre, glowing, and lighting Elliot's face from underneath, was the sun. Small purple lines cut across the screen in perfect maps of each of the planet's orbits. Each line was broken by the planet whose path around the sun they represented, and each of them turned on their axis, real enough to touch.

Elliot touched his finger on the third planet from the sun, and the image zoomed in, rushing through the stars until a three-dimensional perfect earth filled most of the screen. Elliot could see the continents, the ocean, whispery bands of cloud, and when looking closely, noticed random spots of light along the land masses. As Elliot touched one of the lights, the image zoomed further and shifted to the left. The giant mass of current day Africa connected to current day South America filled the left of his screen and on the right, six Anunnakian symbols faded into view.

Elliot jumped as another light globe smashed to the floor, quickly followed by the last. The room took on a sickly green glow as the only light drifted up from each of the puddles meandering lazily over the marble. The room still shook and over the now constant grumble Elliot could hear the baby screaming. He looked up, green faces all staring at him, frightened eyes catching his.

The first strikes of lightning hit the top of the Coliseum and for a second, nothing happened. It was like the old building had absorbed all of the explosive energy and taken it on the chin. But then, starting at the point where the bolts touched down, deep cracks appeared, running down the sides of the already beleaguered figurehead. Without notice, and with sickening force, it imploded. In one choreographed instant and with no warning, each of the cracks detonated what was left of the Coliseum, and broke into a thousand pieces, flying over the city of Atlantis. By now, there were no screams and no sign of life. The destruction of Atlantis was almost at an end.

The noise of the exploding building falling above them, sent chills down Elliot's spine and he punched his hand onto the symbol in the orange sphere on the right of the screen. Each of the diamonds sprung to life. The six symbols were now replaced by a graph shaped axis, empty with a purple line about two thirds of the way up. The graph began to fill and the light beams from the diamonds intensified.

Above, the clouds seemed to sense what was happening and increased its lightning attacks on the rubble of the Coliseum. Elliot could hear rock exploding from all directions now and the violent shaking had already knocked over some of the escapees. The lightning got closer and closer, sniffing out their hidden little room.

The graph reached the line and glowed white. Elliot didn't wait a second and pressed the green triangle that appeared. Then a blinding flash of white light, gave away their hiding place. Lightening ripped into the roof of the room, sending its charge through the walls. Elliot closed his eyes. He didn't hear the final explosion. The bricks and mortar struck him from every angle of the room, and his earthly body was dead before the culmination of forces in the room ripped it apart.

The storm washed over Atlantis, and most of the Earth, for three long days and nights. Despite losing most of its intensity, after three terrifying days, the thick black cloud of smoke and acid rain remained. It Soaked Atlantis, and 90% of the planet alongside it, slowly digesting any evidence that such a place ever existed.

Chapter 1

The Red Shoe

New York Subway
22/02/2022
7 :18am

Theo stood with one arm in the air, holding onto the handrail as he rocked gently in time with the trains movements. As always, the subway was packed with every cross section of society he could think of. The old Jewish lady, tea cosy on her head and angry suspicious eyes. Hispanic woman, young and voluptuous, her shirt read 'Broadway Hilton'. The black rapper slash gangster with big baggy jeans, bandana, the works. Pregnant teenager, Old angry veteran, lots of suits, white home boy, Asian student, the only thing missing was the Asian tourists. He checked his watch, 07:20, it was too early for the tourists.

Theo was about average height and had floppy black hair that flicked slightly over his face. He had good natural colour that made it look like he had a tan, apparently that came from his father's side and although he thought his nose was too big, he also had a very handsome face.

He instinctively ran his free hand through his hair, pushing it back as the train pulled into Cathedral Parkway and checked the knot in his tie to make sure it was straight. Today he had gone for the jeans, white shirt, grey suit jacket and black-tie combo. He was aiming for smart casual. Since he had started his job as the call centre manager at Green Mountain Energy, trainers, jeans and his Knicks t-shirt had to be upgraded.

Theo stepped this way, then that, as the passengers stepped round him to get off the train, flowing out of the open doors like water through a hole. The tide turned and New Yorkers began to flood the train. Then there she was. Stepping on after the large black fella who looked like he belonged on stage with Louis Armstrong and before the young Muslim student. Blonde hair tied back in a ponytail that only used half the hair and red, blue and green ribbons intertwined.

Today she was wearing a black, pinstripe, knee length skirt and white open collar shirt. Silver earrings framed her beautiful full face and a silver pendant hung around her neck. She brushed past Theo on her way to some vacant hand rails and he breathed her in, that same fruity perfume that stirred something in his stomach every morning. He looked down at her legs; today's tights were black with ornate swirls snaking around her calves and as always, her red shoes provided the platform on which she stood.

Every morning for a month she had gotten on his train, at the same station at 07:20 she stepped into his world and every morning his mouth went dry, his palms sweaty and when their eyes met, which they did almost every day, he felt like two hands were performing a Chinese burn on his stomach. She took her station on the train and immediately looked round to check Theo was looking. She smiled and looked down at the floor. He hadn't taken his eyes off her since she got on. They were at opposite ends of the carriage but had good line of sight and as they both kept glancing at each other Theo ran through his opening conversation yet again in his head.

"That's it; I can't go yet another day without talking to you. I'm Theo, I'm gonna get off this train and spend the entire day waiting for 07:20 tomorrow and I'm fed up with it. Every morning you reduce my insides to jelly and I'm not sure why, so I think we should go for dinner and find out."

So simple, not too scary and the way she looks at him, she must say yes, surely. But each day he would catch her eye, they would both smile, then he would look away and that was the best he could manage. If only he had known she thought about him all morning as she got ready for work, that some mornings when running late she raced to the station to get the same train, and made sure to get on the right carriage.

The black jazz player swayed to his left blocking Theo's view and he had to lean to the right to see her. The Muslim student rummaged through his bag and again blocked Theo's view. He pulled his head in and waited for them to move. He caught her eye and this time they both held it. She bit her bottom lip, looked down at the floor and straight back into his eyes. For Theo it was like no one else existed. He smiled and relaxed. They both felt it this morning and once again she playfully bit her lip. It was like a dream and nothing else mattered in that moment, until something broke through the veil.

"Allah Akbar!!" Theo heard from somewhere.

The girl in the red shoes was lucky to be standing so close. The force and the debris from the home-made explosive ripped through her so quickly that she died contemplating the weird feelings stirring in her belly. Not the terrifying explosion contained within her metal coffin.

Moving at 20mph the middle carriage of the 07:50 into Lexington bulged under the pressure of the blast before exploding outwards in a shower of noise, metal and broken glass. The rest of the train shook and in the dark, underground tunnel, the train split into two parts. The front half continued to move forwards, ripped away from the battered carnage behind it, and the rear pushed forward. It's momentum driving it into the smoking, twisted metal, driving the carriage off the tracks and into the solid concrete tunnel wall.

One by one the other carriages derailed, some tilted through 90 degrees and skidded along on their sides, others ploughed onwards searching for a track. Inside the carriage, they lost all power and finally settled, smoking and silent under the eerie and sporadic glow from the external tunnel lighting. The silence was deafening, but was quickly broken by the first wave of groans, screams, and sobs. Small flames and toxic smoke danced around Theo's carriage and hemmed in by the concrete walls it began to spill out into the tunnel.

Theo was enveloped in smoke and darkness and his eardrums felt like they had burst as a loud ringing assaulted his inner ear. Theo felt pressure on most of his body, from the chest down, something was crushing him. He put his hands down, drearily feeling for what it was. It was a person, warm, wet, and certainly dead. The acrid smell of burning plastic stung his nose. Touch was the only sense he had left and even then, adrenaline was surging right through to his fingertips, distorting what he could feel. He wriggled his body and pushed down with his arms, struggling to free his legs. Finally, the weight of the dead jazz player slipped from him and slumped onto the carriage floor.

Smoke burnt the back of his throat and Theo's lungs as he struggled with each short, sharp breath. He had to get out. He rolled onto his side and lifted himself to his knees. Deaf, blind, and running on autopilot, he felt around for something to pull himself up with, his hands gripped around something cold and he lifted to his feet. Everything felt odd, wrong. As he knocked his shoulder into a pole, he realised the carriage was on its side. With his head throbbing, his ears humming, he shuffled forwards, pushing through and stepping on body parts, broken glass and twisted metal. His arms stretched out in front of him searching through the darkness.

The faint glow of a subway tunnel light through the smoky haze dictated his path upwards. He felt what was left of a chair to his right and climbed up, heading for the light, and came to a gaping hole where the window was. He lifted himself up and through and once outside he tried to climb down but his lack of orientation caused him to fall and be unceremoniously dumped onto the dusty floor in between railway tracks. The smoke was filling the tunnel but down here on the ground it was clear and he breathed his first, full, clean breath of air. He laid flat on his back and regrouped.

'What the hell had just happened?' One second, he was feeling giddy as he saw her bite her…. 'Oh shit!'

Theo jumped up like he had been stung or bitten by something. If his ears were still ringing, he couldn't hear it anymore. His head was clear and concise, and he looked at the vast underbelly of the carriage he just fell from. It had come to a rest on its side. He had climbed out of the window at the top and fallen into the mud. He ran round the wreck to the other side; broken glass littered the area around him and he had to squeeze in between the wall and the front corner to get to the roof.

Above where the explosion had detonated the roof had been blown away, leaving a hole for Theo to climb through. The smoke still made it hard to breath and see, but by keeping low, Theo was able to locate people, or in some cases parts of people. He found one older gent, lifeless on the floor. Theo grabbed a handful of the man's jacket and began to pull, dragging him out through the same hole he climbed in through. He emerged, dragged him an extra couple of feet and dumped him on the floor next to the wall.

People were emerging from the rear carriages, most had escaped injury, and many were walking up the tunnel, trying to find help or to see what was happening. They saw Theo sit the man against the wall, turn and disappear back behind the carriage. Only to emerge seconds later dragging yet another humanoid form, this one was well done, the clothes had melted to his body and all the hair was burnt from his scalp. Theo left this one face down in the dirt next to the old man and went back inside. He dragged two more bodies out into the tunnel, including a young child before he found any trace of her.

He spotted it while trying to lift the old Jewish woman, a single red shoe. He took two steps and picked it up, her calf and foot came with it, but nothing more. He paused for a second, absorbing what he had in his hand. Then stoically he removed the shoe, placed it in his trouser band and continued to get the old lady out of there.

This time survivors from the other carriages were waiting and helped Theo. Three pairs of hands relieving him from his duty and another couple to help him climb down. Theo looked into the eyes and around at the faces of the reinforcements, his body went weak as that same determination left as suddenly as it had arrived. He fell to his knees and was helped to the wall where he sat upright on the mud. He looked down at the shoe, it was perfect, so much so it appeared to glow red in the darkness of the tunnel. It dropped from his hands to land between his feet then he rested his head in his hands. Everything that had just happened flooded through him in a wave of emotion, he couldn't hold it in any longer, and he quietly sobbed, his shoulders gently rocking in the chaos surrounding him.

Chapter 2

The White Light

Theo's Apartment
22/02/2022
9 :14pm

On the wooden coffee table, there was half a full bottle of Jack Daniels, with its distinctive square shape and black and white label. A bowl of ice, almost empty with too much water in the bottom, a smaller bowl full of lime wedges, over half of them had been squeezed of all their juice, and a red shoe. It looked similar to a ballet slipper except it had a small heel.

The flickering, changing light of television pictures stirred the room. Theo relaxed back into his sofa, popped his feet onto the table, exhaled deeply and took another sip of his drink. The ice danced against his top lip, and the Jack warmed the back of his throat as it went down.

He was freshly showered after much of the day was spent at the hospital seeing doctors, New York Cops, FBI Agents and some guys who didn't announce where they were from. He had told the same story twenty times that day, with each time playing down claims that he was a hero. They showed him photos of a selection of young Muslim men, and Theo was able to identify the 'student' who had affected his day so dramatically. He wondered, what would drive someone to do such a thing, to rip their body apart for their cause.

Theo had always loved the phrase: 'One man's terrorist, is another man's freedom fighter,' since he had heard it one night, when debating Israel / Palestine issues with his childhood crush and babysitter, Emma Friedman. All stories had two sides, and he always felt, that if someone had dropped a bomb on his family, he would probably want some sort of revenge too.

He remembered the passion with which she defended the Palestinian cause, "These young men were soldiers, fighting against the administration, but the power of their enemy was such that their only way to hurt them was to attack the structure of the core of the powers they fight to resist."

Since then, he had envied their conviction, the fact that they believed in something so much that they were willing to die for it. It reminded him of conflicts of the past, when people were willing to die for something that they believed in, the American revolution was the most relevant example he could think of. Now, however, having lived through a terrorist attack, he wasn't so sure if it was envy or hatred he felt. He was so numb, he couldn't tell.

He flicked the channel, the story of the bombing, and the disruption it caused had been at the forefront of every news channel's daily coverage. Just on cue, the nine thirty NBC coverage was not about to buck the trend and miss out on this ratings gem. Theo turned up the volume. Phrases like, 'links to Al-Qaida', 'Red Alert',

'9-11', and 'Home grown', were thrown around by reporters, Presidential spokesman and so-called experts. Then, they played their trump card. It appeared that one of the passengers from the rear carriages had recorded the aftermath of the attack on his mobile phone. The anchor-man warned of images that were unsuitable for children, which everyone interpreted as 'essential viewing.'

The screen filled with the image of the tunnel, bouncing around in time to the footsteps of the camera man. A young man, who was visiting his grandmother in New York from California, appeared in a small box, at the top left of the screen, over the video as it played out. He started speaking, his excitement was evident in the speed and pitch of his voice. He then told of his horror at hearing an explosion, completely out of nowhere, followed by the lurching, and pitching of the train, the screams of the passengers, and then of the hideous sound of grinding metal, being thrown from his seat and tossed around, and then stillness followed by groans...

Theo had stopped listening before he broke into his tale of the super man who just kept pulling people out of the train. He had put his feet down, leant forward and rested his elbows on his knees and was looking at the screen, brow creased, with a questioning look in his eyes. The shot was mostly still now, just lifting and dropping slightly as Phil Heart, from Wisconsin CA breathed deeply.

The scene was one, straight from any good Hollywood blockbuster movie. Smoke was illuminated by the subway tunnels emergency lighting system and lights in all the train carriages were sporadically trying to flicker to life. Everything: man, woman and machine were enveloped in a small halo of light and dust.

The camera was slowly panning from one side of the tunnel to the other, gleefully taking in the carnage up ahead and all around it. It stopped its rotation and gradually zoomed forward to the carriage that was laying on its left side, and due to the force of the explosion, in Phil's expert opinion,

"Had, listed onto its left side, broken free of the front carriages, twisted to the left, bounced and scrapped along the left tunnel wall, before coming to an inevitable and devastating end to its journey.'"

His excitement almost threatened to spill over but he tried in vain to hide it behind the voice of 'A True American Reporter', strong and confident, he even signed off with,

"Phil Heart. NBC. Diane?'"

On any other day, given any other set of circumstances, Theo would have found the 'try hard,' Phil Heart hilarious. But today, his heart just stopped, his mouth went as dry as flour, and the ringing he heard earlier had returned. What Phil Heart from Santa Cruz, CA failed to report on, was the small white ball of light rising like a phoenix from the same flames that Theo had navigated. Every second it was in frame on its ascent to, and through the tunnel rooftop, Theo had been unable to breathe. It wasn't that he couldn't, he just didn't want to. Now this ball of whatever it was, was gone and was as obvious to him as a siren on the rocks, and yet no one had mentioned it. Theo questioned his drink with a glance, like the owner of a new puppy who finds a wet spot.

'Time for bed,' he said out loud.

He looked over his shoulder at the red slipper on his table and took a moment before he flicked the light and left for his bedroom.

Chapter 3

The Neptune Puzzle

CSIRO - Parkes Radio Telescope
24/02/2022
3 :12pm

Half the staff at the CSIRO's famous Parkes site, were back in the cooler Sydney air, far to the south of the World's largest Radio Telescope. The dry desert air smouldered, in the hot February sun, and with the town being in the middle of the longest drought in living memory, the dust hung, light and arid in the heat.

Emma Tansey was at her desk, at the main control system within the cool, air-conditioned core of the huge Radioscope's main building. The unusual octagonal building at the centre of the Parkes complex, had been her home for 12 hours a day for the last 60 days, and she still had another 30 to go. The calendar on the wall in front of her had a countdown all through the month of February, under a picture of a Fireman holding a puppy, and of course, he had no shirt on. She had dated a firefighter when she was home, up north in Cairns, and each year, she still bought the charity Firefighter calendar as a wink to her past.

She was a born spiritual astrologer, and, with the help of her parents, had studied the planets, the Zodiac's, and Elemental Tarot which unlocked her 'Spiritual Gifts' as she would humbly describe them, if pushed. She was also sharp as a tack and, upon understanding the planets, had decided that she wanted to "really understand them," and was now in the 4th year of her Masters in Astrophysics. She loved the simplicity of Math and laws of the universe; that using numbers, you could pretty much figure out anything and, she particularly loved that she had found the connection between "Science and the Spirit". This spurred her on, and was why she found herself here, as part of her theory into the expansion of our Galaxy and Universe.

On Paper, it sounded like the perfect placement, yet the data-entry role she had volunteered for, had turned out to be mind-numbingly boring, and monotonous. It consisted of combing through hours of recordings from the previous weeks, looking for any basic anomalies as part of the Parkes' role in detecting unusual radio frequencies. While conducting this work for the CSIRO, she was also measuring over 30 specific locations within our Galaxy, going back close to 5 years, and plotting their exact locations, using a program she had developed for her Masters.

The Hubble Constant, surface brightness fluctuations, had provided science with proof that the universe was expanding, which up until now, had only been the only measurable metric and was near impossible to measure accurately. Her hypothesis was, that the universe was in fact expanding. Yet, she was hoping to see a difference in the rates of expansion from one day to the next, by using the radio telescope and the software program she had developed. In hopes that she would be the one to accurately measure the future expansion, and accurately map its past. The fact this would also prove her theories about alignment within astrology and the Zodiac signs, would just be the icing on the cake.

Never, had she been brave enough to mention the final conclusions she was expecting to make once she had all the information. She kept her astrological side pretty quiet around the university, and the CSIRO locations, though she did run her own TikTok and social media pages to share some ideas with the world. Under the pseudonym TanseyMuse, she worked to heal others with her knowledge and her "gift" as it was often called.

All the historical data had been collected and collated, and she was now working on the most recent recordings, as they were available to her. She had just received the previous day's data and was running it through the AI, when her day, and hypothesis changed.

The waves dancing on the screen in front of her were the AI's interpretation of the specific radio waves coming from a region of space, expected to contain Neptune within its scope. It was dancing in what appeared a random way, but when calculated over time it showed a distinct pattern which allowed her to measure points in space. She was running the program through timelapse and at first, she almost didn't notice it as she was barely looking at the screen between measurements, but then during one glance at the screen, the peaks and troughs were getting visibly further apart.

"That's not right," she said to no one revealing her Australian accent and soft tone.

It had her attention now and as she watched the time in the bottom corner flicking through at 1 day per second, it suddenly went haywire with massive spikes occurring for what was just 3 or 4 seconds. It then danced around a little erratically before settling into a simple static pattern almost identical to before.

"The faaaaaaaark?" she exhaled, while tapping her pencil on the desk in front of her, the mouse was held by her other hand, and was reversing the feed as she stared intently at the screen. The light from her monitor reflected in her square black glasses as her nose got closer and closer.

She stopped the feed on the 11th of August of this year, the feed ran at 1 hour per second with the lines and waves getting noticeably wider, and wider before they began to dance all over the screen in the most random way she had ever seen. They were not even waves across the screen showing frequencies, they flew in every direction. All over the screen aggressive, sharp lines snaked everywhere and as the minutes passed, they grew in number filling the entire screen.

"What the fuck?" This time she asked, a little more in her formal tone. She instinctively looked around the room for someone to share this anomaly with because right now, it made no sense. Her best guess was that the AI had malfunctioned in that moment, though that would have shown up on the same day recordings, in other regions all over, and would have been flagged by now, she would have seen it herself. She had covered hundreds of regions of space, combining the data from the last 24 months. This wasn't the AI.

She leaned back from the screen, took off her glasses, and absent-mindedly rubbed her pretty tanned nose as she thought. A habit from when she was a child, which obviously worked as, she had a thought, slipped her glasses back on, picked up the phone to her right and pressed the button on the panel on the side, next to the name Karl.

"Hello, this is Karl." A light Australian accent answered

"Dr Kopek, G'day, it's Emma over at the CC sir." She was using her formal voice and playing with her hair while she spoke; another habit.

"Sorry to bother you on your day off but, I have run into something on the data stream relating to frame NEP04 and, I was hoping to pick your brains for a second?"

"Did you say NEP04?" he asked. She checked the screen grab and looked again at the date, and frame name.

"Yes sir, NEP04." At that second, she gritted her teeth and looked alarmed, she had just realised this was Varun's sector, he was specifically focussed on the planets in the Alpha through Indigo quarter's of the galaxy. She had been so caught up in the excitement of what she had seen, she didn't think about the fact that she wasn't supposed to be looking at these frames. This wasn't exactly classified material; she had told herself when she logged in using the password, Varun had written, on the post-it note under the screen in his office. Besides, she needed to see the planets for her research, and she was running a second program to ensure her workload was up to date.

"Isn't that?" The voice on the phone started

"Yes Sir, it's Varun's project," she cut him off mid question.
"I was just conducting a side project looking into…"

"Emma!" His tone had changed completely, and at the sound of his voice, she sat upright.

"How much of the NEP data have you run so far?"

Suddenly nervous, Emma took a second to think about the obvious answer.

"Um, this is the first one sir, I just wanted to run some measurements to prove a ..."

"Emma, Breathe," he commanded and, interrupted her as she tried to explain herself. Suddenly, Emma felt as though she was in a lot of trouble, and she couldn't understand why. It was his tone, and energy she could feel coming from the phone. She had spent a lot of time with Karl and the team, and he had never sounded nor felt like this.

"What you are doing is of no concern to me, all I can tell you is, that you have to stop."

"Ah, but Dr Kopek, what harm is there in ..."

"Did it sound like I was asking you a question?" he demanded

"Well, no," she protested, "but I was..." Again, he interrupted

"But?" he shouted "No buts Emma, drop the NEP data, this is Varun's project, and his alone. Am I clear?" she couldn't understand where this aggression was coming from, yet he was making himself very clear.

"Crystal Sir," she conceded as she slumped in her chair. "What the fuck" she mouthed at her reflection in the blank screen to her left. There was a slight pause before her boss spoke again.

"Ok," he started in a calmer tone and then began to list his demands.

"Delete the analysis you have run so far, remove the raw data from the AI archives and I want you to be prepared for a conversation when I'm back about how you got access to Varun's files."

"I'm sorry sir, I just was..." she started again to explain, she was sure if he heard how innocent it was, he would understand and could back up from this aggressive stance.

"Emma," he again interrupted, but this time it was the soft tone, and soft energy that she recognised.

"Honestly, in the next few days it won't matter. Just trust me, let it go. Can you please do that?"

She heard the change in his tone, but as the proud empath she was, she also felt the change in his energy. She felt his fear. She creased her brow as she tried to understand what was happening here?

"I can do that sir." She knew he needed to hear this from her right now, yet there was no way she was going to let this go. This was weird as hell in her eyes, and she felt in her gut there was a giant question right in front of her, filling her with excitement.

"Thank you," her boss sighed.

"Now, can you do me another favour?" he asked, straight back to business.

"Of course," she replied, barely listening, and still trying to logically piece it all together.

"When you're done with the Tango twenties, get out of there, and take a long weekend. I have a team coming down from QUT, in Queensland, that can manage your shift for tomorrow."

All she heard was, "long weekend," and she smiled, causing the dimples to appear in her cheeks.

"Of course, sir, that will be great." she said, but in her head all she was thinking was,

'Three days to put together a puzzle.'

She hung up the phone, placed her memory stick into the PC under the table, and extracted the files she needed then left. She had already run all the data Karl had requested, and was excited to get home and analyse the rest of the NEP0-99 recordings.

Chapter 4

The Presidential Puzzle

New York
26/02/2022
12 :46pm

Three days had passed, Theo had taken part in the obligatory TV interview and still didn't like the tag: "hero." Every person he had dragged from the train, was due to an instinct that he couldn't really explain nor control at the time, and not because he had a desire to save them. At the time, each one was a burden, stopping him from finding the girl in the red shoes. He didn't think it was a very heroic moment in his life. Truth be told, he was actually disappointed in himself, that he had been thinking so selfishly in a situation like that, cut him up inside a little.

Today, was the biggest day since it had all happened. The media frenzy surrounding yet another sickening suicide. bombing was still in full force. Like sharks at feeding time, they weren't going to stop until they had ripped every ounce of flesh from this story. All the dead had been named, and sent back to their hometowns, so the process of healing could begin. For Theo, however, it was the day he got to meet The President.

Joe Biden was in New York, meeting many of the banking executives and financial gurus on wall street. He had requested a morning lunch with his latest ally, and Comrade in this everlasting war on terrorism.

Theo couldn't possibly say no. In fact, as he contemplated the phone call to arrange the meeting, he remembered he wasn't asked, rather, he was told that The President had requested his attendance. The flirty belle on the phone had provided details of his itinerary for the day and had commented about seeing him on the news the previous night. She did not at all consider, that Theo may not want, nor be able to attend.

He sat as comfortably as he could, as the world's media struggled outside the hotel, trying to get a shot of New York's hero and the President at a table; that rocked slightly, when Theo leaned forward, and eased his weight onto his elbows.

The president had been held up, and was going to be delayed by a few minutes, leaving Theo to sit with clammy hands at an elegantly laid table. Pearly white, embroidered tablecloths laid as smooth as Lake Seneca on a still day, and the silverware, could have fed a struggling family for a month. An informal 'thank you' is what Theo had been promised by Helena, in and out in ten minutes. A couple of official photos, waffles, pancakes, and coffee.

Despite him humbly saying, yet again, he was no hero, she insisted, 'all the girls in the office thought you was very heroic.' He smiled, despite it all, he did like the way women were looking at him, and he liked any excuse to wear a suit.

The entire front dining room of the 5th Ave. Waldorf had been taken over by Presidential needs. Each corner of the room contained a man in a black suit with an earpiece, almost perfectly concealed. Two young aides, wide eyed on coffee, argued animatedly, over the specific wording of an upcoming speech on climate change. The grand front window, that swept across the front wall, was a sea of faces and cameras, exploding into a fountain of flashes, every time Theo faced them.

He picked up his coffee cup, and took a sip from the dainty bone China, sitting in his palm. Leaning forward, he placed his elbows down, and almost spilled his coffee as, again, the table rocked slightly. Theo looked around, as if expecting some super-human, specimen of a waiter to be watching, and already on his way to solve the problem. After all, this was the Waldorf. Seeing no such thing, he took a spare napkin, folded it a couple of times, and leant down, still sitting on the chair. He took a minute to wedge the leg of the chair in such a way, that the chances of him spilling hot coffee all over the President dramatically decreased.

The blood rushed to his head a little, and he came back up, to see the world's most powerful man standing right before him with a beaming grin on his face.

The first thing Theo noticed was his teeth, and how against his dark tanned skin, they shone with a radiance that pulled you in. The intensity and warmth in his eyes momentarily stunned Theo as he half expected a coldness, after all, career politicians. Or it could have been that the President of the most powerful nation on the planet was standing right in front of him, with his arm extended, ready to sit and dine with him, and he didn't have a clue what to do or say.

The President smiled and retracted his arm.

"Let's try again from the top." Biden's hypnotic Southern tone, broke Theo's awkward trance.

"Theo, it's a great pleasure to meet you. It's men like you, that make my job so much more rewarding." he pulled out a chair and began to sit.

"I've been up since 5am, and all I've had time to eat was a French cheese bagel." he opened his jacket, leaned back a little and crossed his legs, sitting sideways on.

"I've had the pancakes with maple syrup here before, they're exceptional. You fancy joining me for some?"

Biden's attitude and demeanour helped Theo relax, and soon they were chatting freely. Biden opened with sport, it was one area which any American man could relate: and, within no time at all, both joked and traded insults about their respective basketball teams. To Theo, it felt like he was just catching up with an older Uncle or a very astute grandfather. He didn't seem as lost as he appeared on the news each day. Outside the paparazzi flashed away continuously and inside the conversation flowed effortlessly. Time flowed as quickly as the conversation and in no time, Theo had polished off a stack of pancakes and half a litre of freshly squeezed orange juice.

Theo explained to The President, that he didn't think of himself as a hero, he explained in detail the connection he felt with the girl in the red slipper, how horrific it had been and that his thoughts had only been on trying to save her, and not on any anybody else. Biden insisted, that despite his reasons for going back into that train carriage, he had still stopped to pull others to safety, even though it would stop him from getting to her.

"Evil only prevails when good men refuse action," he quoted.

"In you, I see a truly great man, and one to whom I bestow the title: hero!"

Both men laughed, and Biden rose to his feet, getting ready to leave. Theo instinctively stood too and offered his hand, for the first time, to the most powerful man in the world. Their hands clasped in a solid, friendly shake and Biden was half-way through saying what a pleasure it had been, when it happened.

Starting from his palm's centre, Theo's whole hand began to feel as though it was vibrating at a frequency that was very unpleasant. He looked up at Biden, his gaze had dropped to their handshake, and he had the same, questioning look on his face as Theo. Neither man pulled away, instinctive curiosity took them over. He glanced down, small-scale, shaped lines began to draw themselves up Biden's arm, alarmed, Theo looked up again and wished that he hadn't.

Bright yellow eyes with a lizard-like slit pointing upwards at the centre, stared intently at Theo. President Biden was no longer the same, content, and welcoming face he had been for the last 10 minutes. Instead, he now burned with an anger that sent shivers right through Theo's body, yet what he didn't see, was that his own eyes had turned a beautiful pure white, whilst omitting a small cloud of blue light. Theo's arm felt like it was on fire, and a high-pitched screaming seared itself into his ear drums.

It was Biden that pulled away first. His eyes were at their brightest when, defiantly, he pulled his hand out of Theo's grasp. His eyes, and face instantly returned to the normal softness that had earned him so many admirers over the years, and he stepped back clearing his throat.

For Theo everything felt fine. It was as if it hadn't happened at all, the ringing and burning had gone, and there didn't appear to be any after-effects. He looked at Biden, puzzled, what the hell had just happened? Biden was looking at Theo and, had the same look of disbelief. This hadn't happened to him for a long, long time.

No one else appeared to notice what had happened, yet The President's energy had shifted remarkably, igniting a nervous tension, that resulted in a stare down between the too. Theo couldn't look away, he was searching Biden's face, looking for some small glimpse of what he had just seen but everything seemed completely as it had been before.

It was the taller, older leader of the free world who turned away first, worried maybe that Theo might try to touch him again, or maybe his muffled excuse was true and he was late for a meeting.

Theo watched him walk away, his fitted grey suit looked worth every dollar as was the black one his aid was wearing. Biden talked quietly to his staff, before he gestured angrily to two members of his security detail to follow, they jumped in line and followed their president out the door. He didn't look back, but his personal assistant turned, aimed his phone at Theo, and clicked. Taking a photo of the most confused person on the planet, and by doing so, only confusing him more so. One of the female personal assistants was talking to Theo, though he hadn't heard a word.

"I need to go home." he said, cutting her off mid-sentence.

She paused and looked at him. Finally, she decided and smiled. "Yes, it can be a little overwhelming the first time you meet him."

Theo exhaled a laugh, looked at the young looking, forty something, ex beauty queen and then gazed after the president again.

"Overwhelming is one way to describe it," he said half to himself.

Chapter 5

Papal Knowledge

Vatican City – Papal Residence
26/02/2022
3 :19pm

Two members of the Swiss Guard, stood on either side of the heavy wooden door. Like deadly court jesters, they stood solemnly, staring ahead. The long socks up to the knee ballooned outwards at the thigh, into bulbous pants that drew in at the waist, with a tight belt. The same red and yellow vertical stripes, continued upwards through their shirt, stopping at their tanned, muscular necks. Atop their heads, their black berets sat at a slight angle, and their gold crosses hung proudly, pinned to their chest. They were the men charged with protecting the Vatican from its many enemies and, with a little help from God, they were yet to fail.

Neither guard flinched at the sound of a loud bang from inside the room. The sound of breaking glass followed, and the yelp of pain from a woman proceeded a knowing glance at each other, followed by a knowing smile. The guard to the left blinked, though there was something odd about the way he did. Then, the guard to the right followed suit. He closed his eyes and flicked them open again, though, this time, his eyes closed from the sides. Both eyelids swept in from the left and right, meeting in the middle, and then jumping back to the sides. It happened so quickly that unless you really looked, you wouldn't have noticed.

More screaming sounded, followed by a loud bang on the wall directly behind the Swiss guard on the right, and another knowing glance by the two men, then a deep voice sounded, speaking in a language that was unrecognisable and muffled through the 6-inch-thick, solid door. It was silent for a few seconds, then the locking mechanism clicked, and turned. Neither guard turned to look, and the door opened just enough for a beautiful, petite, young, blonde woman to slip out to her freedom.

She wore a short white dress over her perfect, smooth, tanned tight body that was torn from her shoulder, ripped across her stomach, and pitted with blood. Her eyes were wild with fear, tears rolled down her face from her swollen left eye, and blood dripped from her left ear. She held her hand over the rip across her stomach, blood trickling through her fingers, falling towards the inside of her thighs. The door closed behind her, and neither guard acknowledged her presence. She walked tenderly down the corridor, slightly limping, and still holding her stomach, she had been lucky though. The cut wasn't too deep, and she hadn't been sodomized at all, which was rare. All she wanted now was to get clean, to get this creature's seed out of her and to try to forget it had happened at all and, that it will probably happen again soon; she was an Alaha after all.

Chapter 6

Birthday Suit

Theo's Apartment
26/02/2022
7 :02pm

I t was dark outside by the time Theo walked into his apartment, and tossed his keys down onto the table in between the tv and his mole skin, two seater sofa. He looked around his tidy two-bedroom home of two years. Everything was exactly the same as when he'd left it this morning before his 'crazy' day. The red shoe still sat on the table and could be seen in the reflection of his large plasma TV, and his two chilli plants stood strong and healthy behind the sofa.

Theo had been very pleased when he kitted out his second-floor apartment. He had done well in creating a warm, comfortable place for him to be able to relax in the evenings. Despite some suggesting that the chocolate brown and cream combo was a little 'dark,' he liked to feel enveloped by the room, like a warm blanket.

A modest yet modern kitchen was positioned through a door to the right of his TV, and to the left, a short corridor retreated into the two bedrooms. At the very end, was the marble tiled, massive bathroom, slash shower room that had sold this place to him.

The day's events played over, and over again in his mind, as, while on auto pilot, he walked into his kitchen. The white tiles on the floor contrasted beautifully with the dark, granite-effect worktops, and every conceivable gadget lined up in their polished, chrome skin in a symmetrical pattern. He opened his big silver fridge: fresh fruit, a loaf of bread, a dozen eggs and a six pack of Corona, sat comfortably in the cool air. He could still see Biden's yellow eyes, surrounded by a brow of small scales and every possible hypothesis was flashing through his mind. Only one of them made sense, and despite what he had seen and felt, was the one that generated the most fear.

The fresh hiss of gas escaping from the Corona, was followed by the brittle sound of the crown being dropped into a small bag containing many others.

He took a long, thirsty swig; the ice-cold bubbles danced on his tongue and tickled the back of his throat. He took the beer away from his lips, exhaling with the satisfaction that only a cold beer on a hot day can bring.

He was a young 29-year-old man who had witnessed his adoptive grandfather's one-sided battles with Alzheimer's. As a young teenager, he remembered the white haired, cauliflower eared, man mountain, he lovingly called pop, being dragged from the shed in his backyard by police and medical staff. Two police officers, and a nurse ended up in hospital, such was his grandfather's conviction that they were Nazi's, plotting to drag him and his family to a camp somewhere deep in America.

Theo remembered some of the more lucid conversations between him and his grandfather, especially once he was safely in the home, taking his medication.

He had explained to Theo that on that day, as clear and as obvious as he could see Theo in front of him, he could see a woman and two young children cowering behind his lawnmower. He saw the black swastika emblazoned on police officers clothing and was aware, like all Americans, that Hitler had won the second world war, and they were coming for him and his family.

The tears, the fear, and the confusion quickly left though, as he stood angrily, and demanded to know what Theo had done with his grandson. He quickly turned violent, shouting Theo's name, searching for him. Theo had to watch one of the greatest minds he had come across in his 14 years, dragged from him, pleading with the nurses not to give him more drugs, and begging them to find Theo. He protested his sanity, up until the drugs surged through his veins, and cloaked his brain in a warmth that put him into a deep sleep. It was a moment that had stayed with Theo his whole life, and one that had manifested itself in his dreams.

He swigged on his cold suds once more, and made his way through to his bedroom, emptying his pockets on the small table in the front room, on the way.

It was the only conceivable explanation - early onset dementia

He sat on the edge of his comfortable, ornate wrought iron effect bed and sank into his soft mattress and thick white cotton blanket.

He placed the small bottle in his hand on the dark brown side table next to the bed, and as he removed his shoes, he wished he were capable of shutting his brain down like his laptop.

This was way beyond the realms of reality for Theo, and as such, was confusing the hell out of him. For someone so logical, who rationalized everything he saw, and experienced, it was killing him that he couldn't come up with an answer to the many questions he had floating through his head. Then, like an answer to a mathematical problem it came to him. A shower would help.

He stripped down, folding the clothes that could be worn again, sliding open the mirrored doors of the wardrobe, and placing them neatly in a shelf, ready for the next time they were needed. His underwear and shirt got tossed into the straw basket in the corner of the room. Naked, he strode back into the hallway, stopping on his way to check his reflection in the wardrobe mirror. Most of his left side was still bruised from that day on the subway.

"Why couldn't you have just got the bus?" he asked himself. He waited for an answer. Of course, none came, and he left his room, turned right, and walked into his bathroom.

It was a dazzling white room with large square tiles on the floor with cream marble like lines just visible under the bright LED downlights. The bath, sink, and wall tiles were also a clean, and well maintained white with a dark subway style grout, providing the character he loved. The fixtures were polished chrome and reflected like mirrors. The only colour in the room came from the thick, brown towels, neatly folded on the lid of the straw washing basket, and the hand towel hanging from the chrome ring next to the sink. The shower curtain hung alongside the bath, it too was white, and a big man-sized window split in the middle, was next to it. It was frosted all over, and slid up from the bottom, allowing for someone to slip out onto the black iron fire escape that clung to most of the buildings in this vast city.

Theo brushed past the curtain, and turned on both the hot and cold taps, causing the large shower head above to spring to life, and Theo left it to warm.

He stood, and looked in the mirror, the yellow eyes flashed through his mind, and, as he often did, he began a conversation with his reflection.

"After the emotional rollercoaster that has been my life for the last three days, that was the last thing I needed."

He began to list with his fingers.

"I just started a new job, a job that I've worked very hard to get."

He dropped the first one.
"Been blown up!"

He pulled down on his second.

"Oh, then seen a bloody ghost floating up from the wreck which no-one else seems to have spotted."

His middle finger dropped.

"Got invited to meet the President of the free world", he pulled his eyebrows up and nodded, in a very sarcastic 'good idea' pose.

Fourth finger.

"Turns out, that when standing, and shaking hands with the most powerful man on the planet, I see him turn into some kinda lizard, and he stares at me like *he* has seen a ghost."

Theo stared long and hard into the mirror, checking his own eyes, making sure that they didn't change. The sound of the shower, drizzled gently against the hard porcelain bath. steam was beginning to snake over the top of the curtain, yet its advance was wispy and slow. Theo leaned in for a closer look, pivoting against the sink in front of him. He opened his left eye wide with his fingers, and spent a second to stare at his iris, looking deeply into the array of colours in his eye.

His pupil was surrounded by a dark ring of blue which got lighter towards the edges. He checked the other in the same way, his pupils were dilating slightly in relation to the amount of light they both received. He smiled a wide smile, ran his fingers along his gums, and tilted his head back a little to allow the light to reveal some hidden secret, that would answer this riddle for him. Nothing.

He was healthy as an ox. Steam was now beginning to fill the top of the room. Theo abandoned the mirror, deciding a nice hot shower might not give him an answer, though would make him feel a little more human. He pulled back the curtain, and stepped into his bathtub, then turned to let the water engulf his face and ears. Giving him a few seconds of peace.

He put his arm out, and leant forward, using it to prop himself against the wall, water ran down the back of his head, and cascaded down his muscular back. This was like a gentle meditation for him, while under the water he was able to leave his thoughts behind and just enjoy the sensation the hot water gave as it snaked down his spine. He finally turned, after a good long soak, to reach for his shower gel, he filled his palms, and brushed it through his hair with his fingers whilst the water beat gently against the back of his neck. His hair puffed up bright white under the lights, as the soap began to expand. It ran down his face, and Theo closed his eyes. He gently leant back and, while still scrubbing, positioned the top of his head back under the water. Water filled his ears, ran over his face, and consumed his every sense.

After a few moments, he snapped his head forward, pinched the water from his eyes and listened. "Really?" he asked out loud.

Desperately seeking a 'No.' The phone continued to ring, dulled through the walls, and door, and drowned by the falling water, yet he could still hear it wailing from the lounge room table. He took a long, exaggerated breath as he tilted his head back. It wasn't stopping. As if, trying to decide whether or not to get out of bed to run at 6am on a day when the sky was awash with rain, he gingerly and reluctantly made his decision to go for it.

Once his feet had stepped out of the bath, and were on the marble floor, his pace suddenly quickened. 'He had come this far and if he didn't make it before they hung up it would all be in vain.'

Naked, he dashed down his short hallway, past two bedroom doors, and his sofa, to reach the small table in front of the T.V where his mobile phone was resting. The room was soft and lit only by the two lamps in opposite corners, casting the shadow of the chilli plants against the wall behind them.

Dripping random drops of water onto his carpet Theo answered the blocked number that was calling at his rather inopportune time and sat naked and wet on the suede effect sofa he loved.

"Hello?" Theo asked, and despite it all, he was actually happy now, he had made it in time to answer the call. The interruption to his first real moment of relaxation and mad dash down the hallway hadn't been in vain.

"Theo Miller?" The voice on the other end demanded in a soft yet forceful way, already aware of the answer. Theo sighed

"Look pal, I'm in the middle of a shower, are you trying to sell me something? Cos if you are, now's not a great time." Theo stood, ready to dismiss this caller and get back to his shower.

"I understand your meeting today with our President was very eventful." The voice remained calm and assured. it was stating a fact. Theo's pupils dilated; his heart stopped for a second then exploded against his chest.

"Who is this?" Theo demanded, but not loudly. Suddenly he felt like he was being watched.

"You need to leave your apartment, now." Still calm, almost emotionless, it demanded.

Theo pulled his phone away from his ear and looked down at the screen. His brow creased as he looked at the number. The phone spoke again, but it was inaudible, he bought it back up to his ear.

"..... In about thirty seconds. Climb down the fire escape. I'm in a black Chrysler Voyager." Theo tried to speak, to ask what was happening, in about 30 seconds. He never got the chance; the phone was dead. He decided to check something out.

Still naked, he walked back down the corridor to the bathroom at the rear of his building. Opened the big, sliding, bottom half of the window next to his bathtub, and leant out for a look. Sure enough, at the bottom of his winding fire escape, a black Voyager ticked over, ready to flee. Theo's heart leapt into his throat, 'this was real.'

He pulled his head back inside, and immediately reached for a towel which was hurriedly wrapped, tightly around his waist. His mind raced with a thousand questions. 'What's with the black Chrysler?' and, 'what was going to happen in about ten seconds?' The image of Biden's eyes flashed in front of him, it snapped him back to an alert sharpness, and he darted into his lounge to get his phone. He had left it on the coffee table, next to the red shoe. He stopped and thought of her a little longer than he should have done.

His front door exploded inwards, in a shower of heat, and splintered wood, that rode the coattails of a wave of light and a noise that threw Theo backwards into his hallway. The second he landed, the first of six fully armoured, and battle-ready SWAT style officers, stormed in through the man-sized hole that was torn into the wood. A green laser beam cut through the smoke, hunting any moving objects, scanning for life. By the time the third set of feet shot through the door, Theo had already scrambled to his feet and was backing away, turning to run back to the bathroom.

The first shots detonated in the small confines of the apartment, and chewed the ground behind Theos feet, he was just able to keep moving fast enough for each one to miss him. Like the waves at the beach chasing him up the sand. Only this time, he was never going to be caught.

By the time he was fully upright and running, he had slammed through the bathroom door and shut it behind him, which seemed to cease the tirade of bullets. Without thinking, he poised himself to hop out of the window onto his fire escape. He waited, the silence intrigued him, he strained to hear what was going on, desperately trying to control his breathing, it was all he could hear. His eyes very faintly began to glow. Still, he waited, he really didn't want to climb down his fire escape in just a towel.

In perfect unison, two members of the assault team opened fire through the door. There bullets passed through the it like it didn't exist and slammed into the bathtub, destroyed the sink and ploughed through the floor. The room was awash with splinters of wood, fragments of marble and porcelain, a smoke haze of dust and burning hot metal. Green laser beams poked through the holes in the door. Once again in went silent. The only sound was of water spraying from the faucet in the remaining half of the sink.

In the narrow hallway the two men that had rained down upon the door stood upright on one knee, p90's to they're shoulder. They breathed heavily but trained their sights firmly on the door. One mistake here could cost the entire team their lives. Upon instruction a third dropped to his stomach and crawled towards the door, green laser beams covered his advance and faintly lit the smoke from the gun fire.

When he reached the door, still low to the ground he spun so his feet were poised to kick it open, and he sat on his back side. He pulled out his side arm, a colt 45. He cocked it ready for action, then pulled his feet back and kicked out as hard as he could, he used the force to kick open the dilapidated door and slide himself back a couple of feet as he did. He leant back, lowering his shoulders to the floor and brought his gun up, his finger strained on the trigger. He held his breath, two men stepped past him and stormed the room, both swinging their readied weapons in sharp perfect arcs, surveying the room.

Water still sprayed from the broken sink, and big chunks of white debris laid like big blocks of chalk all around the room. Broken glass laid at the foot of the window which was now just like a mountain landscape at the top, and bottom of the destroyed pain. The room however, did not contain Theo.

"Clear!" One of the men declared. Yet, they kept their automatic weapons ready, and upon hearing a sound from the street below, all three men snapped a look towards the window.

The final ladder of the fire escape slid down with a clunk of metal on metal and gave away Theo's position. He had jumped through the window a second before the first wave of bullets poured through the door. Something had told him to go, and go he did. He had jumped each flight of stairs in one leap, using the handrail to soften the effect of the cold metal on his bare feet.

He climbed down the final ladder as fast as his limbs would move. A cold breeze lifted his towel as he crawled backwards towards the ground, and snagged on a rivet that hadn't properly been sealed. By the time he noticed his towel was up at head height. He stopped his descent to unhook himself, just as a tirade of bullets sparked off the metal all around him, instinctively he pulled in his limbs, but a ricochet clipped his left hand. Letting out a loud yell he dropped from the ladder.

Falling backward time seemed to slow down. His hand burnt, his towel fluttered whilst still attached to the ladder, and more boots stomped across the metal frame outside Theo's apartment window.

The first man out had lost his line of sight, jumped the first flight of stairs, and spun to unleash another volley of bullets at the falling Theo. They whizzed past him as he fell. A flash of light exploded from the end of the gun, sending a bullet on a beeline for Theo's left leg. Somehow, he was able to watch it on its path, could see it spinning through the air, like a small golden spear of white-hot metal.

He jerked his leg to the side, the bullet just scraped the inside of his thigh, slicing and cauterizing all in one, and continued onwards to dig into the ground below. Though it hurt like hell, it was much better than a direct hit into the femur.

Theo felt the ground rushing up towards him and braced for a painful jolt.

His head snapped back, and plunged into a black garbage bag, then the bare skin of his whole left side slapped against the black asphalt. Though the fall threatened to break his ribs, it settled for bruising them, and shaking his body to its very core. He couldn't breathe for a few seconds and gasped like a beached fish until he saw the first gun of his assailants searching over the black metal railing of the fire escape above him.

The first of three bullets chewed into the ground.
Thud.
Thud.
Thud.
Right where Theo was lying.

As the second commando poked his head over to take a look, he saw the passenger door of the Chrysler slamming shut as the car sped away.

Inside the car Theo was in the front passenger seat, on his knees facing the rear, looking out through the back window of the car. It smelt brand new, a strong pungent leather and was lit up on the inside like a spacecraft. His rescuer's face was lit up in blue, like an ultraviolet light. Theo stared intently behind them, completely unaware of the blood dribbling onto the chair from his right hand, and leg. His eyes were still glowing a little, and every breath was shallow as breathing deeply was too painful after the fall.

The car made light work of the alleyway at the back of Theo's apartment, and was soon on the main roads, allowing Theo to relax a little, and take stock of his surroundings, as well as make sense of what the hell had just happened to him in the last 5 minutes and 32 seconds.

His first thought was his nakedness, his second thought was the blood, and his third thought: the smell. Though Theo didn't realise, the only thing that had stopped him from fracturing the back of his skull, as he fell, were the used nappies from apartment 13. He ran his fingers up to the back of his head and lo and behold, he felt a creamy past matted in with his hair. He looked up to the God, he liked to blame bad things on.

"Really?"

He looked across at the guy whose car he was polluting with blood and baby faeces, and saw an intent face focused on the road and his mirrors. Unshaven, though in a clean, rugged way, his small eyes glowed under the blue lights of the speedometer, Theo saw a bout of confidence in his every feature, especially in the grin, that threatened to break the stoic determination and focus across every other part of his face. Theo started to speak, though was cut off before he had the chance.

"Hold on son. We are not out of the woods yet." He had a faint hint of an Arabic, or Middle Eastern accent. Theo couldn't tell.

"Reach into the back, there should be a jacket in there." He snuck a look down at the blood pooling in the front foot well of his wife's car, and then back up to the road.

"You hit?" he asked, stealing another look across.

Theo was still searching the back seat for the coat. All the driver could see, in his rear-view mirror, was the naked blood-stained ass of Theo Miller and his gaping hole, quite literally. If the driver hadn't also seen the three black GM vans slide around the corner, appearing as if jumping out at their prey from behind Theo's right butt cheek, it may have been a funny moment.

Theo felt his hand touch what felt like a bundle of wool in the footwell behind the driver's seat, and grabbed it triumphantly. He pulled it up, and as he brought it into view, he spun his body, dropped his ass and sat back down on the chair. He didn't take time to see what he had because the second he looked through the windscreen he was pinned into the back of his chair by the thrust of the Chryslers Twin turbo 512 BHP engine. He looked across at the driver and could see his eyes trained for a few seconds on the road behind them in his mirrors, Theo instinctively turned to look over his shoulder. One in front and two behind taking up the two-lane highway. The lights were at full strength and lit up Theo's face like a Christmas tree. They weren't finished yet.

"I've got a small hit on my leg," Theo said trying to find the arm hole in the black woollen cardigan he had found.

He turned it and looked quizzically at it. The streetlights blurred past and gave him just enough light to see how the garment was made. He pushed his right arm through and leant forward to swing it behind him to get his left arm into position, just as the driver swung the car into a hard left turn. Theo slammed, clumsily against the passenger door, his left knee came flailing up and the cardigan, now half on him, it dropped from his grip again. The car slid around the corner, as if on ice, with the back end swinging around in a large arc, then sideways, the front wheels in full opposite lock. Luckily, the driver managed to realign and correct and the car, then shot off straight like a dial.

The driver stole another glance in his rear-view mirror as Theo once again fumbled for the left arm hole of his newly found cardigan. Triumphantly, he thrust his arm through, and was pleased to see his hand emerge, finally he had something to cover himself. He sat back in his chair while pulling the garment around him, and now he was no longer naked he focused once again on looking over his shoulder at their pursuers.

They had gained a hundred meters or so since he had last looked, but there were still three hungry looking pairs of lights chasing them down. The extra bit of distance seemed to subconsciously give Theo the time and space to feel the sharp pain in his thigh. He looked down to see the wound, mostly closed from where the bullet had burnt him more than cut him, yet blood still gently seeped out.

"Mate, excuse my language, but what the fucking hell is going on? Who are you?" Theo asked, looking directly at the driver. He didn't offer an immediate response.

"Who the fuck are they and why did they just try to kill me?"

He continued, gesturing behind them. He watched the driver, searching for clues. Theo saw his eyes look up at his mirror again, as he swung into a sharp right turn, again sliding the car sideways. The driver offered a fig leaf of an answer.

"I don't think you would believe me if I told you Theo, but once I lose these bastards, I will fill you in on the finer details. Right now, just buckle up and let me drive, ok? This is my wife's car, it doesn't handle the same as mine, it feels like a bloody tank." He looked at Theo, trying to give him a reassuring glance.

"Jesus, are you wearing my wife's cardigan?" He smiled, checked his mirrors again.

"It suits you."

Theo looked down his body to see what it was he had grabbed from the back seat, the engine roared as the driver dropped a gear, and shot into oncoming traffic to avoid a couple of slow-moving NY taxi cabs. The black woollen cardigan Theo had grabbed, was a very feminine, thinly cut, knee length cardigan with very loose thread almost making it see through. Theo swayed from left to right as the car zig zagged through the traffic, horns blasted all around them and another look over his shoulder confirmed that they were still being followed.

The roads were fairly empty by New York standards, they had managed to reach speeds in excess of 100mph at times. Yet, as they reached the suburbs of queens their luck changed, and the road before them became a sea of parked cars. The driver didn't miss a beat, and mounted the curb, blasting his horn as the car jumped painfully onto the footpath. Pedestrians dived out of the way and spun to the sound of a revving engine, and long, loud horn blasts.

Bouncing around in his chair, Theo once again looked behind him to see if it was enough to lose their three followers, only to see bright headlights right behind them, the front of the black van filled much of the car's rear window, and he struggled to see past it, to the other two.

They were right behind them now.

The car darted left and right, narrowly missing old ladies, a couple of businessmen and all manner of Queens' finest. The driver was concentrating intently, yet still managed to send a mailbox sailing into the air, a parked bicycle into the cars on the road and the small wooden tables and chairs out the front of a curb side coffeehouse, into a thousand pieces. Theo instinctively brought his arms up to cover his face, as the latter showered the windscreen in debris.

A sharp swing right, was followed by a full left lock, and the car once again skidded sideways into a smaller side street off Queens Boulevard. The driver had over cooked it and bounced off the corner building's brick wall, though managed to hold it strong, as the car's engine revved hard enough to pull them down the street. Theo's door had taken a large hit and the paint all down the right side was either on the walls, or flaked onto the road under them.

The little jink into the side street had bought them some more distance from their followers. As the speed grew, and building after building whooshed by, the driver began to speak to Theo, who was constantly checking over his shoulder, and wincing as they dodged the many potential accidents before them.

"The guys in the vans behind us Theo, and the guys who shot up your apartment and part of a very select group of NSA agents. They deal with presidential protection orders and are part of a black ops team known only as Ducaz. We have our own agents working in The President's inner circle and overheard the order for your execution."

The car swung right, back onto the main roads. The traffic was lighter, and although the driver had to swing from one lane to the other, he was once again able to build speed. Red light after red light was ploughed through with reckless abandon as they drove and the driver continued.

"That's nothing special though as people get taken care of all the time, but the reasons for it grabbed our attention." He looked across at Theo who was staring back at him.

"How did the meeting with our commander in chief go eh?"

Theo stumbled looking for an answer but couldn't find a sentence or words to begin to answer that one. The driver smiled again as he checked his mirror.

"That's ok, we know what happened, and it is very exciting for all of us. If we make it out of this, you're going to......."

Before the driver could finish his sentence, the black van's halogen high beams, filled the car. One of the vans had somehow broken off from the pursuing pack and cut them off on the corner of Queens subway station. As the driver looked to his left, the two vehicles collided. The force felt nuclear within the car's tight interior.

The front bumper of the black van smashed into the driver's door, the three inches of solid steel, and side impact protection bars in place, had no chance against a 3.5 tonne fist travelling at over 60mph.

At the moment of impact, Theo's world once again slowed as, inch by inch he saw the door encroach, and engulf his rescuer. The jagged metal consumed the driver's seat tearing into the driver with frightening ferocity and ease, killing him instantly. Blood sprayed in every direction, and as the shockwave passed through the car, Theo played back the horror in his mind, each drop of blood floating mid-air, coating everything red.

The impact sent the car sprawling across three lanes and closed the cabin in around Theo. Limbs flew around, as lines snaked their way across each of the windows. Just when the mosaic couldn't get any more complicated, it imploded, resulting in millions of glass shards bursting through car. Theo watched in slow motion, amazed that he was able to bring his hand up and wave away the hundreds of shards, heading for his face.

The car stopped in the middle of the road, his mind was filled with high pitched ringing, causing him not to hear the horn blaring out into the skyline, and bouncing off the buildings around him. Burnt rubber filled his nostrils, and one look at the driver told him, this was the last journey this guy was ever going to take. He looked out of the empty windscreen; small clumps of glass still hung onto the edges as little pieces fell into the car sporadically.

The impact had driven the left side of the car in so far that the dead driver's arms, and parts of his body were pressed against Theo, fresh blood had sprayed over him, and his new black cardigan. He looked over his shoulder through the rear window, which was still intact yet impossible to see through due to the glass having shattered in place. He knew staying here was not a good idea, so tried his door handle. To his surprise the door opened, albeit with a stiff nudge from his right shoulder. He unbuckled his seat belt, and fell out onto the road, still dazed and unable to hear anything above the screeching noise the impact had left in his head.

His eyes worked fine though, and in looking back saw the two black vans that were still behind them screech to a halt and almost immediately the doors opened and feet wearing black boots hit the ground. Theo's survival instinct kicked in and he scrambled to his feet, stumbling as he rose, and of course he made for his escape in the opposite direction. His bare feet slapped on the hard asphalt, cutting themselves on the broken glass that decorated the road like snow. He didn't feel a thing, as the adrenaline was already pumping through every vein in his body. His head began to clear a little as he ran down the road, the sound of the car horn slowly replaced the ringing in his ears. This was then broken by the explosion of gunshots.

Theo didn't even look back, he just ran harder, instinctively he brought his arms up, and tensed his body at the sound of bullets whizzing past him.

The accident, rather, attack, had happened on the intersection of Newark and Red Bank Boulevard, and right there in front of Theo, was the entrance to the subway. He didn't notice all the cars around him had stopped, or that some drivers were starting to get out of their cars, ready to help, only to jump straight back into safety at the sound, and sight of bullets, and heavily armed men. Some had swarmed around the mangled wreck of the black Chrysler; others were raining down bullets at Theo, blood soaked, whilst a handful of others had given chase.

The cardigan was still not buttoned up and as Theo ran, it was splayed open revealing his nakedness underneath, but he had no time for modesty, he was in survival mode, and ran like a man possessed, his body on show to the world. Given the femininity of his attire, one taxi driver would return home to tell the story of the bloody transvestite he had seen emerging from a wrecked vehicle and getting chased by a swat team into the subway.

Into the subway, Theo darted and jumped the stairs two at a time, using the handrail for balance. He left bloody footprints everywhere he stepped, and although most of the glass in his feet had fallen behind him, there were still enough pieces dug into his skin that the slapping of his feet had a small element of a click, click, click.

Fluro lights gave everything a white glow and graffiti rushed past him either side as he bounded down the stairs, not daring to look back. Though he had no idea where he was going, he was determined to get there faster than those chasing him. He didn't take a second to consider what was happening, he just wanted to put as much distance between him, and the guys that had shot up his apartment, chased him through New York at crazy speeds, and finally smashed their van into his car, in an attempt, to stop him.

A few departing passengers were climbing the stairs after a heavy day, pressing themselves to the wall as Theo flew past. They heard him before they saw him, and what a sight it was.

When they looked up from their daily monotony, they saw jumping towards them, two steps at a time, a naked man with a black cardigan floating behind him. Blood running down his legs, and splashed over his face, stomach, and hands. Red footprints followed him down the stairs and his eyes were glowing in a stomach-churning bright white. They were not just white eyes; they were glowing as if they were light bulbs instead of eyeballs.

Still pressed to the wall, they instinctively watched his descent as he passed, only to hear further heavy footsteps from above. Another glance and chasing this crazed man down into the belly of New York, were half a dozen men dressed totally in black with masks covering the lower half of their faces and small helmets, only showing their eyes. Everyone they passed had stayed pressed against the wall, staying well out of the way, and everyone they passed couldn't help but stare back down in amazement at what they had just witnessed.

Below Theo, at the ticket entrance, there was just one guard on duty. It was almost 19:50, the evening rush had abated, and things were beginning to slow down for guard Eddie Gross. The stairs opened into a six-lane turnstile system which would change either inbound or outbound depending on the time of the day, and at this hour, four lanes were dedicated for those returning from the city to their little suburb.

Advertising billboards ran down each wall as well as maps adorned with different coloured lines explaining the train directions, and routes. The white tiles reflected the Fluro lights in the ceiling and a couple of monitors listed the departure and arrival train times. Theo glanced up, and could see platform two was flashing meaning, this train was due to depart very soon. This was going to be his target. He knew he was going to need some luck but right now he just didn't want to get shot.

The guard heard the slapping of Theo's feet echoing in the confines of the underground, and a heavy stampede of thick boots charging down the stairs. He looked to where the stairs opened into the more cavernous area where the gates were situated and out shot Theo. The first thing he noticed was the dried blood on his legs, the flailing black cardigan, and then the glowing white eyes.

Eddie was a movie buff, YouTube addict and had thought he had seen everything on his small screen at home, or on his phone during the quieter shifts at work. He already had his phone in his hand tonight, checking to see if Singlemum81 was online. In the ten years working on the New York tube, he had witnessed every kind of junkie episode, homeless hilariousness, and mentally ill embarrassment. Including at least twenty naked commuters at all stages of mental degradation. His own YouTube account had over 5,000 subscribers and was filled with videos of some of these episodes, he was ready for this one.

Quick as a flash his iPhone 11 was in camera mode and recorded Theo in startling clarity. It captured him just as he entered the main area and Eddie chuckled internally at the crazy naked man in a woman's cardigan, obviously out of his head on drugs or psychosis.

Theo scanned the area before him, deciding how to get through the giant metal barrier in front of him. It was fairly simple, each of the entrances with a red cross was guarded by a simple three-pronged turnstile that he could leap in a single bound. He had never been at this station before, but it was much the same as every other stop along the Central Park line. He just made for the one right in the middle, it was the closest to him.

Eddie was still filming Theo as he got closer to the gates, he had no intention of stopping him, he didn't get paid enough for that, and since the incident last year with the guy on ice and the knife, he had learnt that the hard way. He was watching the whole incident on his small 5 inch" screen, and saw the figure in front of him, steal a look behind him whilst still making for the gates. Then, the figure swung his glance to the left and looked directly at Eddie Gross, and the camera. It was only for a split second and as a result he couldn't be sure, yet the figure's eyes were glowing like two dim white light bulbs. It sent a shiver down Eddie's spine, and he now looked past his phone, looking at Theo leap the turnstile with his eyes rather than through the screen.

It was the arrival of a troop of armed men dressed in black from the stairwell that redirected his focus back to his task of capturing this digitally. In a flash, and seemingly oblivious to his presence they jumped from the stairs and too jumped through the metal barrier as if it weren't there.

Eddie couldn't believe what he had just seen, he thought he had seen it all, but a fully equipped swat team, chasing a naked blood-soaked man in a woman's cardigan into the depths of the New York subway network was a first even for him. He felt a thrill. This was going straight onto his YouTube page once he got home. Subway Stories was sure to get a few thousand views tonight. Little did he know what he had, who he had and the stir it was going to create once it went live.

On the other side of the barrier Theo ran frantically for platform two. He had just passed another couple of screens and saw the words:

Eastern line 7:52 – Platform 2

The time in the bottom right corner of the screen read:

7:51.

He was still in the open space of the main underground as he passed a small throng of passengers that had departed the train he was heading for. Almost to a man they stopped dead and pressed themselves against the wall, getting out of his way and the way of the black clad pursuers. The opening for the platform was about twenty meters away, Theo could see a central ceiling mounted sign with an accompanying arrow pointing the way and the words *Platform 2* above it. Theo ducked in, out of the main tunnel onto the platform, unaware of how far away the swat guys were and could see the train only another twenty meters once inside.

There were a couple of benches lying parallel to the tracks, more advertising billboards all along the walls, and a few trash cans. It smelt dry and dusty as he heard a single whistle blast from the conductor, alerting the train driver, they were good to go. He had barely stepped foot on the platform as the first of the men behind him appeared and dived forward, landing on his stomach, and skidding a few inches to a halt. He already had his pistol in his outstretched arms as he landed and unleashed a couple of shots as his fleeing target.

The shots boomed loudly in the tight space around them, and the metal spears whizzed past Theo as he instinctively lifted his shoulders to protect himself. The first two missed their target and pierced the glass window of the tube train Theo was breaking for. The third and fourth exploded from the end of his gun after an extra second to aim. The small sights at the end of the barrel were directly between Theo's shoulder blades as the man in black instinctively pulled on the trigger, the shooter knew after all his years of training that these two were slamming into the target.

The doors of the train were closed, the rest of the swat team were just an arm's length away, and Theo still had ten meters to go as the fatal third and fourth shots flew towards his back.

The warning from the inside of the train, telling passengers to stand clear of the doors, was cut off by two loud bangs.

Theo was agonisingly close as the train pulled away, he could see the faces of the passengers within the carriage through the window. They were staring in amazement at what they were seeing on the platform. Not one of them noticed the train leaving, they were all too absorbed in the naked man, covered in blood with bright white eyes.

They saw Theo suddenly dart to his right as the final two bullets whizzed through the air past him, and the next thing they knew, as the train was gathering speed and momentum, he launched himself at their window. Causing it to finally give in to damage.

He used his elbows and forearms to break through and fell clumsily in a shower of broken glass, first onto a row of inward facing chairs, then as his momentum pushed him forward, into the centre of the carriage, right in the middle of fifteen stunned passengers. One of the swat guys made a leap for the open window, though as the 320-tonne train was pulled along by its 2500hp engine, it had already built the speed and momentum to outpace his jump, and he bounced off the train and back onto the platform cursing loudly as he fell.

As each of the passengers uncurled from their prone positions following the glass shower, they all just stared and looked down to see Theo. Curled up in a foetal position, surrounded by glass, caked in fresh blood, naked, except for a ragged black cardigan.

He too began to uncurl and for the first time since climbing through his bathroom window, the adrenaline slowed, his eyes returned to normal, and he felt every cut, bruise, and wound. Every part of him hurt, ached, and burned. He looked around, every pair of eyes were fixed on him in disbelief, causing him to feel very, very naked.

Chapter 7

Not In Kansas

Baghdad – Office of Control Risk PLC
26/02/2022
11 :11am

"Since its inception in 1903, Control Risk is a global organisation that has been in the middle of every political and cultural hotbed that can be imagined. We have been on the doorstep of every conflict throughout the 20th century, assessing the political integrity, and security risks that have evolved over time and used this expert knowledge, garnered by immersing ourselves within these lands, to help our clients manage the risks, and opportunities of operating in complex or hostile environments."

Brad Atkins was an old hand at selling the services of his employer, and his presentation was just beginning. His Australian accent was almost gone now, replaced with the kind of accent you couldn't name, though a voice that sounded familiar, soothing and like home. He knew where to pause to emphasise his well-rehearsed and delivered company profile speech and was a dab hand at using the massive 100-inch television screen to run through perfectly built and professionally prepared slides. It helped him to ensure that the potential clients' trip to Baghdad would result in another client to add to the long list of foreign investors, wanting to make the most of what was a fast-growing market.

He wasn't much to look at, at only 5'10, he was shorter than most, had a slight frame, and receding blond hair with small spectacles balanced on the end of his nose. He oozed wealth, power, and confidence, from his Breitling diamond encrusted watch, right down to his $1200 Barker Black shoes. His steely blue eyes shone and pierced through you all at once invoking a mixture of trust, and fear in those he worked with. He had a knack for getting those around him to feel so very comfortable, if that's what he wanted.

Dark wooden floorboards clicked under his footsteps as he walked and talked at the same time. Before him, was a grand boardroom table that could easily seat twenty, surrounded by lush expensive black chairs made from the finest Italian leather. The ceiling loomed high above and hanging from golden chains were large orbs of light that gave the room a glow. They were dimmed as he gave his presentation, three men sat at his end of the table, the end where the tv screen took up the wall. On the other walls hung proud works of art, originals from some of the world's greats and beneath the table lay a thick 19th century Persian rug as long and, as wide as any ever made, and probably worth more than many of the paintings on the wall. This room impressed almost every man that stepped foot inside, it told a story, without words. Once you stepped into the boardroom of a Control Risks office, it was very hard not to put pen to paper.

"We support clients by providing strategic consultancy, expert analysis and in-depth investigations, right through to handling sensitive political issues and providing practical on the ground protection and support," he continued, as another slide appeared behind him. He stared each man in the eye as he spoke, moving from one to the other, but focussing most on Cornelius Van de Berg, the MD of VDB Gas and Oil.

He sat back down at the head of the table, leant in slightly as if giving away a secret. His starched white Egyptian cotton shirt collar touched his well-tanned jawline and the shoulders of his grey Italian made suit crumpled slightly.

"Our unique combination of services, our geographical reach and the trust our clients place in us, ensures we can help them effectively solve their problems, and realise new opportunities across the world. Working across five continents and with 34 offices worldwide, Control Risks provides a broad range of services to help our clients manage the risks you will face in this new market." He paused, leaned in slightly further.

"And not just the risk from the locals."

All three of his guests smiled at this tongue in cheek joke which they all knew also veiled some truth. This was a competitive cut-throat market with very different rules to the rest of the world. They all knew business at this level was dog eat dog, and although this was true back in their domestic markets in Europe and in the US, here there were no rules, no government regulations, and laws were written by those with the greatest desire to write them, as opposed to those with money and power.

He allowed his last remark to sit for a second whilst clicking his button, and behind him a slide appeared on Integrity Risk, within the bullet points were such phrases as:

- Corruption risk assessment and audit,

- Computer forensics,
- Third party vendor and agent screening,
- Forensic accounting,
- Intellectual property theft,

"Gentleman, this is the gold rush of the 21st century, and this is the new Wild West. The rewards for doing business in this part of the world are substantial, and unashamedly substantial. You are going to require a sheriff to protect you from the Indians, and the other prospectors and we will get to that later, but like a middle-aged fat American trying to get to base camp of K2 to raise money for his kid's diabetes medicine. You are going to need a guide."

He had all three of his audience wanting to hear more, these were powerful Europeans, in their homeland there was nothing they couldn't do or buy. Poking fun at the Americans certainly got them on side. The tall, broad-shouldered MD spoke first with a slight hint of an Eastern European accent, his English was fluent and flowed well.

"For how long have you had this office here in the capital?" he asked. Brad smiled and looked at him with a self-assuredness that showed.

"You're worried that we followed the gold rush I see; that we were opportunists cashing in like many other global enterprises. Well Mr Van de Berg, we were here long before the oil began to flow, we are part of the bricks and mortar which built this land. We put the weapons in the Iraqi's hands and showed them where to shoot, and when to shoot. We were part of the ground team that steered this region away from communism and into the waiting arms of glorious democracy. We pioneered this Wild West and by joining us, we can help you find 'gold in them thar hills'. Go it alone and I don't like your chances."

This last comment hung in the air like a bad taste or bad smell, neither one of the guests could decide, but one thing they would all agree on later back at the hotel was that it was a threat. It was delivered while looking directly into the eyes of the MD and It was followed by a show of Brad's pearly whites in a gentle smile, but his eyes had lost that friendly charm and it was certainly a threatening remark that would hang in the minds of all three of them.

At this point one of the double doors that sat about halfway down the table, leading to the rest of the Control Risk offices, opened and in walked Brad's secretary. Natural light followed her crept through the door into the room that was shut out from the sun with drawn, block out blinds.

All four men turned to see who or what, had interrupted the presentation, and without speaking the blond-haired secretary floated down the side of the table and towards them.

"Gentleman, you have met Mia my secretary?" he half asked and introduced in one sentence.

They all nodded and mumbled in agreement; they had met her when she had bought them cold drinks when they first arrived. She nodded politely, though didn't say anything, and continued through the board room until she was lit up a little by the glow of the television. Avoiding looking directly at Brad, she handed him a note, nodded submissively, and turned to walk away.

With the note in his hand, unopened, Brad grabbed her arm, spinning her back around to face his guests.

"Mia and her counterparts in this organisation can be *very,* accommodating of our guests needs while they are so far from home," he said, without mincing his words.

"You are at the Babylon isn't that right Cornelius?"

Cornelius nodded, not sure if he was offended by what he was seeing or excited. This was The Wild Wes, after all. The other two men looked at each other, unsure of how to react. Mia did her best to smile at each of the men, and Brad nudged her away allowing her to float back towards the door, and back to her duties.

"You might be far from your wives and family, but this doesn't have to be a lonely city." Brad commented while unfolding the note in his hands.

A moment of silence followed as he ignored his guests to read, and once he was done, he folded it back up and placed it in the inside pocket of his jacket, smiling at all three of them. This one was his genuine friendly grin. It was amazing how he could jump from one to another so seamlessly.

"Gents, I am afraid something urgent has come up and I need to leave. If you wait here, I will send for a limo, Kirby will take you back to the hotel. From there you can spend the rest of the afternoon doing as you wish, and we can continue this in the morning, just let him know what you desire, and the city will provide."

With that, Brad left without another word and walked out of the double doors after ripping them both open, letting the light flood in.

Cornelius Van de Berg, Dave Smith, and Mark Bakker of VDB Gas and Oil weren't sure what had just happened, they kind of looked at each other in a stunned silence. One thing was for sure, they weren't in Europe anymore, it was time to go shopping for some spurs, and a Smith & Western.

Brad pressed his weight into thick wooden doors that were guarded on both sides, by seven-foot-high alligators, standing to attention on their hind legs, their tails curled up behind them. They had been stuffed with their snouts tightly shut but each of them had their front right leg extended and their thick scaly fingers wrapped around a spear that stood from the ground to be level with their eyes. The doors swung open, and Brad marched in quickly followed by Mia who spun immediately to close the doors behind him. He was agitated and strode with purpose, like a man on a mission into the room.

Though this room was smaller than the board room he had come from, it had similar decor. Orbs of light hung from the ceiling on gold chain and once again, the wood was dark, thick and very old. Old leather-bound books lined the walls, and through the open window the desert air hung over the Baghdad skyline, causing the white buildings and spherical rooftops to shimmer through the dust and heat.

Brad leaned on his hands at one end of the table and looked out of the window, his shoulders were tense, and his face focussed in its glare. Mia pressed a button on the wall and a thick black out curtain began to fall, a gentle hum of its electric motor was the only sound in the room. This was immediately followed by a thick maroon fabric that looked as heavy and rich as the rug in the main board room.

Brad continued to look directly ahead, as the windows got smaller and smaller, and the Baghdad skyline disappeared into a memory. He hadn't moved once since settling on the end of the table, yet behind him, Mia frantically prepared a glass of scotch with 3 large ice cubes, she looked nervous. She placed the glass next to Brad's right hand just as the curtain reached the bottom of its descent. A crystal glass, it was half full, straight up and battled with the books to be the dominant smell in the room.

As the curtains were lowered, the lights on the globes began to glow brighter, as if they knew it was their time to shine, but now the light in the room was a different colour, and then, the bright scene filled with brilliant white light when Brad had entered, had become a darker, more ominous room, where golden light cast shadows across Brad's face. He stood straight, taking his hands from the table and took a deep breath. Behind him Mia stood waiting.

He reached down to grab his glass of Johnny Walker Blue, and in one slow swig, it was empty. Half a mouthful lingered for a few seconds before he tilted his head back to let it fall down his throat, at the same time, depositing the condensation lined crystal whisky glass back onto the table without looking. Mia appeared, as it touched the expensive dark wood, to replace it with his sipping glass, then again retreated behind him. A couple of seconds passed in complete silence before he levelled his head, looked around the table, then placed his thumb onto a golden, decorative circle, embedded in the dark oak.

It shimmered from top to bottom, scanning his thumb print. Once it was done, on each side of the table and at the opposite end, 5 plasma screens rose out of the table, framed in the same dark oak that Brads' fresh glass of whiskey sweated onto by his side. They stopped once they were around five inches from the tabletop, held in place by golden arms that allowed them to turn like a head on a thin golden neck. Once they were at their peak, each one flicked to life and suddenly, five faces appeared. Each screen turned to their left, then their right before all five settled to face Brad. He took a sip of his drink, held it in front of him and nodded to his guests.

"Gentlemen," he gestured.

Each one nodded their heads, though didn't speak.

It was the screen at the opposite end of the table that spoke first. An American accent, though not strong like a Texan, certainly American born and bred. The other four turned to face it, and Brad sat on the opulent table chair that Mia pushed gently in as he sat, bringing his head in line with his five other guests' faces.

"I take it by now each of you has heard we believe we have found the next Heosphorus?" He let the question linger for a second, none of the screens nor Brad answered in time for him to then continue.
"We are waiting for verification, but he has been located in the US and by all accounts just had lunch with the Rephaim."

Brad's eyes widened at this, as the faces on the screens looked notably surprised, the screen to Brad's immediate left spoke first, in a perfect English accent.

"Are we sure? We spend the last decade trying to find the Him and we let him get close enough to have lunch with our Rephaim. What happened? Was there an attack?"

The screens and Brad all looked back to the screen at the end of the table expectantly.

"The pieces of the puzzle are just beginning to fall into place so I don't have all the answers yet. I have a conference call with our security teams here in America shortly where I expect to be briefed on the events. But it appears at this stage to be a chance encounter, it seems the Heosphorus was not even aware of what he was."

"Ridiculous," the screen closest to Brads right exclaimed. All the others turned to look at it as he continued.

"Less than a fortnight until the passing of Nibiru and The Heosphorus appears in such a way. I won't believe this is chance event. They have plan." This member of the table had a strong Israeli accent, with a deep rasping follow through. His screen turned to look directly at Brad.

"What is security in Baghdad now?" he demanded.

With that, all five screens turned to look at Brad. He was confident and self-assured as he gave his answer, looking from screen to screen as he spoke.

"The embassy has all the usual precautions in place as well as an extra squadron of US special forces scheduled to arrive next week. They are all soldiers from the Ducaz program and are led by none other than Ang and Set, two of the last remaining, actual Ducaz. The whole unit has been ready for months now. Their senses are like that of an alligator and their strength matches that of any of our pure Ducaz bloodline. They feel no pain and have a heightened aggressiveness which means we have had to evacuate all other personnel from C block during their stay."

Noises and nods of approval came from each of the screens, other than the Israeli, that spoke before.

"This won't be enough; they will come with everything." he said

"Which is why," Brad answered

89

"Each of the subterranean entrances to the complex have movement sensors that cannot be bypassed, or fooled, and all the subterranean tunnels will be patrolled around the clock by pure blood Ducaz and their units."

"But.." the Israeli tried to interject, though Brad spoke over him, cutting him off.

"The Soteria is contained within the old Roman baths deep underground, behind twenty-four of inches solid concrete which can only be entered from above through a staircase whose entrance sits directly under the Eisenhower Mansion."

"But why have we not just destroyed the chamber?" This time the Israeli punched his question through.

Before Brad was able to answer, the American at the head of the table, again spoke, causing the faces on the screens to turn in his direction.

"We have survived on this planet for thousands of years because we ensure we have contingencies, covering our contingencies. In the past we have used Soteria, one day we may need to activate Soteria again. We just need to ensure it is only the Anunnaki that controls it."

The comment hung for a second, then once again Brad spoke and the screens turned back to him.

"Gentleman, I have been tasked with ensuring the hall around the key to Soteria is the most secure location on our planet," Brad again sipped his whiskey and let this comment settle.

"I have at my disposal unlimited resources and the greatest minds on the planet. It would be easier for a black, armed American with an IQ of 70 to sit in the president's chair in the oval office, than it is for anyone to set foot in the room to activate Soteria."

The room was quiet for a second, each of the men seemed to be contemplating Brad's pitch. Eventually, the screen furthest from Brad on the left spoke.

"Brad, I don't think any of us here in the room doubt your team's ability to keep the device secure." As Brad went to speak over the voice of the American, he was forcefully cut off as the calm, and considered voice turned into one of power and certainty.

"But, none of the people in the room, here today, rose to lead their respective tribes by underestimating the Heosphorus and their blood descendants. If you remember our history, during the last rising we were lucky and we have waited close to 2500 years for this opportunity. We cannot wait another 2500 years to cleanse the Heosphorus and human blood from this planet. By then they will be too strong, too many and we will be the ones in hiding."

"What do you suggest then Soros?" asked the screen that started the meeting, and was at the head opposite Brad.

The response was so matter of fact, so simple to the man providing it. It was as easy to say as "go swat that fly."

"Nuke Baghdad."

Brad could not conceal his surprise, he looked around at the other screens searching for an ally against this act, though each man seemed to be pondering the idea. The contemplation only lasted a few seconds before the screen belonging to the man known as Soros spoke again. It was time to drive home his plan.

"We will certainly not be needing the chamber during this period of Rising. I am impressed by what Brad and his team have done, but I want to be certain the Heosphorus cannot do anything to stop the effects of Nibiru this time and the only way to be 100% certain, as opposed to 99% is to ensure no one can get within miles of the Embassy for the next few years. A ten-kiloton nuclear blast at approx. two thousand feet would do the job and ensure our success."

"I cannot fault the logic," chimed the Israeli.

The screen to Brad's immediate left turned to look at the head of the table.

"Hunter, you spoke about contingencies on contingencies, this will surely negate the need for any further planning and security issues. I and the rest of the Emim would sleep better knowing that Baghdad with Soteria at its centre was a radioactive wasteland."

The screen at the head of the table, referred to as Hunter turned to its left and spoke to the only screen to not yet speak.

"Charles, as the head of the Gibborim you have not given us your opinion today. Where do you stand on this.?'

The response was very slow and deliberate in its speech. The strong English accent was similar to the voice of the other English member of this group. Royal in its nasal delivery and deliberate, slow patterns.

"Today's events,' he started.
"Are indeed very troubling. The Gibborim have too waited 2500 years to take back what is ours. The Heosphorus blood coursing through the Muslim veins is going to overwhelm us unless we

remove them from this planet. What's worse is that we are greatly outnumbered. Our only advantage is the knowledge of who we are and what we can do." he paused for a second and the table waited.

"I agree we cannot have any room for failure, our very existence depends on success, but burning the land, sky and sand, whilst destroying something so beautiful all in the name of certainty is just like the Anakin." His screen looked directly across the table as he spoke to Soros.

"The Gibborim's projections are that The Passing will leave most manmade structures standing, except for the weather patterns which we are still working on. But personally, I would rather not destroy a city that's over 5000 years old, just for some shock and awe."

"You're willing to risk failure for a few sandstone buildings in the middle of the desert." Soros spat back.

"That's the problem with you Americans George, you have no respect for history. It's all about the next meal." Intelligence and provocation lined every word from the posh English lips as he spoke.

"Damn right. It's about our future. It's about your future. It's about the future of every tribe represented today. If you have a problem with how things are run then you have every opportunity to …."

"Gentleman, please." Brad had risen from his chair and stood with his arms raised trying to calm the debate going on at the end of the table. All five screens turned to look his way.

"I may have a compromise if you will permit me." He received a nod from the screen at the other end of the table.

"We have been working with the Israeli Mossad to develop a small scale, nuclear dirty bomb triggered by an EMP. Depending on the size it will irradiate an area up to eighty square miles, wipe out all electronic devices within twenty five miles and likely kill 90% of the population but keep Baghdad in all its historic glory.

We will be able to maintain our position at the Embassy with the pureblood Ducaz and Commander Vos's units on hand. The Ducaz blood will render our units relatively unscathed by the radiation but anyone trying to enter Baghdad will be dead within a matter of hours. Not giving them enough time to make it to the chamber.

The radiation kill zone and window, depending on wind direction and strength should last 50-100 days. Meaning we can set off the device in the next week, and keep the area safe right up until the arrival of Nibiru."

Brad looked directly at Soros's screen. "Mr Soros, would this be sufficient?"

The face on the screen pursed his lips while thinking about Brad's plan, then nodded, speaking while he did so.

"The Anakin will be happy with this solution."

Brad then turned to the screen opposite Soros. The English voice that was against the nuclear bomb.

"Your Highness. Can the Gibborim agree to this course of action?"

"I still feel it is excessive, but given what is to come, there is nothing to lose. We will support his move, but we have Anunnaki in Baghdad that we will be removing prior." His screen turned to face Soros.

"If this goes wrong in any way Soros, the Gibborim will remove our support for you and The Bidens as Rephaim post Rising."

Brad took over again, this time looking at the Israelis screen. "President Herzog? The Avim?"

"Agreed." Came the simple answer.

Brad looked at the screen to his immediate left. "Baron Rothschild? The Emim?"

Jacob Rothschild rubbed his grey beard with his hand, before speaking. "The Emim are happy to see such decisions that ensure our success. We will support it with the media campaign. Brad, expect contact from our team regarding the leaking of the story both in the build up to, and the aftermath of, the attack."

He turned his screen to address the table. "I assume we are all thinking ISIS?"

"We didn't create them just for fun." Hunter joked from his position at the head.

"So you agree as well Hunter?" Brad asked looking to the screen opposite him.

"I would have been happy to nuke the damn place. But I like this compromise. Just make sure Brad you don't fuck this up. Too much is riding on you and your team getting this right."

"So it's agreed." Brad said picking up his glass with a mouthful of whiskey left and presenting it to the room.

"Esto Perpetua"

All five men on the screens, repeated after Brad and turned to look at the screen at the end of the table, Hunter Biden was on the screen and delivered his closing statement.

"Word will be sent once I have my meeting with the security teams and we have verification on the Heosphorus. Make your final preparations for hibernation and I have no doubt he will need to speak to all of you before our meeting post Nibiru. We are all busy men so let's leave it here. Brad, you will make arrangements as discussed. Nothing is to be left to chance and for those I don't speak to beforehand. See you on the other side." With that his screen went blank.

The other four screens blinked out one by one, until it was just Brad in the room with Mia standing behind him. Looking down at the floor, as if she was unaware of what was said in the meeting.

Brad placed his thumb on the golden circle again, and the screens began their descent into the table. He waved his hand in the air, signalling Mia, she flicked a switch, and the small electrical motor in the curtains began to whir turning the light in the room back to white from yellow. Brad watched the Baghdad skyline slowly appear, and shook his head slowly.

"Time to get dirty" he thought.

Chapter 8

Starters Orders

Lugano - Switzerland
27/02/2022
5 :41pm

The flood lights cut a brilliant white glare through the crisp, clean Swiss air that swept down the tree lined hills all around the tennis court. A mixture of Sweet Chestnut, European Larch, and Kaffir Lime filled the air with their sweet scent. The sound of insects, birds and the gentle hum of crickets provided a curtain of noise to frame the tennis lesson, the young prodigy Jane Emmerson, was having with her favourite instructor. 13 years old, already 6 foot tall and with a thin build, no one could believe the Thor like power she had behind each of her well-crafted shots, or the Hermes like speed with which she covered the court at times. It was like the ball and her opponent were moving in slow motion, as she darted around.

Right now, she was working on her serve and reached into a basket of bright yellow tennis balls before returning to the line. She bounced the ball on the ground out of her left hand three times before looking over the net and zoning in on the exact spot in the service box she was aiming for. She rocked back and forth from her heel to the ball of her feet before she tossed the ball effortlessly into the air above her head. Her right hand swung her racket in a slow arc behind her head, her long legs pushed her into the air. Her arm came through in a blur, with all the power she could muster, and exploded through the ball sending it crashing through the air at a cool 125mph. It caught the centre line perfectly as her eyes watched it all the way during her follow through.

It was a serve that most of the men on the pro circuit would have been proud of, as most would struggle to return. Her coach on the other hand, pirouetted across from her, starting position in the middle of the box doing a full 360 and casually caught it in her left hand. Her white tennis skirt flared as she spun, and her long blond hair tossed with the momentum, and landed across her face before falling back to frame her and reveal cheekbones you could sharpen a knife on. She tossed it a few inches into the air while looking at Jane and nodding.

"Good. Again," she said loudly, in a soft Russian accent, then tossed the ball into the fence behind her.

Jane smiled as she turned to pick another ball from the basket, she didn't know how Kira did what she did. When she played in the adult super league across Switzerland, shots like that hit nothing except air, and drew murmurs from those watching.

Jane grunted loudly as she struck the next one, getting it up to 127mph, attempting to get it passed her coach, yet it snapped into the white tape at the top of the net. She exhaled disappointed with herself.

"It's ok Janooska" Kira called from the other side of the net.

"Just keep your head level, you dropped a couple of centimetres to your left that time."

Kira used her right hand to pull the hair from her fringe over and out of her face revealing a tightly shaved Viking cut, hidden by her long locks, and waited for the next bullet to come her way. This was a great way for her to stay sharp as well.

Both were dressed in upmarket, white tennis attire: expensive trainers, thick cotton socks, bicycle shorts under a plaid tennis skirt and a singlet made of the latest breathable material. The only noticeable difference between them was the Nike, Black headband Jane wore. It stopped the sweat from dripping into her eyes and tucked neatly under her tightly pulled ponytail.

The sound of the next serve echoed off the trees around them, and yet again, snapped into the tape, Jane looked at Kira questioningly. Kira animatedly put her hands to the side of her head to try to mime keeping it level. The Viking cut was now visible on both sides, shaven around her ears and the sides with long flowing blonde hair at the middle, that when down hid what was underneath.

Behind Kira there was a line of yellow at the foot of the fence which contrasted brilliantly with the bright blue of the court. They had been going for close to 40 minutes and Jane had already unleashed a full basket into the backhand side, there was only another ten to the forehand before they switched it up and worked on her booming backhand down the line.

The next ball skimmed over the net, landed plum on the line to Kira's left and once again she caught it cleanly in her left hand, this time without the theatrics. She raised her right hand to Jane with her palm to her, indicating she should wait, tossed the ball behind her into the fence, and looked past Jane to the gravel road behind the court. She could hear the scratching of tyres on the loose stones as two beams of light approached.

Kira recognised the black Range Rover that was pulling up as belonging to her boss Desta Toure and the smaller Toyota Hilux ute as that of Edmund, the young English boy that lived and trained with them. If he was here during a lesson, chances are she was needed. She indicated to Jane that she should continue and walked over to the small hut that housed the changing rooms and massage table for the players.

Kira walked through the courtside door and in walked her boss. He was a tall thin man of African descent, in his early sixties though, was athletic and fit which we always hid with a frail walk and posture. He had well-groomed grey hair which was tightly curled like a short afro and a little shorter was his grey beard which covered the lower half of his face with the same tight curls. Every hair looked perfectly in place when he offered a wide and inviting smile as he walked through the door. As always, he wore his perfectly tailored suit and his white button up shirt, an interesting dress choice as it was crisp enough for a white scarf around his neck.

"Evening Kira," he offered, his voice, smooth as a melted chocolate.

"Is everything ok Desta?" she asked, showing her concern for this visit.

Desta walked over to her and she went to meet him halfway, he placed his hands on each of her shoulders and kissed her on both cheeks.

"Everything is fine Kira, but we have a situation in the US that needs our immediate attention," he said, looking her in the eye.

He took two steps back and perched himself on the massage table ready for Kira's trademark inquisition and resistance.

"Can't it wait, I am in the middle of a lesson right now." Her sentence finished as the air carried the sound of the ball spearing off of Jane's racket, followed by the rattle of the fence at the other end.

"We have found him, Kira." Her eyes lit up.

"Well, more specifically, *They* have found him. Somewhere in New York during the past 24 hours, but they don't have him which means the race is on."

"Then let's go," she replied as she began to march past him to the roadside exit. Desta laughed his soft, gentle laugh and pointed back passed Kira, to the court.

"I think maybe you should get your student home first, I have brought Edmund with me to drive her home."
"Oh, yes." Kira replied, refocusing on the present rather than the future.

She walked over to the edge of the court; the sound of her Russian accent carried through the air as she practically barked at Jane.

"Jane, lesson is over. Edmund will drive you home now." Jane looked back questioningly and shrugged her shoulders as if looking for a reason.

"What, you want hug? I have to go save world." She turned to look at Desta who was still leaning against the massage table with his hands in his lap.

"Ok, now we go." she demanded, as she walked past him and out of the door.

Desta smiled and shook his head, her bluntness never ceased to amaze him, and was one of the reasons she was one of his favourites.

She marched out of the door and looked over at Edmund who was casually standing next to his Ute. He waved and said 'hi', Kira reminded him that Jane was only 14 and walked over to the Range Rover that still had its engine humming. In the driver's seat was the giant member of the team known as Simeon. Neither he nor the others knew his real name, this was the one he had chosen upon joining Desta's team over a decade ago.

She opened the back door and stepped up into the leather interior as classical music played. The interior lights reflected off the grey leather seats and caused the windows to become faint mirrors. Her mind was awash with a thousand simultaneous thoughts, broken by the deep resonance of Simeon speaking. He looked at the rear-view mirror as he spoke to her.

"Don't forget your seatbelt, Kira." He had a soft, simple accent, not from anywhere in particular. It was also so deep, you could feel his words as well as hear them. With the blackest, darkest skin, and at almost 8 feet tall, he was gawked at everywhere he went, though he knew people were thinking, no one had the courage to speak.

The door on the other side opened and in stepped Desta. With this, Simeon turned and smiled his beaming white smile, it contrasted so brilliantly with his brown skin that when the door closed and the interior light flicked off, his teeth were still almost glowing.

"Ok Simeon, take us back to the mansion,' Desta said as he clicked his seat belt into place.

"Yes boss, but I can't go till Kira has her belt on."
Hearing her name again snapped Kira out of her thought pattern.

"C'mon Kira, you know how serious Simeon is about road safety." Desta smiled and looked at Kira as he said this. They both knew it was less than a mile away, along this gravel road with no other cars, Kira also knew it was pointless to argue. She apologised to Simeon and buckled up. Once he was satisfied, he had heard the click, he reached down and popped it into drive making their way back to the mansion entrance.

During the three minutes it took to get back, Kira tried to quiz Desta on this development, though he refused to go into detail until the entire team was present.

Chapter 9

The Rephaim

Presidential Limo – Washington D.C
27/02/2022
10 :03am

The thin lips of Presidential chief of staff: Ron Klain, spoke as his prominent cheekbones cast shadows across his thin face. His sunken eyes stared defiantly at his President as their conversation continued to go downhill. His eyes flicked back and forth from their normal light blue to a golden yellow as he once again tried to convince his Rephaim that the situation was not as bad as it appeared.

"It is only a matter of time Sir. We have already located him, and we have men on route as we speak to ensure this goes no further."

He was leaning forward as he spoke, and gestured animatedly with his hands, something he always did when nervous. He stared at Biden, waiting for a response, not sure if he should speak again.

An orange light flicked through the tinted windows on either side of the cabin. Biden's face was drowned in shadow as he sat deep in his chair, looking deadpan at Ron, then a wave of orange light illuminated him for a second or two, before retreating from the cabin as if scared away by the tension within. Each time his face lit up, the President's eyes didn't look right, they were going pale and getting the yellow hint that pre-empted an explosion. Ron looked away from them for a second and took in the scales forming around the president's face. He flicked back to the president's eyes at the next pass of light and felt a chill as he looked straight into those bright yellow orbs with the black slit across the middle. The light disappeared and Biden spoke again, his milky smooth voice was quiet though still clear.

"We had him located and isolated before, and yet somehow he ended up naked on the floor of a subway train, naked and covered in blood, and yet still not in our hands. 8 of our finest hybrid Ducaz team were not able to bring him in but I am now to believe everything is ok because we know where he is? The most wanted man on the planet has placed his dirty, Heosphorus hands on my skin, has placed his hand in your Rephaim's hand and not one of you had any idea. I tell you Ron, I am not filled with confidence at this point."

Ron tried to speak again and plead his case, yet a calmly raised hand from Biden cut him off. There was a long silence, as the gentle hum of the tyres on the road, filled the cabin. Biden crossed his legs, pointing his toes in Ron's direction.

"The heads of all five tribes have already met and no doubt are making changes forced upon us by the ineptitude of you and your people, changes that divert us from our plan, and changes move us into the unknown. As you know Ron, I do not like the unknown. The certainty and stability I bring is why I was elected your Rephaim during this most crucial period."

Biden looked at his nails and let this comment hang for a second before continuing. He didn't look at Ron as he did.

"In three hours, I have a meeting with the head of the Emim tribe and I expect to be able to tell him that this issue has been dealt with. I expect to be able to tell The Rothschilds that our new friend has divulged everything he knows about us and his dirty friends and that we have nothing to worry about as we wait for the culmination of over 5000 years work."

He looked up from his nails as he delivered this last sentence. He looked directly at Ron then dropped his leg to the floor and leaned forward just as another wave of light flashed across the cabin. The demonic mixture of scales across his face and his egg yolk yellow eyes flared in the orange light and pushed Ron back into his chair.

"Let me be clear here Ron, that's one. If you make it to three, I am going to ensure that you spend the final days of the Passing front and centre on the surface of this God forsaken rock." Ron swallowed hard and sat back further as Biden leaned in closer still.

"I will ensure that your existence in this history is forgotten, forever, as your entire bloodline joins you during the final moments. You will have never existed." Ron nodded weakly and Biden slowly sat back into his chair and once again crossed his legs. Turning to look out of his window at the last moment.

"I am glad you understand what is at stake here."

"Yes Sir." Ron replied, obviously shaken.

With that, he reached into his pocket and pulled out his cell phone, and placed the first of half a dozen phone calls as they drove.

Chapter 10

Kaleidoscopic Haze

Metropoliton Hospital — New York
27/02/2022
3 :13pm

Theo hadn't been given a choice by the armed transport police that met him at the next station, they didn't carry guns like regular police officers, only the tasers they pointed at him which left little to the imagination of what would happen next. He had been arrested and taken to the local hospital to get cleaned up. He had pleaded the fourth thus far, and he lay in his hospital bed with two police officers outside the door. It wasn't ideal but he now felt safe, everything he had been through was playing through his mind as he rested.

His thoughts were a little sporadic and he was finding it hard to keep focus. He had dislocated his shoulder, perforated an eardrum, had to have pieces of glass removed from all over his body including from near his femoral artery meaning an hour in theatre and a general anaesthetic. Everything had gone smoothly, and he was in a post op recovery room by himself, overlooking the East River. He had awoken from the operation and had been given a large dose of Demerol to help with the pain. He was trying to stay awake, though kept drifting in and out of consciousness.

His breath became a little heavier as the drugs washed through the base of his spine and trickled through the back of his thighs, releasing the tension from his adrenaline filled muscles. His eyes flickered slightly as his mind took the moment to process everything, the only way it could. His whole body relaxed as images began to pass through his eyes in a kaleidoscopic haze like dream.

Like images in a flick book, they started slowly at first, allowing him to look, study and assess each frame from the selection he was being shown. It started with 'her'. She was staring right at him, he could see her so clearly, he wanted to reach out and touch her face. Her soft skin surrounding still blue eyes that had a hint of turquoise at the edges, as she stood on the train.

Then his mind was filled with the sight of his hand holding President's, the scales were appearing again causing his heart to beat faster as the president's, cold yellow eyes entered his dream, they blinked, closed from the sides and as they opened, they were replaced with the high beam lights of the Black Dodge van slamming into the side of his getaway vehicle earlier that night. As the van hit, he was thrown backwards across the car and his head snapped back into the window, hard.

He opened his eyes to him falling backwards from his fire escape. Bullets passed him in slow motion on either side, and he could see his towel, still fluttering in the soft breeze as it clung to the metal railing. Red Shoes on a table made him gasp. A white haze drifted up from the shoes and in it he could see the boy from the train, the student with the backpack. Then, an explosion engulfed him. Hot, red, and orange. Red Shoes again. Biden's eyes appeared with a high-pitched ringing.

He looked down at his hands in awe, they didn't feel like they were attached to his body. The ringing had gone and now it was like he was under water. The centre of his palms began to throb with a soft pain that grew in intensity. He fell to his knees, completely unaware of where he was, and cradled them as the agony grew. Small wounds began to form right where the pain was as the skin began to turn black. It was decaying and falling away to leave a hole that was growing outwards.

Eventually, Theo could see a white light shining through the small hole in the middle of his hand. The pain didn't stop, he tried to scream yet nothing came out. He drew all his energy into one giant breath, pushing as hard as he could, every muscle in his core pulsed, tossing his head back as he screamed in agony. The scream left him as a blaze of hot white light shoot from his mouth. Then silence and no pain. He was staring at himself, his feet were bound, and had his arms, outstretched on a large wooden cross. He was battered, bruised, burned and almost dead. He began to walk towards the gruesome sight of his own corpse, getting closer while looking intently at his own dead face. Suddenly, bright white eyes opened and stared directly at him, and Theo woke from his dream.

His temples throbbed and a foggy headache prodded at the back of his head. He was still groggy from the Demerol as the light from the room began to take shape through heavy eyes. A warm orange sunbeam cut through the window that took up half the wall on the room's riverside. His bed lay along the left wall, centred and pointing into the room, allowing access to both sides. The bed was big and heavy with a thick mattress, and sheets, hemmed in both sides by anti-roll bars. Given the circumstances, it was quite fitting for a deranged nut job that runs through the tube in the nude.

Since he had been picked up, he had been taken straight to the hospital a couple of blocks over, and with no ID, and no conversations thus far, the cops had no idea who he was or what he was doing being chased and shot at through the underground station. They had reports of a SWAT style team chewing through the city, firing automatic weapons at will, and causing all manner of accidents. Vehicles had been left burning in the middle of one of the busiest cities, and thus far, the footage circulating on some of the news channels, and YouTube, showed a war zone unfolding and some crazy camera flares on one guy's eyes.

Every trace of the armed soldiers or SWAT team had disappeared, and the cops were keen to know what was happening in their city. The decision was made to take Theo to the hospital where he had required surgery on a deep wound on the inside of his thigh. Once he was cleared by the doctors, he would be straight down to the station to answer about a thousand questions that half of New York was also asking.

He looked at his left arm, it had the usual array of small tubes and valves to allow the bag of saline, and fierce antibiotics to drip slowly into his bloodstream. His lips smacked together, and the roof of his mouth felt dry and dusty. He tensed his core, as if to sit, yet struggled to will his body and the best he could muster was to raise his right arm about six inches, before letting it fall. He sighed a little in frustration and decided to at least be thankful for the amazing richness of the light from the vibrant afternoon sun that was now booming through, reflecting off the white hospital walls.

The door opened, and Theo's gaze rolled to his right to see the young nurse walking in. Both the cops at the door to his room had stood as she approached, and one had turned to stand in the doorway after she entered to keep an eye on her and Theo. Their prisoner did not appear dangerous thus far, though it would be foolish not to be cautious.

She came over to Theo's bed, pulled up the clipboard from its plastic sleeve that was draped over his bed, near his feet and took a quick look. Through his heavy eyes, he observed her silently, watching the light from the sun cast across her pretty face as she studied his notes. She looked up at her patient and could see his eyes blinking as he looked at her.

"Afternoon Mr Doe." She said with a smile
"Surprised to see you awake so soon after your op."

Theo tried to reply yet it came out more like a loud exhale of breath. Although his mind was alert, his body needed more rest.

She placed the wooden clip board down, face up on the bed and walked round to the drip hanging from the frame on the left of Theo's head. His eyes followed her, and his head slowly rolled over to watch her check the valve controlling the flow, she seemed happy with the current levels. She looked at Theo and placed her hand on his forehead, an old habit that she picked up from her mother. Afterall, his heart rate, blood pressure, and temperature were all displayed on the small LED screen next to her. She felt it always provided a personal connection and believed it helped her patients feel the warmth of a maternal touch.

She looked into his eyes, and with her hand still on his head muttered, "I hear you've been a naughty boy." She moved her hand as if gently wiping his brow and looked him dead in the eye.

"You'd better behave in here though if you want us to help you get better." Theo tried to nod, it was a failure, yet he did enough to appease his Carer. She gently slapped his cheek as she stayed bent over him to declare he was going to be fine in a couple of days.

She stood and turned to pick up the clipboard again and reached into her breast pocket to pull out her little silver pen. She clicked the end and scribbled a few numbers down before placing it back into the plastic sleeve and turning to walk out.

"See you in four hours Mr Doe," she declared, turning to look over her shoulder.

The door to the room was at the opposite side to the bed, and as she left, the officer that had remained standing stepped inside and walked over to Theo's bed. He too, was bathed in warm, orange light as he stood looking Theo over. Then, whatever thought he must have had, passed and he turned and took a couple of steps to the window to gaze out at a glorious afternoon across New York City. In front of him, was the wide bay where the Harlem and East Rivers meet and water was as still as ice, reflecting the orange sky as the sun hovered alone without a cloud. Mill Rock stood proudly right amongst it in the middle of the conflux like a blister on this perfect surface.

He leaned in to look at the source of a thudding sound out over the East River to his right. Theo had heard it as well and, gradually opened his eyes to look over at the officer. Outside, he could see a couple of army helicopters, obviously on a training exercise, flying low up on the opposite side of Roosevelt Island. They were low enough that he kept losing them behind the structures blocking his view of that stretch of the water. They looked quite menacing as they appeared, disappeared, then reappeared again. Both were jet black, which did strike the officer as unusual, and he rested his arm on the window above his head as he readied to watch them burst into the bay in front of him. And appear they did.

It looked like nothing Spence had seen before. They swept past the grassy point of Lighthouse Park, and suddenly they were fully exposed, and a lot lower than the officer had thought. Barely fifteen feet from the surface of the water, they came out together, side by side with a flurry of noise, power and a dazzling display of waterspouts that spun up from the river below them. Officer Spence chuckled to himself and nodded, he was impressed, thinking: 'if only I had my phone to get a video.' They glided across the still water of the bay, turning as they did towards the hospital and the window Spence was standing in front of.

Behind him, Theo's eyes were wide open with the familiar white glow that made it seem his eye sockets were completely empty. He laid flat on his back looking directly up at the ceiling, stiff and rigid. His heart rate on the monitor was climbing each measure; quickly rising from in the seventies to well over a hundred in no time at all. Theo felt his body coming to life; starting with his hands and feet, and quickly spreading down his spine, like someone had injected pure adrenaline into his core. It spread through his body like a ripple on a pond, moving outwards, hitting his chest, activating as he sat bolt upright on the bed breathing in like he was emerging from a deep dive in the ocean. With a clear mind, and an amazing energy coursing through every sinew of muscle, he looked directly out the window past the police officer, at whatever was coming.

Spence hadn't noticed Theo behind him. He was still fascinated by these two helicopters, which had completely banked around, and continued directly towards him. Within seconds, the larger of the two choppers, a European Augusta Westland Troop carrier, broke off the current path and sharply rose exposing its belly to the now mesmerised spectator. The other slowed its forward momentum and slowly began to climb towards the sky above the hospital. As it climbed it slowed further until within seconds it was settled no more than fifty feet from the window of Theos hospital room.

Like a moth staring into a flame, Officer Spence stood hypnotised, his only movement was to lean back from the window and stand with a puzzled look on his face. He was staring directly at two men, sitting one in front of the other in the cockpit of one of the world's most deadly attack choppers. They were staring directly back, though the helmets and dark visors gave nothing away. The sun was sitting directly behind the chopper, illuminating it. In the street below, there was already a commotion as this chopper hovered level with the third-floor window, directly over the gusty road beneath.

Theo couldn't see the chopper from the bed, he saw the shadow sweep in across the room and stop. An ominous dusk replaced the orange glow, as the roar of two Augusta A129 Rolls Royce, engines sounded off. Officer Spence broke his spell for a second and looked over his left shoulder at Theo, and this was just as shocking as the fully armed attack chopper hovering fifty feet away from him. He was ripping the IV's out of his arm, though it was the eyes. He looked like the demons he imagined all those years ago at Sunday school. It took him a second, then instinctively, he turned to stop whatever this was, from getting out of his bed. It was like the chopper disappeared for a second.

All this had happened so quickly the officer outside the room had only just opened the door to see what the noise was, and as he did, the pilot of the Italian built killing machine pressed down on the small red button in his right hand. The centre mounted M197 three-barrel Gatlin cannon spun to life and white-hot metal 2cm wide and 5cm long exploded forth with overwhelming force and an impact that ripped into the side of the building and into the room. The door handle was still in his hand as the window and officer Spence both exploded in unison in front of him.

The window and everything behind it for about twenty feet became a blur of colour, heat, noise and energy as wave after wave of giant bullets ripped through the space. In front of Theo, it all seemed to fall apart into a thousand pieces, and then burst into the air like confetti. With the outside wall and window gone, the ferocious wind from the rotors and roar from outside followed like a concussion wave from a bomb, further adding to the kaleidoscopic chaos.

Before the pilot had played executioner, Theo had rolled off the right side of his bed onto the floor, away from the window. From there, he could see the carnage unfolding directly between him and the door on the opposite side of the room. He saw the first shell en-route before it had broken through the glass. He saw it break through with a white-hot point, shattering the glass the second it touched but punching a thick hole that left a wake of nothing as it continued through and passed through the cop at the window as if he wasn't there.

The second, third, and fourth shells all appeared immediately, smashing their own holes in the already falling glass. Each one had a tail of energy warping the air around it, as Theo watched them on their relentless path of destruction. Soon he could barely see through all the debris floating around him, and despite the fact his world was moving so slowly that he could see each metal fist advancing at about the average jogging pace of an adult male. He was trapped.

He couldn't make it across the room to the door, it would be like jumping into a giant metal blender with your fingers crossed and the huge hole the deluge of bullets was creating, well, was full of bullets and death. His mind raced to come up with something.

Something above them all, from the roof of the hospital suddenly flared. Theo couldn't hear it above the cacophony of noise in his room, yet the pilot heard it and so had his co-pilot. Worse still his co-pilot had seen the source and opened his mouth to shout and yanked hard right on the stick in front of him. He didn't get to finish his warning and the yoke of the chopper haven't even moved when the world around him turned into a bright white, fiery hot inferno.

Down on the street, most people had already run away as far as they could. A brave few couldn't look away, as they reeled in horror when the chopper had opened fire. Now, this white finger of smoke had weaved drunkenly from the roof top, right into the glass protecting the pilot at the front. The chopper nodded forward like a dog that's been tapped on the nose before instantly bursting into a giant fireball, followed by a thousand deadly pieces of flying metal and hot liquid.

A wave of heat and flames from the exploding missile slammed the already wounded building in front of it and the room shook violently before the walls themselves exploded inwards under the onslaught from outside. Theo had pulled the bed over with the metal wheels up in the air so it was now laying on top of him, the final explosion collapsed the outside wall and he became pinned under the bricks and dust.

The room around him had gone from a tranquil place of healing to a horror movie scene. As the dust settled, from his position under the bed Theo was finally able to look around. After a quick examination he was able to view the gruesome nightmare the officers experienced just before their death, the officer originally standing at the window was lying on the ground, his chest looked as if someone had taken out his organs, blended them and put them back. Lucky for him he got a quick, the second officer that had entered the room as the chopper began firing hadn't been so lucky. Like stapling two pieces of paper together one of the chopper blades had pierced his gut and stuck him to the wall, with a painful groan, Theo realised he was still alive, slowly losing his light.

Down on the street it was bedlam as the main chassis of the chopper remained intact and spun wildly, in a ball of flames towards the ground. Its entire nose section containing the two pilots had exploded towards the building and up through the rotor blades, lifting them clean off the top. Those that remained, ran for their lives, except for that one person, stood there filming it on their phone. They were watching in awe, not looking ahead, but at their small screen and what it was capturing. By the time they realised it was coming straight for them, there was no time to run.

Up on the roof, it was a lot calmer. The second and larger chopper was in the process of landing on the large helipad up there for the Emergency Helivac Patients. Its massive crest of metal blades was fifty-five feet across, slicing through the air, slowly lowering the large metal carcass down onto a huge white H. The slick black wheels kissed the tarmac as they heard the explosion from the other chopper and as the suspension in the thick metal legs eased them to a full stop, a secondary explosion rang out and shook them and the building with the force of a small earthquake.

Inside there were a few looks between the passengers. They remained steely eyed, experience and wisdom showed in all their faces, they were right to be prepared. If they had just lost Falcon 1 then the Zeta must be here, and if the Zeta was here then that meant He was the Heosphorus.

Sitting along the benches, they reached down to grasp their Magnapulse, P90 replicas from their laps. The cutting-edge weapon was unlike anything available to the public. It was an exact copy of the shoulder-fired, personal defence weapon commissioned by the U.N for its peacekeeping missions, however it had been modified and used a battery to power an electro-magnet that was used to propel its specially designed rounds. As a result, it was a lot quieter, had almost no recoil which also meant it could fire its projectiles at a rate that could almost touch the bullet in front, if fired in a straight enough line. When the trigger was depressed in full auto mode, it was literally like a spear of bullets flying.

More importantly, for the eight men in the passenger section of the chopper, it meant you could fire a line of bullets while strafing, impossible to dodge, even by the Zeta and Heosphorus.

The suspension ceased the craft, the man nearest to the door grabbed the large white, and red handle. The modified sliding allowed him to open the entire left side of the chopper, aiding in a speedy exit for all on board. He looked across his unit around him, all were now standing in unison, as his hand left his side. He nodded once and with a defiant snarl, each man nodded back in unison.

Their skin was getting darker as they did, then the skin around each of their eyes went darker still, like a chameleon changing colour when on the hunt they all transformed in a matter of seconds. Small lines were appearing in the wrinkles and old skin around their eyes, they looked scaly as the afternoon sun reflected off them. Again, as a single organism, they all grunted loudly, their eyes glowed with a new yellow colour, washing away the white. One soldier blinked away some dust, yet something was different, and strange. Then another soldier blinked, and there it was, his eyes closed in from the sides, from the dark corners and met in the middle.

The big man at the door pulled down on the handle and let in the New York air. It was crisp and surprisingly clear and as he pushed it back along the side of the chopper, the gusts from the rotor roared into their world.

The leader at the door saw him the second the door opened. About 30 feet away on the edge of the roof overlooking the river was a man dressed all in black, including the balaclava over his head. He was standing, holding something on his right shoulder. Behind him, the smoke and flames from Falcon 1 could be seen rising into the air, behind the mask a cheeky smile appeared.

The cockpit lit up like a Christmas tree, and a loud warning sound filled the chopper. The pilot was shouting something to those in the back as the soldier at the door brought up his gun. He didn't even get to finish that thought. From the visitor's right shoulder, a large plume of smoke shrouded the green and yellow projectile as it flew low, straight across the roof of the Hospital towards its inevitable end. It entered the wide door that was anchored in place to expose the inside of the defenceless craft, it slinked like a snake and exploded right in the middle of the heavily trained soldiers.

It was unavoidable, viscous, and instant. As the blast wave rustled the clothes around him, the black clad soldier on the roof, stood like a golfer admiring his drive down the middle of the fairway. A secondary explosion ripped the already tattered chopper into hundreds of smoking hot metal shards that flew into the air. The man quickly lifted the Javelin surface to air missile from his shoulder, folded it into the shape of a large metal briefcase and made towards the door leading down to the emergency stairwell.

As he entered the door, Mina (Mark) Yakoub removed his hood with his free hand, he peeled it off, shaking his head to flick his hair into shape over his square and tanned face. Thick, perfectly shaped eyebrows sat neatly over his glowing white eyes and as he descended the stairs, he could hear the shock waves from the carnage he had caused outside as numerous explosions rumbled through the air and the walls around him.

Outside was pure carnage, and inside it was pure chaos. Theo had seen the blades from the helicopter fly into the room, witnessing, in horrifying detail, how it had pinned and eventually killed the second police officer. As he realised the worst of it may be over, the immediate noises in the room were now dominated by repeated detonations happening outside, all around them. Car horns blared up from the streets along with all manner of alarms from the hospital, and surrounding buildings.

Theo tried to shuffle his way clear of the bed, only to realise that his hips and legs were trapped between the heavy bed frame and the floor. The dust in the room made it hard to see, though a large support beam had fallen when the walls and accompanying vertical beam had been destroyed only minutes before. It sat across the back of his upturned bed and the thick frame had buckled under the weight, pinning Theo's bottom half so tightly he couldn't even feel his legs. There was no pain because the thick mattress and sheets were between the metal and the lower half of his body, but even as he tried with everything he had, there wasn't even an inch of movement.

A dusty haze of noise was all around him as he began to feel for something to grab hold of to try and pull himself free. He was face down, reliant on his shoulders, he was able to lift off the floor, his hands scrambled out in front of him, and his right hand found something metallic, cold, and solid. Though it wasn't attached to anything, it might work to help lever some of this weight from on top of him.

Though his ears were not ringing, the noises all around him were just as deafening as he dragged the thick metal pipe towards him. He had no idea where it had come from. Half of the walls and floor had fallen into the street below and there was debris all through the room, which may assist in his escape. He twisted the top half of his torso to the left, holding the metal pipe in both of his hands, almost like a kayaker holding their paddle. Then, dug the point under the bed frame and lifted the other end with his left arm, pushing up with an unusual chicken wing style motion. Though it was useless, he refused to give up, his left arm burnt as the lactic acid filled it, and his eyes glowed the brightest white they had ever done. Seconds became minutes around him, as he felt a strength flowing through him that he hadn't before. The pipe suddenly bent and became useless. Dejected, he fell onto folded arms in front of him. He needed a new plan.

"Ok Theo, pull it together,' he said, lifting his head yet again and keenly looking around the room. As if taking it in for the first time, the whole room looked different.

"How are you going to get out of this?" he asked slowly, his eyes scanning everything around him.

Every object held a clue, a plan, he just needed to find the right object. The noises around him seemed to dim to a background hum, as Theo thought of ways to get his legs free. The wall behind him, and the long one that used to contain the window were pretty much gone, and the scar from the wound went deep into the building. Of the four walls that were originally keeping Theo in, only one of them resembled what it did when he first was checked in.

To his right, there were more rooms, exposed now. Before this, he couldn't see them through the dust, though he heard screams of panic, and pain deep into the building. Theo always thought of himself as a good problem solver, yet as alarms blared all around him, his mind became panicked as his brain couldn't settle on anything that was going to get him clear. Theo knew this was no freak accident. Whoever was chasing him on the train, was here to finish the job, and these seemed to be the type to be very thorough.

He caught a whiff of burning rubber in the air, carried in on the smoke coming from the street below that was blanketing the side of the building. He looked sharply to his left, looking over his shoulder as he lay pressed against the floor, at what was left of the long glass window at the front wall of his room. Small pockets of light shone in, beaming through the dust. One of the beams suddenly darkened, as a shadow cast across it, Theo saw the small change out of the corner of his eye and looked back to where the door used to be.

Two figures cut through the smoke and dust, standing in the gaping hole, leading to the concrete emergency stairs they had just ascended. Theo's chest exploded, as a burst of adrenaline surged through his prone body and instinctively, he tried again to drag himself free... still useless. He was trapped and here they were, whoever they were, and he didn't like his chances. He thought he felt his legs move... nothing, he looked over to the two men. He could barely see their features, only that they were dressed in black and both wearing black hoods. Only one of the men had stepped fully into what used to be his hospital room, with the other standing a few feet behind, looking around and behind them occasionally.

The one inside the room removed his hood and Theo watched him carefully as he stepped further inside. He was scanning the carnage around him, he couldn't believe the amount of damage done in such a short space of time, and as he inspected the room, Theo saw the man's eyes for the first time, glowing through the haze in front of him. Theo's face took on the expression it did when he first saw two girls one cup, he couldn't understand what he was seeing. He went numb in disbelief. Then the eyes stopped scanning the room, because they were looking directly at Theo's lost expression from barely ten feet away.

"Simeon, come lift this beam from him." He raised his voice over the alarms, it was English with a hint of an African accent. Soft and warm, even though the shrill, wailing sounds in the room. He looked over his shoulder at the second man, as if to confirm his order, and stepped forward, dipping as he did to his haunches in front of the frightened, and confused captive. He had found what he was looking for and a content smile spread across his face. Theo laid prone on the floor, lifted his shoulders, and perched on his arm as he looked the dark-skinned stranger in the eyes. They were a soft, glowing white, that quickly dissolved into a rich dark brown iris with a jet-black centre.

"Are you here to kill me or save me, cos either way, I'll take it." Theo said with a defeated look and tone.

A baritone laugh rolled gently from the man, as he looked over to the other figure in black. He was a hulk of a man, adjusting his grip on the huge metal beam pressing Theo's bed against him.

He looked back down at Theo, as he extended his right arm to cup his left cheek in his hand.

"We are the good guy's Theo, and we are here to save you. So you can save us all."

As he smiled, his eyes began to glow white again and a warm tingle grew across Theo's cheek. It was like a smooth hit of dopamine pulsed gently through his body and peacefully without a single care, he fell into the first decent sleep he'd had in a while.

Chapter 11

The Vault

Forbidden Library – Vatican City
28/02/2022
8 :51am

C ardinal Pell's rounded shoulders rocked in time to his shuffling footsteps, as he walked along a stone tunnels. One of many that lead to the vast haul of treasures buried beneath the Vatican. Despite his half-smile, he had the usual look of concern, doubt, and confusion he had become famous for. He was well regarded in Vatican circles as one of the smartest men in the city, and his photographic memory was one of the reasons he was appointed as the youngest Keeper of Artifacts, in the Churches history. He had now been in the role for a long time and his earthly body was ageing, and under the weight of his genius, so was his mind.

As he shuffled deeper into the Vatican vaults, his lips continued to jolt with little ticks, and as was almost always the case when he was alone, he was mumbling something to himself, or to God, as others had speculated. His red zucchetto ticked left to right as he continued to waddle forward, the light from the candles on the walls reflected off his glasses, both the lenses and the frames. In the shadows of the flickering flames, a few beads of sweat were beginning to form on his forehead.

He cruised quickly down the long corridor, 300m lined with bookshelves, that lead to the main desk in the entrance. The massive circular desk behind him was receding, and as he marched forwards, the darkness in front of him sensed his arrival, and glowing orbs illuminated his path and the corridors of books.

At the very end of the tunnel, there was an already open, thick, wooden door, and as he approached, the lights behind him, in the main library hall, appeared to have gone. He stepped inside, the far end of the forbidden library and once again disappeared into darkness, not even visible from the desk near the main entrance.

Pell shuffled on, and after passing a couple of old wooden doors, cut back into the thick stone walls, he came to a T junction and without looking up, or even breaking his rhythm he cruised around to the left as his mumbling continued.

Ahead of him, at the end of this tunnel was a large wooden door, about twice the height of any man with was what looked like an Alligator statue, standing upright, in front of it. He kept shuffling forward, passing ornate torches that caused the light to dance around him and as he came closer to the door, what looked like the statue from the other end stood to attention and took a step to the left and turned to his right, to face the Cardinal as he passed.

The Ducaz was tall. At least eight feet when fully unfurled. It had a head almost exactly the same as a croc, but it bent at the neck like a snake and a long, muscular torso had evolved to allow the creature to stand using its two strong legs and short tail as a support. His arms were much more like that of a human, still covered in scales and about double the size, but they hung from the side and gave him complete flexibility. His hands were a genetic combination, he still had the nasty claws and thick scales, but they had developed an opposable thumb allowing them to hold weapons and operate machinery just like us. They had been built by the early Nephilim to act as their warriors and just like most humanoids they were made in a lab, splicing DNA from different parts of two or three species and experimenting with the results. If he wasn't such a terrifying concept, he would have looked almost comical in his Swiss Guard Uniform.

Pell swung a quick glance and a louder mumble in the direction of the Ducaz as a show of gratitude as he passed him and without doing a thing, the large wooden doors began to open together. Pell didn't miss a step and with a twitch down the right side of his face he crossed the door sill into the room. The Ducaz immediately took up his position in front of the opening and the thick wooden doors closed behind him with a click, and once again the tunnel was silent.

Inside Pell had now stopped and he wasn't mumbling anymore either. Every time he stepped into this room it was like all the madness and voices in his head silenced, at least for a second. He had stepped into a stone room, resembling a very small church vestibule. To the left and right, there were a couple of rows of very old wooden pews, leaving a small aisle down the middle that led to a wooden pulpit, draped in the colours of the Vatican. The ceilings were high enough to give the room an echo when you spoke, and a quiet hum of prayer bounced around now as Pell looked directly ahead at The Cross of Christ hanging proudly on the wall above the pulpit.

As one of the Church's greatest secrets, the Cross sat secured in this most holy of prayer rooms, deep within the Vatican tunnels and catacombs. Only the most trusted members of the church knew of its existence, and only a handful had seen it. As The Keeper of Artifacts, Cardinal Pell had spent the last two decades looking after this, and many other equally interesting Church treasures. This, though, was one of his personal favourites, not because of the history or story behind it, though rather how he felt when he looked at it.

"Cardinal Pell!" A chirpy voice cut through his concentration and the spell was broken.

A young bishop popped up from behind the pulpit, looking back at the cardinal with a big grin on his face.

"Bishop Maris." Pell replied. Lowering his gaze from the Cross to the fresh-faced monk.

Maris was only in his mid-twenties, had a very slim build with dark hair, and what would be a beard if he were able to grow one, rather it was a collection of whiskers across his chin and upper lip. His dark, thick eyebrows lifted as he asked.

"What brings you down here your eminence?"

Pell didn't answer as he began to shuffle forward.

"The plans for the move are on schedule. Your Eminence, my team will be here this afternoon, all the preparations are done."

Maris wasn't nervous as he spoke, even though Pell was a difficult man to communicate with.

Pell grunted several yeses as he nodded repeatedly, circling the pulpit, past Maris, and stood in front of the cross looking up. Several of Maris's tools were sprinkled on the floor, it appeared as though he had been doing some restoration work. There was a moment of silence while Pell looked up at The Cross, and Maris looked at Pell, it hung in the air for a moment before Maris tried again.

"Cardinal?" His question hung for another second before Pell turned to look him in the eye. As was always the case, Pell seemed to find clarity for a moment.

"Maris, wonderful work you and your team do, but the Cross will be remaining here. Please cancel the arrangements."

He turned back to the cross which stood proudly on the wall, illuminated by warm yellow lights pointing down at it from the ceiling. It didn't resemble any of the stories he had read, or heard, about the crucifixion of Christ, and it certainly didn't look like a standard crucifixion cross from the time. This wasn't just solid wood carved together, it was far more intricate. The wood itself formed the base of the structure; it was made of petrified wood that had been carbon dated to be close to 30,000 years old. The grain was thick, and clear and ran from top to bottom. Upon further inspection, there appeared to be a metallic element within, providing a shine to the wood, reflecting a green hue at certain angles.

At the base of the Cross, there was a structure made of metal that shone like black polished stone it was to stand on there was also a second piece on a hinge to enclose the feet. Up where the hands would be bound were similar metal structures, though this time it was moulded to fit a human hand with the clamp fitting around like a strap, that was retractable. The carving of the metal was flawless, the fixtures were technologically impossible for the time, and as the Keeper of Artifacts, Pell also knew about the carbon fibre tubes that ran from each of the metal fixtures, down through the centre of the cross to the metal base that formed the foot of the main wooden stem.

Most importantly, Pell knew what it all meant. He knew what the Cross was, what it was for and why the Church kept it. He also knew what it meant if it wasn't leaving which was why when he turned back to Maris, a tear was brewing in his left eye. Maris could see it. Though, he was a bit confused, it was best not to ask.

"As you wish Your Eminence," he said, looking down at the floor.

Pell paused for a second as if finishing a thought, then snapped his eye to the door, grunted his yesses again while nodding and passing Maris, he made his way back up the aisle and away from the Cross Of Christ, and the slightly confused young Bishop.

Chapter 12

Two Out Of Three

White House Rec Room
28/02/2022
7 :12pm

R on stood in front of the door to the president's gaming room and took a deep breath, as he exhaled, he brought his hand up and knocked twice before reaching for the handle and clicking open the door. As always, he wore an immaculate black suit, white shirt, and a blue and red tie with a silver tie pin across it. On his lapel, was the standard American flag, a badge of honour.

"Mr President," he announced as the door opened and he stepped inside.

Since taking office earlier in the year Biden had set up the 'Presidential retreat' within the White House, allowing him to relax with some of his favourite pastimes. Dozens of the President's favourite video arcade machines had been flown in to aid in his downtime. All along one wall were 6 red bucket racing seats, all linked to an individual screen, linking them together. Above them, on the way, was one giant screen which showed the race to any spectator. The screens were all on, showing live game footage, switching to leader boards as it advertised for more quarters.

The left wall had a basketball game, a booth to climb inside covered in Dinosaurs, and 3 different Time Crisis shooting booths. In the middle were an air hockey table and some sort of mechanical horse racing track where you could bet on the winner of each race before each of the horses shunted backwards, to line up and start again.

The air was thick, filled with cigar smoke, and the sound of various games announcing their place. A short fanfare came from the horse racing game, followed by the announcement of 'no more bets' as Ron walked through the room.

On the wall opposite the door, was a giant screen, in front of that was the President's favourite game. Tiger Woods Golf. This was his true sanctuary.

Here, he could come and get away from all the noise, and just focus on his thoughts. Plus, he could take part in 18 holes of golf at any course worth playing, right from the comfort of his thick leather armchairs.

President Biden was sitting in one of those chairs to the right of screen as Ray approached. Standing in front of the screen, holding a controller in his hand, and scrolling through club selection was the president's son, Hunter.

Hunter ignored their guest, as did the president, as he took a few greedy puffs on the thick Cigar he had imported from Cuba last month. Thick white smoke swirled around his lips, then out into the air in front of him as he savoured the taste.

Ron could hear the thwack of club on ball, signal a gentle applause from the game as he entered the golfing section, stepping down into the 'play zone' as the president dubbed it.

President Biden put his cigar in the ashtray on the small table to his right and turned his body to look at his Chief of Staff, while remaining seated. Hunter, having finished his shot, walked over, and sat in the chair to his father's right as the two men talked.

"I take it you have some news for me then Ron?" The president asked.

As he did, he placed his hands in front of him and touched each of the fingertips together and sat back in his chair, crossing his legs. His perfectly pressed navy-blue suit pants creased over his knee, and the crisp white of his shirt reflected the colours, and lights of the machines around them.

Hunter, wearing practically the same outfit as his father, picked up his cigar from the ashtray, and looked at Ron as he sparked the end, waiting for the response as well.

"Unfortunately, sir, I do. The extraction team was ambushed, and the target escaped." Ron looked down at the floor as he finished his statement, he couldn't look the president in the eye and tell him he had failed.

Biden stared blankly ahead, absorbing this new information, it was Hunter that chimed in first, letting out a small cough before struggling through his statement.

"You fucking what?"

Ron was about to answer when Biden held up his hand.

"Hold on son," he said with a quick glance to his right. Then back to Ron as he slowly lowered it.

"Ambushed? by who?" he asked, looking rather accusingly at Ron.

"We are still going over the data from the attack sir, I am hoping."

"Hope?" Biden cut in. "Fuck hope! And fuck the Data." The words hung in the air for a second as he reached over to pick up his cigar again.
"We both know who this was, and if they have him, then it is time to deploy the contingencies." He lit his cigar again.

His mind was deep in thought as all the connotations began to roll through one by one. Both men, either side of him dared not speak, they waited patiently before.

"Fuck!" The president exclaimed again, this time to himself. "Ok, convene a meeting with Control Risk immediately, I guess we're gonna have to get dirty."

With that, he stood whilst using his left hand to grab his small white controller. Ron was still looking at his leader, waiting for instructions.

"What the fuck are you waiting for, you want it in writing? go, get it done."

"Yes sir." Ron replied and turned to leave. Biden continued a few steps until he was front and centre of the giant screen. He stood in front of a picture-perfect replica of the 8th hole at Marilago, bringing his cigar up to his lips, pursing them around it, as he brough his hand down to form his golf grip.

Talking out the corner of his mouth as the cigar simmered, he left one final warning for his Chief of Staff.

"Oh, and Ron? He paused for a second, just long enough for Ron to turn and look again. Biden didn't even look back as he said it.
"That's two. you know what happens at three."

As the words left his lips, he swung hard, the sound of club striking ball peeked through the noise of the room once more. Ron knew what it meant and walked straight for the exit to set up an emergency meeting as instructed.

Chapter 13

White As Snow

Air Above Atlantic Ocean
28/02/2022
9 :42pm

The table in front of Desta, hummed at the same frequency as the giant Pratt and Whitney engines that were pushing them through the air from the back of the customised Boeing 727. The luxurious cream leather recliner he sat in, transferred that energy through his body as he sat looking out of the window deep in thought.

In front of him, on the polished wooden tabletop, sat his open laptop, two glasses of neat whiskey, and a small glass bowl of Gummy Bears. He was in one of the two chairs on this side facing forwards, and opposite him, sitting in the window recliner, looking out of the window was the giant figure of Simeon.

Along each side of the tube-like room, they were in, were the unmistakable windows of the airplane, interior was a very modern and smooth upgrade to replicate the feeling of a luxury hotel lobby. Desta and Simeon were sitting at the table near the back of the plane, continuing towards the cockpit were more executive style recliners, and the whole right side of the plane was filled with tables with chairs. The left side was double recliners, again in cream and at the foot of it all, was a soft brown and tan carpet that Simeon hugged with his bare toes under the table.

In the recliner on the other side of the plane to Desta and Simeon was the snoozing figure of Theo. Still in his hospital scrubs, he nestled under a thick, white blanket with one bare foot poking out the bottom. His head was held back as he slept in the chair, and the rhythmic sound of his breathing was slow and deep. He had been through a lot and was finally getting the time to recover.

Scattered around the other chairs of the plane, were the rest of the Zeta team that had raced to America to get to Theo before the Anunnaki could. Behind Desta, and around a table placed longways down the plane, sat Kira, Deena, and Raquel. They were perched forward in their chairs, leaning on the table, and placing cards down one after the other. Further forward again Mina and Edmund sat in the two front recliners directly in front of a giant flat screen TV built into the wall. The screen was split horizontally, and they used the controllers in their hands to guide their soldiers around the screen whilst killing Nazi Zombies. Every now and then, they would mutter instructions to one another as they collaborated in their favourite game.

'He's cuter than I thought he would be." Deena said, laying down a 10 on the small pile of cards in front of her and the other female members of the Zeta team.

"Ten, close." she announced and in a single move she picked up the deck of cards and flipped them, discarding them to the side.

The three of them often played cards together, it was cathartic, and allowed them to work on some of their intuitive skills whilst having some simple fun. All three of them were still in the slim fitting black jumpsuits that they had been wearing when rescuing Theo. Kira had undone the entire top half of hers and had tied the arms around her waist leaving just her white vest over her tanned skin. Deena still had hers zipped up to her neck, and her hair was still taught and tight in her high braid. Her flawless coffee coloured face sat perched atop her slightly elongated neck, she looked like she was always sitting with perfect posture, though it was just her build and gait. She oozed femininity and grace; the exact opposite of Raquel, who was sitting to her right and facing backwards down the plane.

Kira glanced over her shoulder, looking back down at the plane's cream, and brown interior. Theo was sleeping facing away from them so she could just see the top of his head and nose poking out past the side of his chair.

"He is a lot whiter than I thought he would be," she said to the table, with a squint in her nose and a smile on her face.

"He's a lot softer than I thought." Raquel chimed in. Her tough Australian accent cutting through the engine noise and hum of the carriage.

"Two fours," Deena announced, laying two cards in the middle of the deck face up. Her soft Saudi/American accent barely audible away from the table.

"One nine," Kira followed, now with no cards in her hands, just three laid out faced down, ready to be used.

"Two Kings," Raquel said, looking at Deena questioningly, hoping she couldn't play.

Deena paused, looking at her cards, trying to decide.

"I wouldn't kick him out of bed if he farted, but I don't think he would do it for me, you know what I think about the useless thing attached to the end of a cock." Raquel continued

"Two sevens," she placed her cards down and looked at Raquel,
"What's at the end of a cock?" She asked. Her innocent tone set Kira off and she burst into laughter.

"The rest of him," Raquel said over the sound of Kira and her own pending laughter. Deena looked confused for about a second before she smiled, showing her perfect white teeth.

"The rest of what?" They heard Edmund's curt London accent coming from the seats at the front, behind Raquel. He was still playing the game, though both he and Mina were listening over their shoulders.

Raquel jumped up onto her knees on her chair and spun around playfully, though she was a tough Aussie, these were her brothers and sisters. She flicked Edmund on the back of the head. He flinched, then she scolded him for interrupting their conversations.

"He's just not what we were expecting Raq." Mina said, whilst rebuilding his wall defences one plank at a time.

"He's white as snow." Ed joined in. "Isn't the Heosphorus supposed to be from the purest lines? Back exit, Back exit" he suddenly barked.

"On it." Mina replied

"I promise, I'm as excited as you guys, it's just weird, now that we have him, it's kinda like."

"An anticlimax," Mina finished for him.

"Yeah, exactly. Plasma gun." he finished.

"One six," Raquel heard Kira say excitedly from behind, and both the boys were determined to get past level nine so weren't going to offer any more.

She turned back around and placed her last card. "One Ace." she said, with just three face down cards in front of her remaining.

With that, the pilot's voice came over the ceiling's built-in speakers. The soft American Israeli accent of Nadev, the final member of the team, paused the game on the screen and at the table. It also snapped Desta out of his daydream, bringing his attention back to the plane.

"Ladies and gentlemen of the HMAS save the world. We are now starting our approach into Lugano Switzerland. We do have some pretty sharp cross winds, so please put things away and put on your belts. We would like to thank you once again for choosing to fly courtesy of the Shikh Mahammed Oman and remind you to check out the Duty Free as you pass through the airport terminal."

Desta had a wry smile on his face as Nadev finished his announcement. He reached forward and grabbed a couple of gummy bears from the middle of the table, and as he brought them to his open mouth, he looked across at the Heosphoros sleeping soundly in the chair to his left. It was Simeon that broke the silence.

"It's almost over Desta. Two thousand years and more and we are lucky enough to be the ones to see it through." The depth of his voice resonated when he spoke, echoing through his giant frame and enormous, muscular neck.

"You know that's one of your best features Sim." Desta's voice rolled back.

Simeon tilted his head slightly to ask the question, his bright blue eyes shone, and creased slightly as he tried to understand what his leader and friend was referring to. Desta chuckled and reached for another couple of gummy bears.

"In this moment, at this precipice, through your world's eye, you still see the joy in our mission. Don't ever change my friend." With that last sentence he reached his right hand across the table onto Simeon's and gave it a gentle squeeze.

Simeon looked down and what looked like a child's hand on their father's. He brought his right hand over placing it top of Destas. He looked up at him and smiled as he spoke.

"You can't teach an old dog new tricks Desta, and besides this, I doubt I can change that much in the week that we have left together."

Desta broke into a sad smile and looked solemnly at his companion. An unspoken moment connected them, as they were reminded briefly of their mortality, and what laid in store for them all over this coming week. Since locating Theo, the mission had been so consuming, they had both almost forgotten the fate they shared. They pulled their hands apart, then chuckled together in unison. Desta picked up his glass from the table and raised it in front of him. He looked at Simeon.

"These next seven days are going to be, well, interesting. But I couldn't think of a better man to be facing this down with."

Simeon smiled and picked up his own glass. Both men drank as the moment stuck with them for just a few more seconds. When Destas' glass hit the table, he stood where he was and turned to speak to the rest of the team.

"You heard the captain team, were nearly home. Let's lock everything down for landing."
"What about sleeping beauty?" Mina shouted over his shoulder while head shotting a Nazi zombie officer

Everyone, except the men at the front, instinctively turned to look at the newest member of the team.

Desta looked at Simeon, Simeon just shrugged his shoulders.

"We will wake him when we get to Lugano, until then we let him sleep."

Chapter 14

Order Up

Baghdad – Office of Control Risk PLC
28/02/2022
9 :46pm

Brad sat behind his thick wooden desk with a big smile on his face. In front of him, sat the head of the Iraqi Army, and the Defence minister he had appointed only a few short years ago, with a few strategic "accidents" along the way. The three men went back a long way and had been an integral part in the rebuilding of a friendly presence in the region, a presence under US control, and as such, under the control of the Anunnaki.

All three had drinks in their hands and were informally dressed, although Brad still had his expensive suit on. He liked to keep the windows open in his office, something about the smell of Baghdad reminding him that this wasn't home, and to stay sharp. In the cool February evening, the desert air floated up into the elite offices of Control Risk and meant Brad's jacket was still sitting casually on his shoulders. Thick leather office chairs held each of them in place, and on the desk between them, were three manilla folders, each one containing the same literature,

Brad looked down into his glass and watched the ice cubes chase each other around the edges, as he swirled the dark liquid gently.

"So, understand.", he said, addressing Al Harabi, the head of the army.

"No unit placements outside of what is already scheduled. I don't want any questions coming up that may jeopardize the launch."

"What about the ISOF we have in the blast radius?" The head of the Army asked, in English, but in a thick accent.

"The ones with access to the Hibernation Protocol will already have their instructions, what remains, remains." He paused and looked at Al Harabi to emphasise his unspoken instruction.

"Understood." He replied whilst dropping his gaze in a show of submission.

"We do have important civilians in these places." The defence minister added in much better English than his countryman.

"Some we cannot afford to lose." He took a long sip of his drink and the two other men waited.

"But some we cannot trust with this new information."

"To be fair Nahir, that sounds like a 'you' problem" Brad replied.

"Anyone cleared for Hibernation in Baghdad, should be out by the third. If you get stragglers, or people left behind that's on them and you. We all know what's at stake. You don't need my advice on how to get your people underground."

145

"What about you, what about here? If the projections are correct this building will be safe from the blast but well within the radiation radius?" Harabi asked

Brad exhaled and smiled again; he had a plan for everything.

"Now that, that is a "Me" problem, and one I am all over. Everyone here that is cleared, will be on US soil or deep under Control Risk by the time of Passing."

"Will you be coming back here after?"

Brad began to chuckle at the question, he wanted to tell them how much he hated 'The Arab world' as he called it. Their smell, their music, their clothes, their food; he hated everything about this place. The people, and the culture he was forced to endure as part of his role on the Anunnaki council made him sick.

"The world post Nibiru will be very uncertain." He warned before bringing his glass up to his lips for another sip of his smooth brown whiskey.

Chapter 15

Neptunes Answers

**Goonumbia – NSW Australia
28/02/2022
10 :10pm**

The chirp of the Black Ring Crickets hung on the warm breeze as it gusted in through the open window of the small sized caravan that Emma called 'home,' with her boyfriend. She always opened the window at each end to create the flow of air she loved. The energy she drew from it, as it flowed around her, was part of her connection to nature and the ley lines. She loved sitting out on the small wooden balcony near the front door and listening to the crickets singing at night. This, along with her boyfriend, had been her haven while working over at Parkes, she had turned it into a home away from home

"If we are going to be here for three months, best make the most of it," she had said when moving their two suitcases and one box with them.

There were now candles everywhere, along with a multitude of incense burners that were scattered in between. A smiling Budha in the corner of the room was almost waist height while he sat, and he still had the Santa's hat on, from when they celebrated their first Christmas together. Along with the yoga mats rolled up in the box under the Yoga positions poster, there were seven bowls, each one designed to cleanse a particular "Chakra Point".

When she wasn't working at Parkes, her and her boyfriend would go to the local markets and farms to collect fresh produce for her boyfriend's: 'Cooking with T' Tik-Tok page and, testament to that, was a large bowl of chopped mango that Emma absentmindedly reached for as she sat in the middle of the carpeted floor. She was surrounded by printouts of what looked like very similar screen grabs to earlier in the day and as she stared at this one, a small drop of mango juice fell and landed silently on it.

The candles next to her were almost burnt out and the glow from her laptop was the only other light source in the caravan, she had been so consumed she had forgotten to turn on the lights. The small printer over on the table, where she and Terry ate each day, continued its relentless drone as it continued to print and feed paper through to its tray.

She was sitting crossed legged, hunched over, intently watching more lines dancing on the laptop when she seemed to come back to reality. She took a deep breath, looked around the floor and at all the paper around her and checked her watch. She was buzzing with excitement and couldn't wait for her boyfriend to get back from his shift at the local pub, so she could tell him everything she had discovered.

"What the fuck?" she asked herself, as she realised, she had not moved for almost four hours.

She was still wearing the same clothes she had gone to work in, and had only taken a break for bathroom visits, and to chop her fruit: Mango and Pomegranate. Her hair was still tied up, but more had spilled from her bun during her intense afternoon researching and hypothesising. She looked a little like the scarecrow from the Wizard of Oz when Terry, her partner's keys, finally hit the latch.

"Hey Baby Doll." came the familiar English accent of her 'King of Swords,' as she would often call him.

With the sound of his keys hitting the door, it was as if a small pressure cooker finally released some of its steam, and the excitement she had been stifling in favour of more analysis and research was finally free, as she was able to share it. She jumped to her feet excitedly with a giant smile on her face and skipped the six or seven steps across the floor to get to him as he entered. As he did, he saw her smile and energy, and held out his arms as she jumped at him. She wrapped her legs around his waist and held herself in place as he linked his strong arms under her bum and held her there to give her a big kiss.

Tonight, he got a quick peck on his lips and a flurry of information, words and 'sciencey stuff,' which he had little idea about, and at this pace, could never understand. He smiled at her though as she hung from his neck with her arms behind his head, and he let her flow, joyous that she was so excited about something. What that something was? He had no idea, though it sounded big. He leant forward to kiss her, and to shut her up for a second.

"Baby, my feet are killing me, how about I get sat down, I pack a billy, and you tell me what it is that has you so excited."

"Oh my God, Baby, I'm sorry." she said dismounting.

"No need to be sorry my love, that's how I want you to great me every time I come through the door. I've just been on my feet all night, and I really have been looking forward to a Billy or two with you." he finished, winking, and kissing her again on her lips.

He released the kiss, and her bum, then walked past her to sit on the small couch in front of the coffee table speaking as he did.

"Ok, so a bit slower this time, but what did you do today? He asked, beginning to sound a little excited himself now.

"You are not going to believe it." she said proudly.
"But I think Neptune is gone."

"What, The Greek God?" he asked, with a very questioning tone.

"No, the planet dickhead." she laughed in reply. Terry instantly laughed too. A wide smile filled his handsome, bearded face until he realised the actual words she had spoken. He squinted his eyes and furrowed his brow.

"Hold on, what do you mean Neptune is gone?" he asked?

"Like, Gone, Gone. Like I think something hit it or moved its orbit around the Sun gone?"

Terry smiled at this doozy, by now he was sitting on the sofa while Emma stood in front of him, gently shifting her weight and rolling her body as she tried to channel her energy. She looked at Terry as she said the words again.

"Look at all these printouts." He bent down to grab a few and bounced over to him, slapping it on the table.

As she slipped the screen prints down, Terry had grabbed a small wooden box from under the table and placed it in front of him, as he reached under for their small glass bong, Emma continued to explain.

"These pictures here are the Radioscopes readings run through the A.I. and translated as visual radio waves right, you've seen these before?"

Terry looked up and saw the picture, he waved his dark hair from his eyes as he lifted his gaze from the table.

"Yep, you showed me some of these before."

"OK good.'" she said, her excitement growing.
"Well look at this one here." she questioned, flicking through and pulling one out to show him.

Terry finished sprinkling some chopped green herb into the top of the glass bong on the table in front of him, then took a good look at the picture.

"Ok, what am I seeing?" he asked. Staring intently and quite excited to learn.

"This is the Radioscope image of the sector containing Neptune, on August 11th, pretty normal right, nothing special there?"

"Yeah, looks just like the other ones," he replied.

"Well check out this one from the following day." With that she handed him the second image.

"Whoa, that's different," he gasped, unsure of what it was, but it had drastically changed.

"Then the next day." She handed another printout down to him.
"And then again the next day." Another printout which Terry took, and studied.

Though, he wasn't as educated as Emma, she had fallen in love with his mind. He was just as sharp as she was and seemed to understand most things, she showed him from her time at Uni. As he studied the pictures, he knew that the A.I. program, she had developed, used this information to measure points on the waves to measure points in space.

"Then finally day five." she finished and handed him the last image she had. It looked practically identical to the first one she had shown him, he thought.

She looked at him, waiting for the big 'aha' moment. She bounced in front of him, such was her energy right now. He looked up, not sure exactly what it was but not wanting to disappoint her, he just nodded and asked:

"So, what caused it? Are you sure it's not just a computer glitch?" She was ready for this.

"Well, that's what I thought at first." she said, leaping back to the carpet and grabbing another small handful of pictures. This time she handed him the whole stack at once just stating.

"Same Radio Scope, same date and time, perfect signal."

"Ok." he said, nodding again. He reached for the small glass bottle in front of him and brought it up to his lips, his right hand reached to the top with a lighter and a quick flame followed by an inward breath caused him to sit up right whilst holding his breath and listening as Emma got into the interesting part.

"So I ran the AI over the radio waves images from before and after it went haywire aaaaaand," She held the A for far longer than necessary, she had a flare for a dramatic reveal.
"Neptune was no longer even in the sector square. Soooo, I checked the other 16 sector squares in the quadrant and it was nowhere to be found. Like Gone!" she explained, making a clear reference to earlier and giving Terry full Jazz Hands.

Terry exhaled and a thick stream of white smoke came from his mouth and swirled into the room, he gestured to the billy causing Emma to shake her head while still holding her Jazz Hands up.

"Where did it go?" he coughed and asked all at one.

"I don't know for sure." she said.
"But I have a theory." She paused and pointed to the glass pipe on the table.
"You should probably pack another one of those for this part cos its gonna sound pretty out there."

"Oh baby, you speaka my language!" he announced in homage to her favourite song and reached to top it up for a second hit.

"Ok, so after I unscrambled this data, I ran the same sequences for the other squares in the sector and found the same anomaly on each square, but it starts and ends at different times for each. I ran it through a few algorithms we use up at QUT and was able to surmise it is a moving object, working its way across the sectors and along the way wiping out Neptune?"

"An Asteroid?" Terry asked just finishing the top and looking up at her.

"I thought so, but whatever this is, it didn't hit Neptune, because it hasn't changed its trajectory or speed in any of my measurements across the full quadrant. It looks like it flew through the measurement field and kept on going, but along the way has had enough energy to move Neptune from its orbit around the Sun."

"For real?" he questioned before again, lighting the top of the pipe and taking a deep breath.

"1000%," she replied confidently.
"But it gets better, well, or worse actually depending on if I'm right or not." She got lost in that thought for a second before snapping back to the conversation again and looking right at him.
"I think whatever it is, is on a trajectory to pass within 5 million km of Earth."

"Is that bad?" he asked innocently, still holding his breath.

"Well, whatever it is passed within about 10million of Neptune and where is Neptune." She held up both her hands and shrugged her shoulders.

The second the words left her mouth Terry exhaled, and like the smoke leaving his lungs, her words hung heavy in the air between them. It was the first time she had said it out loud, it was the first time she had contemplated what it meant. Up until now, she had been so obsessed with solving the puzzle, without fully grasping the overall goal. She brought her hands up to her face, as she gasped at the prospect of whatever this is, coming to Earth.

"Oh God no." she said, the fear in her eyes, real and evident.

Chapter 16

Pass The Test

Baghdad – Babylon Rotunda Hotel
01/03/2022
1 :03am

Cornelius stood tall in his Executive Suite on the thirty third floor of the Babylon Rotana. His expensive, tailored suit still clung to him as he stood in front of the wall to floor window and looked out at this wild frontier city before him. He was on the riverside, and it was almost midnight as he sipped his 4th glass of Glenfiddich, looking down at the lights of the American Embassy, just on the other side of the water in the Green Zone.

His net worth stood close to $1.3Billion and right now, he was contemplating all the things he had done to build this vast fortune. It was harder for him as he aged, because there were times where he felt he didn't deserve it all. The people, businesses, and friends he had trampled on in the early days had earned him the nickname the Hydra. Although, hundred-hour weeks for over a decade didn't hurt, it did cost him the one person he had ever loved, as well as his two children. This was the curse of age; reflecting on the wrong choices all those years ago; and fear that history will repeat itself now, and for what? Shareholders?

Cornelius had arranged business deals worth upwards of $1Billion on almost every continent on Earth, though something about today and Control Risk seemed off. He switched his gaze to the large suspension bridge crossing the river to his right. The lights outlining the structure were slowly changing colour. The word Slaves hung in his head.

He turned away from the window with that thought, and slowly retreated to the cream, modern sofa in the middle of the room. As he stepped down into the sofa area, he put it together. He had been struggling to understand why this felt wrong compared to so many other business meetings, with some horrific people over the years. He had been offered whores pretty much everywhere he had gone, but these girls were not whores. They were slaves, he could see it and sense it in them. As he sat it still, thoughts fluttered through his mind, as it didn't make sense. When he had done the work with N'tali in the Congo they had been using slaves and child soldiers, yet, it didn't feel like this. He held his glass up to see the light through the rich, golden-brown whiskey.

"Maybe you're just becoming an old sentimental fool." he said to himself, then threw it back in one. As his empty glass hit the table there was a knock at the door. He looked down at his watch and turned slightly so to face it.

"Come in." He said turning to look.

The door opened and in walked a stunning young woman with long blonde hair and piercing blue eyes. She closed the door behind her, looking over at Cornelius. Even though, there was about twenty feet between them, he could smell her instantly. It was a slight floral scent with something he didn't recognise mixed through it.

He couldn't have known it was a strong pheromone used by the Alaha, and it certainly sent a cloud around all his senses as he breathed her in. Her white outfit was brilliant white and contrasted against her rich dark tanned skin that exposed ample cleavage.

Silence settled in the room before she felt comfortable and took a step towards Cornelis on the Sofa. Her movement seemed to knock him out of the trance he was in, as he stood up quickly from where he was, apologizing as he did. He held up his hand as if to indicate she should stop when he finally managed to mumble out some words.

"Not tonight, I think you have the wrong room." he said, knowing this was not the wrong room.

He also already had a rock-hard erection from the pheromones and was unbelievably desperate to have her. This wasn't him though, luckily, he was still sober enough and conscious enough to remember his values, and despite all the bad things he blamed himself for, whores and women were never something he felt drawn to. This felt even more wrong than before.

"Please Sir, I am Your Alaha, I have been sent to you to give you all of this." With that she lifted her hands to her neck and unclipped something causing her white robe to drop completely to the floor.

It caused a new wave of her perfume to float into the room and Cornelius felt his mouth begin to water, his palms were suddenly very sweaty, and his erection throbbed. She took another step towards him.

Cornelius's hand came up again and this time he even took a small step back. His mind was racing, he hadn't had sex in almost four years, he never thought about sex, in his whole life he had only done it a dozen times. He had never felt the desire, ever.

"This isn't right," he said, taking another small step back.

She had her right hand covering her vagina and her other one was cupping her breast as she looked at him. She slid her middle finger inside herself and smiled.

"This is my only purpose." She drew her right hand to her lips and placed her middle finger deep in her mouth.
"I taste right." she said with her finger resting on her tongue.

Beads of sweat were now forming on Cornelius's forehead as his erection twitched in his pants. His mind was screaming at him to go and taste her. He stood locked on, unable to move or find a rational thought. It was when she pushed her finger back inside herself and moaned that he came to life and strode towards her. She smiled; he was coming.

He took a dozen strong steps across the room and towered over her as he stopped right in front of her. He could smell her perfume, he could smell her womanly scent. She looked up at him with such a trained innocence then bought her right hand up to his lips. Before she could touch them, he dropped to his haunches and grabbed the fallen gown she was wearing from around her feet and pulled it back up around her as he again stood. She was shocked, unsure what to do now. As she started to protest, Cornelius shushed her and clasped the clip at the top, clothing her again fully. He looked down at her stunning face and full luscious lips.

Each time he stopped for even a second it was like the trance was starting again, he had to keep on moving. He put his hands on her shoulders and guided her to turn, she complied and walked towards the door, he stepped in front of her to open it for her. He couldn't look at her as she left, he didn't trust he would let her go and once she was gone, he closed the door and backed against it, tilting his head back and taking a deep, deep breath to try and get his conscious mind back. He had taken ecstasy as a youngster, and this had felt very similar. He didn't like it, and he didn't trust it.

"Something is wrong." he said out loud to himself.

One last deep breath and he trusted himself to step away from the door. He still had a raging hard on, and the room still smelt of her, though somehow, he could think just as clearly as before she entered. He was a smart man and begun to put the pieces together pretty quickly. Obviously, there is something in that perfume that makes men a little crazy. A very powerful weapon if you can get your enemies pictured doing things, or women, they shouldn't be.

'Air, need air.'

He walked past the sofa, and past his empty glass to the large sliding door that opened onto his small balcony. When he pulled it open the sound of Baghdad buzzed in alongside the smell of a cold desert evening. He took a deep breath and went to step outside before deciding he needed another drink in his hand after what had just happened. He was also very aware of the bulge in his pants that had not yet left so he turned back to the table and just as he grabbed his glass there was another knock on the door.

He was stunned for just a second, and then everything that made him Cornelius kicked in and his mind cleared, ready to take complete control of whatever was behind that door. He strode purposefully over and took a deep long breath as he opened it.

"This better be important." he barked, taking charge before he met who was on the other side. He opened the door sharply. Another Alaha stood in the hallway.

"It's past midnight, what do you want?" he demanded. She attempted to enter the room, yet Cornelius stepped across the doorway, stopping her.

"I assure you my motives are not like the last girl." she said looking up into his face.

This one smelt different, was dressed differently, and unlike the last girl, there was fear in her eyes. Although, Cornelius was a little confused, he did what felt right and stepped aside to let her in.

"What's going on?" he demanded, as he closed the door and turned to look at her.

She was equally as perfect as the previous girl, she too wore white, though, it was a little more conservative and her hair was plaited, not flowing. It was just as she was about to speak that he recognised her.

"Mia?" Cornelius asked, taking a closer look, and stepping towards her.
"You're the girl from Complete Risk, from Brad's office?"

She smiled. "Yes sir." The warmth in her smile and her smell had Cornelius completely at ease, his shoulders visibly relaxed as the tension running through him disappeared.

"What are you doing here?" he asked while walking past her to the table to grab his empty glass. He certainly needed another drink now.

"Sir, I saw you today with Brad and could sense your unease. I wondered why that was?" She didn't move from her spot. Holding her hands together in front of her stomach, she watched him, her gaze followed him across the room to the bar.

Cornelius took the time to pour his drink, three fingers deep in the expensive crystal tumbler before turning and looking at her, propping himself on the bar as he did.

"Who was that girl here before you, and what did she do to me?" He finally asked, politely. Taking a long sip on his drink as the word 'me' left his lips

"She was an Alaha, she was coated in a pheromone created by Complete Risk in the 1970's which is a modified version of the female Silk Moth's pheromone, Bombykol. It has been used to lure many great men over the years. Yet not you. Why?"

He looked at her, took another sip, his mind calculating everything he was hearing, seeing, smelling. It still wasn't making sense and it was rare that he couldn't see a situation for what it was.

"I have many questions too, but rather than skipping through them all, let's circle back to number one. What are you doing here?"

"The Alaha was a test." she said as she decided it was all or nothing.

"If I am right about you, then you are one of them, and I need to give this to you. Urgently" She reached into her robe and pulled out a manilla folder.

Cornelius watched her from across the room as she stepped forward and placed it on the table where his empty glass had been.

"Please be the One." she said looking him dead in the eye. Then she turned to leave.

That jolted him to life at the bar and as she was walking to the exit, he strode over, asking her to wait as he did. As she opened the door his long arm reached over and closed it again. He stood over her, tall and tanned. She looked up at him vulnerable and still obviously scared.

"Please sir, look in the folder and do what is right, but I cannot stay here any longer. Each minute I am here brings you closer to danger."

"I have so many questions," he said

"There is no time," she replied, putting her hand on the door handle again and gently pulling. This time Cornelius let her go.

When the door closed, he looked behind him at the empty apartment suite, a myriad of smells including the warm Baghdad air wafted through. His now half empty glass hung casually in his right hand and right there, on his table, a cream folder, no more than a half inch thick. He looked at it for a second, everything else in the room blurred. Then he smiled. A genuine, deep smile. He thought he had seen everything in all his years. He had been involved in some very interesting situations and really did think that as he got older it was all done. Now, he was in his own spy novel, and the thought made him feel twenty-one again.

Without a single shred of fear or doubt, he hopped down the step to the sofa, sat down right in front of the folder, put his glass down, took off his jacket, flung it behind him, and without a thought, he picked it up.

He opened it up to a wad of printed A4 pages held together with a bull clip at the top. The first page had some computer jargon he couldn't understand in a light grey box, it referenced specific IP addresses, secure server ID codes. It appeared to be validating the sources of the documents enclosed. Then on the bottom half of the page was the first email.

It was from an unusual email address, one that didn't look like an email with the @ symbol, and it matched some of the numbers in the box above.

It was only two lines of actual communication amongst more computer jargon, yet, as Cornelius read them, he felt his stomach tighten, and his mouth suddenly felt very dry.

Embassy ready for radiation event.
Proceed as ordered.

Then he saw the date, which was sent today!

Everything about him suddenly heightened and as always when under pressure he became the best version of himself. He flicked to the next page, then the next, then the next. Skimming through email after email, picking out certain lines as he went.

```
Authorisation from the Council.
Arrival and destruction of Nibiru.
Radiation Cloud 50km approx.
80% mortality within 7 days
95% within 21 days
Protect Nibiru passing
Control Risk Management
Increased Ducaz unit placements
Embassy awaiting Ducaz
Evacuation orders rescinded -
Dark operation, friendly casualties expected
```

Then four in a row all referenced Babylon Mall - 03/03/03 - today was the 1st of March.

The names he saw referenced, and obviously emailing back and forth, scared him, because these were the most powerful people both here in Baghdad as well as over in the US.

AMT was quite easy, it was Ambassador Matthew Tueller, it was his email at the very beginning. It was easy to find Brad from Control Risk throughout, Al Harabi was mentioned as well as Sheikh Al -Muhammed, but then one email from Brad to what appeared to be an email address off the network, Ron Klain suddenly made all the RK references make sense. He swallowed. The President's Chief of Staff?

Cornelius heard his own voice in his head, above the noise. "Action" He didn't need to pick this apart and figure out all the pieces. His gut was saying this is really happening: on the 3rd at 3pm. Two days from now. He then realised it was now well after midnight.

"Shit, tomorrow!" he said out loud.

What could he do? He stood up and began a gentle walk around the table. He used to pace slowly to help him think and now he needed to more than ever. He was listing all the people he knew, that might be able to stop this. It was a long list, being compromised by associations with some of the men in the emails. Then, he centred on the Dutch Embassy, he had visited as their guest on his previous overnight stay, spoken with them many times regarding setting up his business, and even bumped into an old Krauvbaul teammate from his time in college; one of the security team that checked him in.

He stopped his walk, looked down at the floor, and looked straight through it as his mind settled on Sigrid. Tall, played hard, played to win, yet played fair. It was worth the risk.

Back to action, he scanned the room, looking for his jacket, he needed his phone. It was lying in a heap behind the sofa, and he strode over, picked it up, pulled the phone from the inside pocket and let it fall back to the floor without a single care for the handmade silk lining, or expensive merino wool fabric.

Sigrid had sent him an email as a way of sharing his details. Cornelius, at the time, had been too busy to reply, but he knew it was there somewhere, and he was pretty sure his email signature had a phone number for him.

He was sitting back on the sofa in front of the manilla folder as he flicked through his phone, getting to his emails, then swiping over and over to recede back in time. 'November last year' he thought to himself as he scrolled down. He slowed; he was in November. There were hundreds of emails on his personal account, his eyes catching key words as they rolled down the page.

Sigridblacke@ned.emb.org popped into view and, he clicked immediately to open it.

My details – Sigrid Lowen

It read in the body of the email, yet below this was the Embassy signature, and...

"OK, yes!" Cornelius said as he looked at Sigrid's mobile number here in Baghdad, right in front of him. Without a second thought he clicked on the number, and his phone began to dial.

Cornelius already had a plan; have Sigrid meet him at the Dutch embassy in the Green Zone tonight, grab Mark, and Dave from their rooms, and bring them with. Get it all done and together within the hour. Then get out of Dodge.

His phone came to life as he connected to Sigrid in his apartment near the Dutch Embassy.

"Gude Morgan, wie est das under diese hur?" The sleep was clear in his voice, as was the irritation. Cornelius jumped into fluent Dutch and explained.

"Sigrid, this is Cornelius, from Van de Berg Oil and Gas, but also your team mate at Koog Zandjik."

"Cornelius?" he knew exactly who it was, though it was still a surprise to hear from him.

"It is past 3am here in Baghdad, can you.." Cornelius didn't let him finish.

"I know the time my friend," he cut in.

"I am staying only across the river from you, I am here in Baghdad and I need to meet with you."

"Well surely it can wait until the morning." came the reply, the sleep had already cleared from his words and his mind had already been stimulated to attention.

"I am sorry, but this is a matter of life and death, potentially the death of everyone in this city. I will be at the Embassy within the hour, you need to get there. Can you get there?"

"Well yes, I can, but what's going on? What do you mean the death of everyone? Where are you?

"Sigrid!" Cornelius cut through the questions.

"The clock for me is already ticking, you trusted me as your Captain for two seasons, I need you to trust me here. Get to the Embassy and tell no one. I will call you when we are close by."

"We?" came the reply

"My team from V.D.B." There was a big sigh on the other end of the phone, Cornelius waited.

"OK, I'll head there now. It will take me about 20 minutes, meet me at the service entrance you left through last time."

"Thank you Sigi. Remember, don't tell anyone, I have no idea how deep this goes."

"How deep what goes? Cornelius, are you sure you're ok?"

"No, I am not OK, and neither are you, or any of the people in this city if you don't get to the Embassy. I will be there in 45 minutes."

He didn't wait for a reply, and hung up on Sigrid, he was going to be there.

Next, he needed to get Mark and Dave together, so he tapped his phone twice, and pulled it to his ear, tapping his foot as it rang and a loud "damn it" when Mark's voicemail kicked in. His phone read 03:13, they would both be out cold. He stood up where he was and tapped his back pocket to make sure his wallet was there. On his phone he dialled Dave and put it on speaker as he walked to the door and left to go and wake Mark. They were both two floors down from him in their own suites, and around Cornelius, the halls were empty, apart from the sound of the phone ringing through his speakerphone.

"C'mon. C'mon, C'mon," he muttered to himself as he walked down the lush red and gold carpets on his way to the elevator.

Dave's voicemail kicked in just as he pushed the button, frustrated, he hung up, and put his phone back in his pocket. He looked up to see the lights behind the numbers moving, showing the elevator's arrival, he looked to his left, then to his right. A gentle 'Ding' chimed in, and the doors opened before him. Empty, aside from his own reflection in the giant mirror covering the whole back wall of the lift. He stepped inside, pressed thirty-one, turned his back to the mirror and took a deep breath.

Cornelius stood at suite 3102, his phone in his left hand with Mark on speaker just ringing out. Inside the room, Cornelius could hear the phone chiming. He banged on the door, loud enough to be heard, though not too loud as to arouse suspicion. He was beginning to feel nervous. He had called Mark 3 times now and knew that he wasn't a deep sleeper.

He decided to try Dave's number, and room and slid down to the next suite while dialling his number again. Just as the speaker phone came to life and the dial tone rang out, Cornelius noticed the door was open, not by much, it just looked like it hadn't been closed properly. The hairs on the back of his neck stood upright, he disconnected the call, put his phone in his pocket and eased open the door.

"Dave?" he questioned, as it opened, and he stepped inside. The sound of the TV and the light from it flickered through the suite. As the only lights on, all the shadows danced a little, animating the entire room.

"Dave?" Cornelius hoarsely whispered, stepping further in, scanning left to right. It wasn't until he took a few more steps he could see Dave lying on the sofa, his phone was on the table in front of him, flashing a tiny intermittent green LED to show the missed calls. Cornelius could feel it immediately, the smell blood of entered his nose, when he reached over the back of the sofa to shake Dave on the shoulder, the TV screen lit up with a beach scene, illuminating the room. Now, it was clear to Cornelius that his friend, and business partner of over thirty years had been shot right through the head, execution style, probably while he was sitting here watching the News. Judging by the splatter behind the sofa, it would appear Dave had been shot, point blank, by someone standing in front of him.

Cornelius's mind went blank, without a single thought to hold onto. Seeing his friend laying here dead had taken the plot of the fun Spy novel, spinning it into a horror story of life and death. His mouth was dry, yet he needed to swallow. As he did, the tragic truth about Mark hit him as well. 'If Dave has been executed, then Mark will be gone too.' This hung in the air along with everything else. Mark's new baby daughter...

"Action Cornelius"

He snapped back into life, and realised he needed to get back to his room, grab the folder and get out. There was nothing he could do here anymore. He turned to leave, poking his head out and searching the hallway before stepping through the door and away from his dead friend. His heart was racing as he attempted to walk calmly to the elevators, to go back up to level thirty. The doors opened immediately, he stepped in again, turned his back on the mirror and this time, went back up.

The adrenaline was rushing through him, as the fight or flight response flooded through him, he felt alert, quick, and strong. He was nodding to himself as the elevator rose, convincing himself he could do this, and live through this, he was going to the 'One' that Mia referred to. Grab the folder go.

Unfortunately, the adrenaline and racing heart stopped Cornelius from properly contemplating what might be waiting for him up there. In the movies the good guys always made it somehow, and that was basically the plan. The elevator stopped, the same 'Ding' chimed through, he held his breath, listening intently. He heard nothing, so with a light sigh, he stepped out. There appeared to be nothing to his right, and nothing to his left. His heart pounded in his ears, though, he just had to keep moving, so he did. Everything in him tensed as he walked down the hall to his room. He got there, and there was no sign of anything out of the ordinary. He looked around one last time, while grabbing his wallet from his pocket. Still nervously checking the hall around him, he scanned it against the panel, and he heard his door unlock, one final glance and he pushed open the door, relieved as he was one step closer.

As the door opened, he could see the suite before him, a man dressed in black stepped in from the balcony, and a second one stepped out of the bedroom. They were almost as shocked as Cornelius was because who knocks on the door of your own execution? It gave him the fleeting second, he needed, to get a head start.

Suddenly every limb, muscle strand, ligament and bone were filled with adrenal fluid, and Cornelius moved just like he did all those years ago when he and Sigrid lifted the Dutch National Trophy together. Like a gazelle, he launched away from the door and made his way back to the elevators, he was just approaching them when lift number four arrived, announcing itself with the usual 'Ding'. Out jumped three men, all dressed identical to the men in his room. It didn't matter, the emergency stairs were right there, and he burst through the door, almost breaking it. The sound rang, and echoed through the white stairwell, as too did the slap of Cornelius's shoes on every fourth stair as he fled like a ninja, away from the men above.

They were already in the stairs, jumping down to catch him. They were talking to each other, reporting what floor he was on, where they were. Though they were coordinating, he didn't have time to care. He was slowly pulling away from the men above him, his long legs and adrenaline filled body was making light work of the concrete steps. He was just thinking about getting to the basement, and car park, there were plenty of places to hide.

"That's correct – Twenty-four" he heard from above.

He looked at the number that zipped by his right side, twenty-six. Rhythm.

Speed.

Step.

Step.

Jump - he just kept repeating, as he found an amazing way to descend, he was getting further ahead of the men above, he could hear them losing ground. Twenty-five. He wasn't even feeling tired yet.

Step

Step

Jump - and he landed again, grabbed, with his left hand onto the rail, jumping again, using the rail to balance, he cleared twelve steps in a bounce.

Step.

Step.

Jump - only for the door of floor twenty-four to fling open, just as he passed.

The man that stepped through, took the full force of a man 6 foot 5 inches, weighing 110kgs, leaping almost into his chest. It smashed him against the wall with a brutal force that cracked the back of his head against it, hard enough to knock him out cold, a vacant confused look filled his eyes as unable to move, he slipped away.

Unfortunately for Cornelius, it sent him sprawling too and after bouncing off the first guy, the two that were coming through next, were able to grab hold of him, and deliver a nasty elbow to the side of the head. It dazed Cornelius enough to knock his vision for a second, and he could just feel himself being dragged up to his feet. Eventually he found himself pinned against the wall.

"He fucking killed him." he heard.

The corners of his lips lifted in a bloody dazed smile. It earned him a sharp blow to his ribs from the man holding him, breaking at least two, immediately, Cornelius found it hard to breathe and tried dropping again, yet he remained held against the wall, slouching. He could hear the echoes of the footsteps getting closer from above, and finally as his sight was returning, he could see one man on the floor, with another kneeling in front of him, and three men arriving from the levels above. He looked at the face of the man holding him. White, they had American accents. This wasn't going to end well.

Though the men were dressed in black combat fatigues, they were neither hooded nor masked. It looked like they had rushed here for some reason and were not fully geared up. It might also have been because their only prey tonight were a few overweight, and over indulged businessmen. Each of them had pistols on their hips, wearing bullet proof vests. A few flash bangs, smoke grenades and actual grenades hung off a couple of them. Including the man holding Cornelius.

The leader was obviously from the group above because he quickly checked the man on the floor, congratulated his men then turned his attention to Cornelius.

Meanwhile, his head finally had time to fully clear. These bastards killed his two best friends and were intent to kill thousands more. Although, he may not have been able to be the 'One' that Mia had requested, he could certainly make a difference. As he looked at the grenade hanging on the jacket in front of him, he couldn't help but tell himself…

"I should have just fucked her."

Everything he had ever regretted doing or saying all meant nothing now, he lifted his left hand quickly enough to meet no resistance, and grabbed the pin, yanking it out. Just as he did so, the men realised, and for a horrific second, all lunged to stop him. Cornelius smiled a bloody smile.

"Motherfuckers" he gargled through blood and broken teeth.

Suddenly, he, and five members of the Control Risks security detail, disappeared to become a memory.

Chapter 17

Feeding Time

Baghdad – US Embassy
01/03/2022
1 :56am

Macintyre, or Mac stood looking at the orange and white cones he had placed to close the wide road leading towards the Tigris on the southern border of the Embassy compound. 'Nothing flash, and nothing fancy,' were the last words his commanding officer spoke to him as he left his office. He oversaw the North; he had put Cleave on the Eastern exit and Bridgman covering the South. Though, it was obvious to him, a VIP was arriving at the road heliport, the lack of fanfare, and the specific orders to *not* engage with the guests was highly unusual.

He looked back down towards the river; four wide lanes of concrete stretched down a gentle hill away from him. About a quarter mile down the road, adjacent to the vacant building, was a giant H with a white circle painted around it, another quarter mile there was a second one, this was all on top of the basic road markings for the day-to-day use.

It was 2am and 99% of the compound was sleeping, the other 1% probably had their hands on their guns. The cool wind carried the desert air through the darkness, and through the silence, Mac could hear the gentle fray of the sleeping city all around them.

His radio cackled to life on his belt, and he reached down pushing a button transferring the noise to his earpiece.

"What time are these guys supposed to be getting in? I've been on since 6am" Mac paced along his cones smiling, as he heard the voice of Bridgeman moaning and pleading to get to his bunk.

"Oh, one thirty" he replied
"C'mon Bridegeman, shouldn't be much longer now."

"Anything from the CO yet? You can't tell me he doesn't even know who it is, He knows whether I had a crap in the morning or not, is he still playing dumb?"

"It's a need-to-know Bridgeman, and I guess we don't need to know."

"There's not much that Bridgemen needs to know." Cleave chimed in and chuckled in Mac's earpiece.

"Eat a dick Cleave." Bridgeman piped up.
"Hold on." Cleave cut him off, "Blades approaching, southern Tigris."

Mac turned to look down the hill and over the city of Baghdad, to see if he could spot the choppers.

"Twin blade, Wester house, troop C." Cleave continued in his ear. "ETA forty-five seconds"

"How many?" Mac, asked.

"Looks like two Sir."

"Okay, look alive, and remember do not engage." Mac signed off, took a deep breath, and stood with his back to the helipads.

Behind him the familiar hum of chopper blades echoed off the water and city, it grew louder and more aggressive until two huge, twin rotor Westinghouse 476 choppers hovered in together, kicking up a storm of wind and noise as they floated in perfect unison onto their landing pads in the middle of the street. The high-pitched mechanical wain and roaring wind was punctuated by loud shouts of inaudible instructions.

Dozens of pairs of boots hit the ground hard, exposing almost 30 men, all dressed in black under the blades of the choppers. Mac could hear more instructions being shouted and, as curiosity got the better of him, he turned around to take a look. It didn't seem that remarkable, just two units of what appeared to be special forces, disembarking a couple of copters.

He knew that 'do not engage' meant he should not even look, and then something caught his eye. Stepping out of each chopper almost in unison, were two men that stood easily two feet above every soldier around them. They made the rest of the unit look like children. But it wasn't just their height that captured Mac's attention, it was their outline, their stature, and the way they moved. Mac couldn't place it but it just seemed off, not human.

Bridgeman's voice over the radio shook him back to reality as he was staring hard, trying to figure out who or what that was. He turned with his back to the choppers again and asked him to repeat himself.

"I said, "who's carriage just arrived at the ball? Can you see who it is?"

"No Bridgemen" he replied.
"Do not engage means no pictures, no autographs and trust me, I don't think we want to know."

"Oh, but you do know." A deep voice spoke.

Every hair on Mac's body stood up all at once, and a shiver ran through his spine. The breath of someone still hung on the back of his neck, and his ear tingled with the close sounds of the last syllable. Bridgeman was saying something in his earpiece, yet Mac couldn't decipher his words, he was slowly turning around to see the presence, stationed behind him.

Looming over him, stood one of the tall figures from the chopper. It wore a black robe with a hood that covered its head and face, and behind its robe, something stuck out: The tip of a green tail, slumped on the floor. It rose another foot taller, straightening its stance as it did. Mac had turned completely, at his eyeline he could see the torso of what looked like green scales, yet formed into a strong, muscular, human shape. The rasping sound of its long breaths was in Mac's face as he turned to look upwards. He wished he hadn't.

Two yellow eyes, with black slits through them stared deadly, at him. He could see himself reflected in the centre and could see a shocked, confused soldier of the US army. He opened his mouth to speak, though. like a snake, the monstrous jaw, scaly green skin, and alligator-like head launched forward and slammed shut around Mac's exposed face. With a quick twist, it yanked off his head and released it to fly down the street towards the choppers that were now preparing to leave.

The blades picked up speed, and in perfect unison they lifted into the air, filling the street with further gusting winds. The Ducaz walked casually towards the rest of his men, as they gathered up their bags and began their short walk to the accommodation unit they had been assigned.

Chapter 18

Order Up

Vatican City - St Peters Basillica
01/03/2022
1 :38am

Pell and Maris stood under the marble eaves, surrounded by the milky white columns at the front entrance to St Peter's Basilica. Behind them, the three, big wooden doors all stood open with the light peering through from the inside. They were looking out into the square, framed by the historical masterpiece surrounding them. They appeared so small and insignificant as they both looked out at the rain gently washing through the colours of the lights in the town square

Pell was in his full official attire and as the keeper of artefacts he was here to welcome the new security team. He shuffled from his right foot to his left, and seemed to be grumbling about something, but that was normal for him. His eccentric nature was famous, or infamous throughout the church and his young prodigy Father Maris stood quietly by his side ready to support Pell where he needed.

A gentle rumble of thunder started in the sky to the East and slowly moved across the priests' paths, echoing off the century's old buildings around them. Sheet lightning flashed like a quick burst of strobe and for a tiny second the whole square was lit up like it was daytime. Pell let out a small tick like 'yip! and continued his shuffling. Maris didn't even seem to notice, as the hypnotic sound of the rain caused him to daydream.

"Ha!" Pell exclaimed, quite loudly this time, he looked down at his 1st generation Casio digital watch. 01:38 it read.

"Late, late, late, he scoffed, flicking a glance at Maris."

It brought Maris back to the present, and now above the rain, he could hear the low, mechanical hum of the approaching choppers. He couldn't see them yet, as the grey sky was low and thick with rain though he knew that they were coming from the right. Maris searched the sky looking, for the approaching lights to punch through. He then turned to his Cardinal.

"Shall we head down to the pad Cardinal?"

Pell didn't answer immediately and looked up into the sky as he scrunched up his face. He didn't like to get wet. He sighed las if he was accepting a fate, or a truth, he wanted to deny, and with his hands tucked into his robe he stepped forward, descending upon the famous white steps into the open Vatican skies and gentle rain of the square.

"Come Maris, let's welcome our guests."

Maris followed Pell a few steps behind, it wasn't expected or even customary, yet for Maris it just felt right and respectful. Watched over by the marble saints above them, they crept out into the rain and into the vast space before them. There was a couple of hundred feet where the basilica stretched forward either side of them with a series of pillars and buildings that then opened into the famous Colosseum style, Saint Peter's Square. Stunning Roman style buildings forming a giant circle around one of the most famous sites on earth.

They were approximately halfway to the main square when Pell pulled his right hand from his robe and clicked a button on a small device held within his grasp. Immediately that he did so a dozen lights in the shape of a circle blinked to life where the walkway joined the dark grey stones of the main square. Then a second circle appeared immediately behind. He placed the device back in his pocket and continued his shuffle.

To perfect circles were now clearly visible from the sky, as were the blinking lights of the two helicopters sweeping down as they cut through the rain. The hum of the rotor blades was now loud enough that it dominated the sky and Maris looked up to the right to see the giant underbellies and blurry lights of the two twin blade Westinghouse choppers. They floated into position, one in front of the other, perfectly aligned and above the circles. Maris's robe was beginning to feel the wind from the blades above, he held up his hand to protect his eyes from the rain as it intensified, charged by the pounding energy of the helicopter blades.

Pell shuffled forward as if nothing had changed, though, it appeared to look like he'd prefer to be anywhere else than here. He hated getting wet, and he despised new faces, and certainly didn't want to be dealing with both in the dead of the night when he should be tucked up listening to the rain. He strode forward, Nibiru's Passing was close at hand and 99.9% is not enough if it can be 100%. He tried to avoid the 1:30AM arrival, yet he was one of the loudest voices when advocating for the additional Ducaz units to protect the key to Soteria, or the Cross of Christ as it was known to his understudy, Maris.

The two choppers touched down, lightly bouncing on their wheels and with a rumble from the engines, dropped an octave and went into standby mode. Immediately, troops began jumping onto the ground, their feet pounding into the dark tiles as they did. One by one, dressed all in black, eventually, 30 men had jumped clear. Just when Maris thought all the men were out, two final figures stepped out of each chopper. Dressed all in black, though this time with a robe-like hood, were two figures each clearly two feet taller than all the others around them. The smaller men were each grabbing bags and slipping them over their shoulders while the two taller figures began to walk towards Pell and Maris.

Maris looked at Pell, the water was running from his papal robe, and shone in the light around them. They were only 50 feet from where the choppers had landed, and he could see these giant figures and a whole army of soldiers coming towards them. The soldiers didn't worry him, but under the hood of each of the giants, he didn't see anything that looked remotely human, even the way they moved felt wrong.

The two giant hooded figures were at the front of the group, thirty men walked behind them. The lights of the first chopper meant everyone had a silhouette, but then the pitch changed and the rear chopper, then the front, lifted into the air. Both banked backwards, moving away from the group before swinging to their right and shifting to leave.

Pell squinted through the rain at his visitors. The men had stopped as the two larger figures approached the two tiny members of the Church.

"Catholic pigs." one of them barked in a deep guttural voice as they drew closer.

"Get us out of this rain and bring me something to play with." As he finished his sentence, both figures drew back their hoods to shock their hosts and he laughed a deep, Barry white style chuckle. Maris was certainly shocked and took an obvious step backwards as he stared at the face of an alligator, with a shortened jaw, unmistakable yellow eyes, and row after row of teeth bouncing as they laughed.

Pell followed suit and drew back his hood, he wasn't shocked at all. All Ducaz had zero regard for humans, especially slaves, and as far as they were concerned the Churches and those working in the institutions were just slaves of the Reptilians and Anunnaki. He knew what to expect, and the second they saw his face, and his eyes, they did exactly what he expected and both dropped to their knees, unable to even look at him.

They both began speaking, or rather pleading in a foreign tongue that Maris didn't recognise until Pell said something angrily in their language and they both immediately stopped, climbed to their feet and stood in silence with their heads bowed. Waiting for instruction.

"With me Maris" Pell said to the rather stunned student of his.
"Keep close" he said, looking him in the eye, which was rare, and with that Pell turned and began to lead his guests back to the basilica and to their new home for the coming weeks.

Chapter 19

Pancakes and Truth

Lugano Switzerland – Zeta Mansion
03/03/2022
6 :22am

Time felt fluid, one second he was laying on the hard stone floor, flat on his back, staring up at the mouldy stone ceiling. The next, he was jumping for the plate of food, slid under the solid wooden door. Hunger and thirst were all he could feel, through bleary eyes he shovelled food to his face and as it hit his open mouth it disappeared, it was gone, no plate, no food. He bought his fingers up to his lips and could feel the pain and crispness of the skin as he explored his face. A long thick beard parted his fingers as they searched. It didn't feel like his face.

With no windows, the only light source of his cell came from the torches in the hall, poking under the door. He was on his knees, in front of the door, he felt naked as the cold stone pinched and squeezed at his skin. He began to lean forward, bringing his head down to the stone floor to peek under the door, his hair touched the ground first, the light intensified as he got closer. His head met with the cool stone, and his left eye caught a glimpse of a brilliant blue sky; bright, with a midday sun. As his eyes adjusted to the light, he could identify a town square, filled with people.

Things looked incredibly dated, everyone dressed in periodic clothing, yet, as everything was tarnished by the glare of the sky, he couldn't be sure. They were all facing a stage, with what looked like a man sized, wooden cross, cheering. Under the door, he could see a man being dragged onto the stage. He was naked, except for a simple white loin cloth, had a slim build, warm, brown skin, long hair, midway down his back which flowed into his matching beard.

When he reached the stage, the two Roman looking soldiers either side of him let go and the man turned to look over the crowd, right through the town air and straight at the man looking under the door. As he did, every single person in the scene before him, suddenly spun in unison to look right at Theo, as he spied under the door of his cell. He felt like him again, he just began to form a conscious thought when a horrific whipping sound shocked his system, and a huge wound ripped through the soft flesh on his back.

Instinctively he arched his back as the overwhelming pain of his skin tearing apart burned every nerve ending in his body and as he fell to the floor, another loud crack pierced his ears, and a second gash appeared from nowhere. A third crack was so loud, Theo brought his hands to his ears and squeezed his eyes tightly. Blind, deaf and unable to move due to the pain.

Then silence; as white, blinding light, filled his eyes. A growing murmur of a crowd could be heard, as gradually the light gave way to a group of men, bearded, robed men. Now he was on the stage, the crowd he could see under the door, were now directly before him.

He began to lift his right hand to his face, though, only got half-way. It was tied, tightly, to the wooden cross on the stage, he darted a look to his left arm, then pulled at it, only to discover, it is just as stuck.

He opened his mouth to shout, for help, though as hard as he screamed, nothing came out. The crowd got louder, cheering, and chanting in a language he didn't know. Roman soldiers lined either side of the stage, he looked around helplessly, and amongst the cacophony of noise and hate, there was one face in the crowd that locked onto his gaze. Suddenly, the noise stopped. The arms waving in the air, slowed completely and, a calm feeling of peace washed over Theo as he stood on the cross, bound, and naked. A smile spread over the face in the crowd, it spread to the corner of Theo's lips as he shared something unspoken for that second.

The arms all fell, the crowd all stood in silence and all-around Theo, small worm-like metal snakes crawled out of the wooden cross and began to search for him.

As if thinking with one mind, or one purpose, all the snakes stood as one, then in perfect unison each one dived towards the prone victim. There was a second of burning pain, then like a startled rabbit, Theo jumped up from his sleep, clutching at his face and chest as he struggled to get a breath and find reality.

"Oh, hey lover." A female voice cut into his thoughts.

During his dream, Theo had scrambled to the head of the bed, waking now he found himself at the foot of a vast bedhead that stretched to the ceiling. White, soft, and pocketed with buttons, squeezing into the fabric, he pressed his back firmly to it, finding himself sitting on top of thick, white pillows.

"It wasn't that bad, was it?"

This time he heard the voice and darted his eyes down to his right to see Raquel laying seductively on the mustard throw, laying across the downy white blanket that Theo had been sleeping under.

Theo's eyesight was a little blurry as he looked at the dark-haired women lying next to him. His knees were almost at his chest as he tried to collect his thoughts and

"I heard that men with big beds had big..."

"Who the fuck are you?" Theo interrupted, as he did, he put out his right arm, to keep her away and he began to slide his back up the wall to stand. He blinked his eyes hard as his vision came into sharper focus and finally, he was able to take in his surroundings.

Bright morning sunlight shimmered through the gossamer white day curtains, glowing a bright white as the light got caught in the rich thread. The curtains covered the huge floor to ceiling windows facing the southern Alps and Theo squinted to adjust to the early-morning sun. Rich wooden floors ran away from the foot of the curtains to disappear under a lush brown rug with light blue concentric circles through it. The smell of lemongrass puffed into the air from a small diffuser on the African style wooden chest of drawers that practically covered the other wall of the room. Above it, hung a painting; circles on a brown and gold background, that covered the rest of the wall. The size of the painting was impressive enough, yet the way the circles were animated, with their golden trim and raised position was stunning in this bright sunlight.

The bed was huge, the pillows thick and this woman was laying on the opposite side of the bed to him with a big grin on her face. Laying on her side, with her head propped up on her left hand and her right leg extended, hugging the bed next to her. Her dark hair was tied up in a tight ponytail, it fell framing her sharp cheekbones and a cheeky grin. Her black cargo pants were skin-tight and flexible, her white singlet hugged her tightly, displaying her athletic, strong shoulders. She spoke again and Theo heard her strong Australian accent.

"You really don't remember me?" She poked her bottom lip out to make it clear she was sad and looked at Theo, trying to make herself cry. Theo lowered his arm and looked at Raquel.

"Last thing I remember is all hell breaking loose in my hospital room, a face, then," Theo paused for a second.
"You." Disdain spread over his face.
"Who are you?"

As Raquel was deciding if she should keep playing with him, the door to the suite clicked open. Theo tensed briefly, looking to his right at the large double door cracking open. Raquel rolled onto her back to look over her right shoulder behind her to see who was coming in. She continued her roll and swung her legs around to a seated perch on the edge of the bed when she realised Desta was here, and as always, Simeon was just a step or two behind.

Both doors opened simultaneously, and upon seeing Desta's face, Theo finally took what he felt was a full breath of air and realised he was safe.

"Raquel, please stop playing with our guest, I think he has been through enough." Desta said softly as he entered.

"You know me D, life is for the living, and what's living without a bit of fun." As she finished her sentence, she turned to look over her shoulder at Theo and brought her hand to her ear in the shape of a phone and mouthed the words 'call me.' She then popped off the side of the bed and walked past them to make her exit. Simeon had a wide grin on his face, he loved Raquel's nature and she constantly reminded him that she gave zero fucks. She either bought out your best or worst, but it made her an interesting friend. He held up his fist for her as she passed, and she gave him a gentle bump and a cheeky grin.

"Theo my boy," Desta started.

"I'm sure you have a thousand questions, and I promise you we will answer each and every one of them for you, but let me start with the top three."

Desta had stopped about six feet from the bed, he was wearing a well fitted, three-piece, dark blue suit, minus the jacket. His light blue shirt was snug over strong arms, and the waistcoat hugged him tightly.

"Number one, you are safe. Number two, we are the good guys. Number three," there was a slight pause.

"We need you to save the world."

Practically standing on the pillows of the bed, Theo began to laugh gently at first, though, as he appeared to absorb the information his chuckling grew. He gently shook his head, almost accepting his bad luck. He was hoping all of this would just go away, and that the president didn't turn into, well... something he shouldn't be. He hoped when he was in the hospital as John Doe, he could slip away. Yet here he was, not only was this not going to go away, now there was Number three. Now he's responsible for saving the world!

He took a deep breath, the victim in him left, he smiled and looked right at Desta.

"There's no getting away from this, is there?" he sighed and asked all at once, Desta smiled back.

"Once you know why my friend, you won't want to get away from it, this I promise."

"What's going on? Where am I?" Theo quizzed.

"Right now, you are in Lugano Switzerland, in approximately five days a rare event known as the Passing of Nibiru will occur causing almost all life on earth to end."

"Of course, it is." He quipped back.
"What else could it possibly be?" Theo shrugged his shoulders and stepped forward, twisting to his left before letting his legs drop out from under him. He dropped on to the edge of the bed then used the momentum to lift him forward to land gently on his feet on the floor. He turned as he did, and stood looking at Desta and Simeon before him, in the beautiful soft setting of this beige themed room.

His soft socks and grey sweatpants were comfy, he thought; he had only now taken notice of what he was wearing. The soft glow of the sun tingled on his skin, his athletic shoulders and arms poked out of a singlet like Raquel's.

"Who changed me?" he asked
Simeon bellowed a laugh from behind Desta and Theo looked past the familiar face for the first time and saw the mighty Simeon properly. Almost eight feet tall, practically as wide but he projected a light from his smile. He had no hair on his dark brown skin and

from his thick muscular neck rich baritone laughs resonated and tickled the air around it.

"All in good time Theo, for now, please come join us for breakfast, I want you to meet the team." And with that, he turned and gestured with his hand towards the exit.

Simeon had already turned and was walking away, still chuckling gently to himself. Theo looked across the room, straight into Desta's eyes, he didn't know what to believe, who to trust, but something in his smile felt right and Theo decided there and then. Either these people were certifiably insane, or he was about to go and save the world. Both options scared the crap out of him, yet he had come this far and was still breathing.

"You have any pancakes?" he asked with a smile, as he made his way round the bed and out of the door.

Theo followed Desta from the bedroom, down a short hallway and into a vast open area, almost three stories high. The Cathedral ceiling above, provided an aesthetic feature and very strong finish. Huge glass panels climbed from floor to ceiling in a mosaic of giant rectangles. Through the windows Theo could see the stunning reflection of the sky on the glass topped water, stretching through the multitude of rich green foliage as far as the eye could see. In the middle of the room, was a giant fireplace, with the height of a man. It was a large, grey stone wall, wide at the bottom as it surrounded the giant simmering fire and then at about the same height as Simeon, it narrowed and formed a chimney.

In front of the fireplace, the floor had sunk, and within it, there were soft cream and dark brown sofas around a small reading table made of glass. They continued through this area and as they approached the edge of this wall Theo could hear the rest of the team chatting, clinking cutlery on plates, and generally chirping together as they ate. They stepped up a couple of dark wooden stairs and rounded the edge of the fireplace wall into the kitchen and dining area hidden behind.

Suddenly, all the clinking and chatting stopped, everyone in the team turned to look at their guest. Soft early morning sunlight poured in through the giant glass windows and with the lake as a backdrop, a large wooden table stretched away from Theo and Desta, running parallel to the giant fireplace and grey stone wall. It was close enough to feel the gentle warmth of the fire and sat proudly on a polished concrete floor that stopped at a large sliding door that led to a wooden deck outside. To the left, was an island bench with a large sink, and stove top, behind that; the first splash of white in the polished cabinets used through the modern styled kitchen.

The centre of the table was the same dark timber used through all the shelving in the fireplace wall and in the stairs. It was cut into a lighter wood which was covered in half eaten plates, serving dishes and glasses of all manner of juices. Around the table still looking at Desta and Theo were the rest of the Zeta's or Bringers of Light as they had been dubbed since before civilization.

Theo was thankful when Desta spoke for him and to the group, it was getting a bit awkward just standing there and having the whole table staring.

"We have a lot to get through Theo, but first we eat and introduce you to the team." He smiled with a reassuring wink and made his way to the seat at the head of the table directly in front of them. There was an empty seat on its left which he gestured Theo towards with his right arm.

"Hello again lover." Theo saw Raquel sitting at the other end of the table on the opposite side, she blew him a kiss as Kira who sat at the other head pushed her arm down to stop her.

Theo smiled back, he felt at ease as the gentle murmur of laughter and disdain, chewing and clinking of cutlery returned to the table. He could still feel all eyes or thoughts on him but he felt comfortable in their presence, which made him suddenly realise how hungry he was.

As the thought entered his head a hand dropped an empty plate into his spot, another left behind a glass, then a third poured water. Seamlessly the team stocked up their guests without even thinking about what they were doing. Conversation flew around as decisions were made about what he did and didn't *need* to taste and before he knew it, his plate was stacked high with pancakes, and bacon drizzled in fresh Maple syrup. Fresh orange juice sat in the glass to his right and at that very second, someone appeared over his left shoulder, reached onto the table, and dropped off a steaming hot mug of thick, black coffee.

"Thank you Nadev." Desta said to the bringer of coffee behind Theo.

"Come join us if you will." He gestured to the empty chair opposite Theo and the chef and pilot happily came round to join them.

"So, is this it D?" The South London accent asked excitedly above the group? Theo looked to his left and on his side of the table at the other end was Edmund leaning forward over his plate, looking down the table at Desta.

"You gonna tell him, like, now?"

"There is a lot to tell Edmund, as you well know, but yes, it starts right now." His gaze slipped to Theo as he finished his sentence.

Edmund and the rest of the team, all drew in a breath and mocked fear for Theo as if on Jerry Springer and he was about to get a giant reveal. It spilled into group giggle and some fun accusations.

"I'm pretty sure it was you that threw up when he told you" Theo just picked up through the light banter.

"Let the man get some food in his belly first," said the soft Deena as she looked at Theo and caught his eye. She was wearing her traditional Najib and a light blue flowing gown, it was her long thick eye lashes Theo noticed, and the blue makeup that framed them. It prompted him to pick up his knife and fork and he cut into his pancakes and eagerly tasted his first food for what felt like weeks.

The pancakes were light and fluffy, the syrup sweet, and just sticky enough. Though Theo wanted to savour the flavours, he was so hungry, he practically inhaled the first few bits of bacon and pancakes and was just having his first mouthful of hot coffee when Desta began to speak to the table and the light conversation around him ended.

"Theo?" He asked strongly, yet in a playful manner.

"How would you feel about joining us in saving the world?" He finished the sentence with a joyful grin, and the table of people erupted into a loud but quick cheer.

Theo couldn't help but smile at the question, and the energy with which it was being delivered.

"I'd love to." he replied,

"But I am not sure how or why I can help."

"You're the chosen one, that's enough, isn't it?" came a curt question from the voice next to Edmund. Mina threw out the statement like a little slap in the face and Desta countered.

"It isn't what they call us Mina, it is what we do." He turned to speak with Theo.

"As I told you earlier Theo, in five days, an event known as Nibiru Rising will occur in our galaxy which will kill almost 95% of all life on earth. We have been assembled and tasked with stopping this from happening for the last 40,000 years."

Theo almost spat out his coffee. "You're 40,000 years old?"

Desta's gentle laugh was lost in the tables, each of the members couldn't contain themselves when Theo asked the question..

"No Theo, our organisation, the Bringers of Light, has been entrusted with this task for the last 40,000 years. I am only 62."

"What task, what is Nibiru?" Desta reassured Theo with his eyes.
"Let me start at the beginning." Desta Replied

"Approximately 200,000 years ago a species of aliens descended onto earth with the intent of pillaging its resources, mostly water and gold. However due to certain Galactic Charters they had to keep this very quiet as it was also very illegal to harvest a class three planet."

Theo took a long deep breath as his brain was in overdrive, deciphering between what he knew, what he has seen and what he believes. Then, he just decided to be like water and flow with the story.

"I know how this can sound Theo." Desta diverted in response. The rest of the table sat in silence, watching their newest member hear the truth for the first time was 'one of the perks of the job,' Kira used to say.

"Don't worry about me." Theo replied, gently nodding his head as he did.

"Tell me it all." All the laughter and fun had left the room and the way Theo looked Desta dead in the eye as he said it, told him all he needed to know.

"200,000 years ago, the earth was lush with life, lush with clean crisp water and it existed in a perfect balance. For every action there was a perfectly weighted reaction, for every poison a perfectly weighted antidote. Nature existed in the ground, above the ground, in the sky and in the minds of every creature. Evolution of species and habitat had meant that over millions of years, the planet and every living organism had evolved together to create a place of perfect harmony, perfect balance. The idea of greed, fear, anger didn't exist, it wasn't even an idea. If ever a Garden of Eden existed, this was the time.

This balance all changed forever, the day The first Reptilians or Anunnaki as they named themselves arrived. Three large 'Hive' class vessels settled in orbit around the Earth, each one big enough to look like a small moon in the sky to the creatures below. Silently they sat dominant, looming, then after a few hours, like a swarm of angry bee's charging out of their hive, small ships fell from all three towards the planet's surface.

The politics of the vast Reptilian Empire was complicated. On board the Master Hive ship sat the Reptilian Queen of the Fang Dynasty, the civil war back home was engulfing her family and the larger and now combined forces of the Naga and Chimera Households were ripping through the hundreds of planets they controlled and harvested. It was threatening to spill into Federal Alliance territories involving the Zeta's.

The Zeta Reticulans, were the self-proclaimed Galactic Police and involving them was at the very bottom of all the Reptilians lists. They were an ascended species of Greys, with technology and weapons beyond anything the Reptilians had achieved. Their only chance was to outnumber the Zeta ships ten to one

The Queen of the Fang, like all Reptilians needed water, lots of it. Abundant on earth, throughout the rest of the universe it was as precious as diamonds. It fuelled their cities, their ships and sustained their 'Hoard'. After losing the ocean planet Re-Atung in a devastating battle, they had no choice but to risk harvesting this little-known class three planet. She knew it came at risk, Class threes were rare, and protected by the full weight of the Federal Alliance, and more specifically the Zeta.

The water alone might not have been enough, but previous scouting parties had returned with gold, a resource used to protect the core of the reactors in all their energy production, but also in the making of their most potent weapon. The Zettara - similar to the modern human Nuclear Bomb, the gold was used to prevent corrosion within the arming mechanism. This too was rare in the universe and pushed the risk to reward ratio in favour of setting up orbit.

The earth was indeed abundant and they found all the freshwater they could transport as well as more than enough gold to fuel the effort for control of the Empire and its power. The indigenous species on earth were so primitive they appeared to lack ego, awareness, but most importantly consciousness had not found its way onto the lush green ball, three planets back from their Sun. There was no resistance from any angle and for almost 100 years the Queen, and her two Hive sisters enjoyed the earth and all of its fruits. It remained the best kept secret in the Galaxy. Until it wasn't.

A Chimera Hive ship stumbled across the Class three in the Milky Way System but within seconds of coming out of warp their sensors lit up and they were immediately attacked. Unfortunately for them the Three Hives under the control of the Fang Queen were all set in a tight orbit around the Earth and as the foreign ship appeared they were within striking distance without even having to move. They were also drilled and prepared for this eventuality and the response to the visit of a foreign ship was brutal and shocking.

Before the Chimera Hive even had time to raise their weapons The Fang Ship's lit it up and under a barrage of missiles energy pulses, an explosion was triggered within, it bulged under the weight of heat filling it from its main engine core and split along its main hull before exploding outwards in a violent, silent ball of flames. They weren't even able to get a message out that they were under attack, so swift was the encounter. That didn't mean their whereabouts was unknown. The Queen needed to prepare for scouting parties looking for a lost 'Hive'.

In less than 7 days almost 30 Hive vessels, aligned with the Queen and the Fang Households were lying in wait. She had given up her secret but it was necessary to get the help needed to defend it. It wasn't certain that anyone would come looking for the Chimera Hive, but it was better to be prepared and not need it. In the end there was almost a month of silence and extra harvesting of the Earth and its resources as they took full advantage of the extra ships in orbit. Almost, because just as the Earth's Moon passed into a new phase, the skies of the earth burned as an Armada of Reptilian ships dropped out of warp and straight into the fight of their lives.

30 Ships, the size of small moons, loyal to the Fangs. 40 Loyal to the Naga claim. Thousands of Dart fighter ships from both sides, leaving the Hives, buzzing like angry bees. Bedlam, and confusion reigned in the vacuum of space around our fragile planet. Explosions seen from the surface, so violent and bright, the dark night sky would flash with hellfire for days at a time. On Earth, even the plants seemed to stare at the glowing night sky.

The war was huge and vast and stretched through countless galaxies and systems. Here in the Milky Way, the battle raged on countless plains. The Moon's surface and atmosphere buzzed with light, energy pulses shot though the sky and exploded in pockets of dust from the surface. The same dog fights were happening as ships and units burst into the Earth's atmosphere to take the planet. Thousands upon thousands of Darts, darkened the skies and screamed at each other as they took aim and the battle for Earth intensified.

It raged for weeks, most of the Hives had run or crashed onto the Earth or, as a last resort, the Moon. Communications were disrupted as almost all the debris and radiation in the Earth's atmosphere blocked vital signal patterns.

Reinforcements from both sides were on the way, but the huge battle was having effect on the effects of the Universal energies, and this had been felt by the Zeta. The Zeta were the unofficial partners of the Federal Alliance and took the protection of non-conscious planets very seriously. Their arrival changed the complexion of the situation and united the remaining Reptilians, and the arriving Hives against their common foe.

Without much time to stop it, the entire Reptilian race found themselves pitted against the Zeta and the Federal Alliance, all over a simple Class three planet in the Milky Way. It should have been a simple act of diplomacy to end the Alliance's involvement, but the stubbornness of the Reptilians is only second to their cruelness and all the houses united to take back control of the Alliance territories for themselves.

The next 50,000 years that stubbornness almost wiped out all advanced life in all the known planets as the Reptilians almost destroyed their own species as they took the Zeta to near extinction and took back partial control of the Alliance territories. However, their numbers were so depleted no one was really in control anymore and desperate lawlessness took over in the pockets where life still existed.

Through it all, the Earth was forgotten, this Class three dwarf planet was so far away, on the fringes of the known universe that even with the warp engine technology it was a fair trip. Through the literature and records kept on all sides the Earth was remembered, but each record that mentioned this small dwarf planet more accurately described the Earth's Moon rather than the Earth itself. The resource rich Eden remained hidden, remained lost, and Nature once again took back control. Although this time something was different.

The innocence of nature, the balance of nature was going to be tested. All across the surface, surviving, and thriving, were survivors of the wars. Some civilisations were already thousands of years old. Grown on the back of Reptilian technology early survivors had found in a downed Hive ship that was almost fully intact. They had been able to use it for a number of purposes, but none more significant than the genetic lab they used to begin to make the first humans.

Work had already begun prior to the war, but using this ship they were able to continue its work and within two generations had been able to add intellectual and universal awareness to the basic, man like creatures we know today as Homo Erectus.

They experimented with all manner of variations and created the basic tapestry of genetic variation we see today. These first civilisations were based on the Reptilian Deity Rule and the hundreds of thousands of slaves created, breading and thriving all worshipped their Reptilian 'Gods'

They also experimented with combining the Reptilian and Human Genome, through a number of means, including insemination and over the thousands of years they ruled, the Human - Reptilian hybrid became just another part of the variation of life on earth they had created. The Immortal Reptilian masters ruled, the hybrid humans became the elite, the ruling class. The rest of the 'pure' humans were just animals.

This disease grew as the consumption and selfish ego of these new creations took over from the balance that once existed. Consciousness and ego began to take hold and spread.

Thankfully, other survivors of the great battle were also thriving. On the very top of the planet a small civilisation had been growing, started by surviving Zeta and grown with small pockets of reptilian created humans and thousands of years to evolve. The Zeta, like their Reptilian foes were immortal. Time was kind and as more humans left the Reptilian controlled lands and found their way to

Zeta their numbers and power grew and from the first few Zeta, their genes were passed to their followers and the BOL were born.

Technology was abundant, but powered by a type of energy lost to the war, almost nothing worked and overtime it all was lost, to become part of myth, legend and magic.

The Civilisations grew and thrived, but every 2144 years, a cataclysmic event would throw the planet into chaos. Giant tidal shifts moving the oceans clean across continents. Volcanic eruptions from the very core of the planet would erupt, choking the planet for decades. Earthquakes would shake the whole planet and giant storms would tear the surface apart as energy flew around like the Earth had been tossed into a washing machine.

Time after time as any civilization was reaching a peak, again it would be torn apart by something they couldn't see from the surface. As each civilization reached closer to the answer, their research would all be wiped clean to start again every 2144 years.

Human life is resilient, often compared to a bacteria or virus and each time the Reptilian Masters would survive with a handful of slaves to start again. Around the planet, countless pockets of other human civilisations would also find a way to start. The Zeta too would face almost extinction, but they had come to the Earth with the knowledge of the great shift that occurs every 2144 year. The reason this planet has not been colonised and why the federation had decided to class it as a protected Class three.

The Milky way is at the mercy of an Iron Giant. A failed star called Nibiru. It was close enough at the formation of Earth's Star to get trapped in an elliptical orbit which it has never been able to escape from. Every 2144 years it whips through the Milky way over the course of 10 days, creating a giant gravitational vortex.

Depending on the specific location of the planets at each passing, it causes unbelievable gravitational and electromagnetic energy disruption. Turning planets on their axis, or sometimes even changing the orbit of an object. In 19BC it is believed to have moved Mars by 6 degrees.

The effect on the planet's surface is unpredictable and dependent on the Earth's position relative to the Sun when it arrives. Some years it passes close enough to shift the orbit and Axis, causing catastrophic change, others the earth is protected by being on the opposite side of our light source.

As a rule, if Nibiru's passing comes in winter, the effects are strongest, if in Summer it may barely be felt.

This Catastrophic celestial event was soon understood by the surviving Reptilian and Zeta refugees surviving on Earth. After losing to the planet again and again they finally understood why. The Reptilians charted Nibiru for thousands of years into the future and knew and planned their survival accordingly. The Zeta however stumbled across a much better idea at some time in history and using a technology lost to their history, were able to build a machine from old ship parts to use the earth's core to fuel a powerful electromagnetic field generator. Effectively the same technology they used as shields for their ships was re-engineered to put a huge shield up over the earth. It would protect the earth from gravitational shifts, electromagnetic changes and any and all of the effects of Nibiru but when building it, they decided they couldn't risk the machine falling into the hands of the Reptilians so it was decided to build a trigger that no Reptilian could ever fire to start 'Soteria' as it became known.

They designed a key to start the shield which would be triggered by the blood and willing sacrifice of a Zeta descendent. This way a Zeta would always have to give their life willingly to start Soteria and save the Earth. Something no Zeta would do under Reptilian control. Unfortunately, the Zeta under estimated their Reptilian foes and as human civilizations numbers grew, the Reptilian masters began to dominate the planet and its millions of slaves. They were able to seize control of Soteria and to fit their own wicked agenda were able to control the minds and humans on the planet. Through the grandeur and deceit of religion they were able to find Zeta bloodlines that could be persuaded to sacrifice themselves for the good of the people and in the name of their worldly Gods.

Through 200,000 years of human evolution and history the battle for the conscious minds raged and the Reptilians remained strong, using their power to control and dominate. Their immortal Masters did begin to reduce in number and over time the Zeta Greys that crash landed during the great battle, too began to fall away. The history was lost further, held by just a precious few minds, warped by hundreds of thousands of years of whispers and stories.

As the modern age began and mankind finally was flourishing, the True Blood Zeta Greys were all gone. All that were left were descendants and bloodlines that had mixed with the human genome whom all had a limited understanding of their heritage. Over centuries and through countless generations the blood and stories from the Zeta Greys spread through the early Muslim world. Stories from the ancestors morphed into religious doctrine and was used as a way to bring together the millions of Humans living and working together whilst carrying the Zeta gene. Religion grew as a way for the people to belong, it gave them answers to the pit they felt in their stomach whenever they listened. The Muslim faith allowed the Zeta, without knowing their history to unite against the Reptilians and they battled for their freedom and for that of the humans as well.

Only three True Reptilian Masters were left but beneath them was an army of powerful families all throughout the globe and all throughout society. They quickly learned the power of a God in the sky. It was a common tool used on many of the Harvest planets hundreds the Reptilians controlled before the 'Great War' that ended all of that.

The Reptilian religion evolved with the planet over time and since the 117th Passing event the Judeo-Christian faith has been their most effective and fruitful version. They started by making the 117th Zeta sacrifice the means to create Christianity. Jesus, or J'ou as was his actual name did in fact die on the Cross, it was done willingly, but it was in fact to start Soteria and prevent the planet's collapse. As a member of the dedicated Bringers of Light, J'ou was part of a small group that existed to remember the Zeta and the power of the Greys. It was also their job to make sure the machine was turned on if the Reptilians decided not to.

By creating an acceptable alternative to their already successful Judaism they guaranteed their success for the next Age. The Reptilian control through the Roman Empire was beginning to fail, and the only solution was for a Church to take its place. The Dark ages and the Crusades followed in the most horrifying period in our history but as the new Christian faith battled the infidel Moore's to the East, the Catholic Church tightened its grip around Europe and the centre of the known world fell deeper into their grip. The Zeta blood line still flowed through the Muslim world and through many other people on the planet, but the Reptilian resilience and patience had meant complete control of the Western world.

The Zeta story was relegated to folklore, conspiracy theories or to terrible books and movies. To all except a handful of decedents charged with keeping the story alive, and they had just one purpose. Find a Zeta sacrifice and start Soteria before the arrival of the 118th Passing.

The Reptilian strangle hold continued well into the industrial revolution. They had formed vast nations like the USA, countries, families, dynasties and through the British Empire and European Royalty controlled large parts of the world. The Muslim and Zeta issue was far more complicated than they would like to admit, millions upon millions of men, women and children all with the Zeta gene in their bodies, all the bad guys in the new global narrative.

Huge pockets of Human run nations and wealth was accumulating and was starting to threaten the power of the Reptilians masters and their Anunnaki followers. The Asian genomes were all free completely of any Alien DNA and a large pocket of Human countries in their Reptilian heartland in Europe almost ripped them apart as the humans came together to try to wrestle the planet free from their control during the 20th Century.

Adolf Hitler led a revolution by the Human factions that almost freed the world in what was the last Great Battle. For the first time in history, civilisations had been allowed to develop to the stage where Humans had large countries of their own, and through some very determined work, the young leader of the German Nazi Party had become aware of the Reptilian curse on Earth. It became his obsession to remove every Reptilian from the planet, and to remove anyone carrying their DNA to ensure they could never return.

Further dark days continued as Hitler and a coalition of human forces tried to wipe through Europe to remove the Reptilian blood line and Anunnaki decedents, along the way slaughtering millions of Jews to ensure their eradication was complete and Final. In his obsession to remove the Reptilians, he and the humans became worse than their enemies and as is often the way with Universal law, in the end the Reptilians rose strong. The Human nations of Russia and China backed the powerful Reptilian Masters and together, the nations they controlled *defeated* the European and Japanese Human uprising's all the while completely unaware of what Hitler and his forces were truly fighting for.

The end of the second world war allowed the Reptilians and their nation puppets to finally take control of the entire planet through a number of initiatives, but ultimately, they were finally able to position themselves as the world government with just a handful of countries, led by humans or Zeta aligned Muslim countries standing in front of them. Such was their power, they knew they would never be threatened again, not before the 118th Passing anyway.

Now, today, Earth is infected by the Reptilians and their influence. Not only do they control the most powerful countries on the planet, but they are the movies, the tv's, the news channels, the streaming, they are everywhere. Humans and descendant Zeta's live as the slaves they have always been, the owners are just smarter and the illusion, more complex.

This period has truly been spectacular by the Reptilian standards, they have numbers they cannot even dream of and almost 100% control and the freedom to take more. However, the human threat has become too strong. The Chinese can no longer be trusted and The Muslim countries are now to many in number, and a simple Crusade will not work. So this time, they have decided to allow Nibiru to pass without the protection of Soteria. Millions of the Chosen will disappear under the surface in huge Ark style cities that have been secretly dug, then emerge 10 days later to a new world. A world where the Reptilian mind and consciousness can again rule without resistance." Desta paused

"We are the BOL Theo. We need to start Soteria and save 7 billion lives. You are the Heosphorus Theo, the only one we have found with enough Zeta DNA to activate the machine." A smile creased over his lips.

"It's also not a coincidence we finally found you five days before the end of the World Theo. The universal energy is at play." Desta finished, locking up in acknowledgement of the unknown that is known.

Theo sat stunned, visions created by Desta's words had flashed before him, he felt like he had seen the Earth's history in person, and what a history it was. Darwinism and his 10th Grade history teacher had been a long way off yet, then again practically everyone was living a lie. The vastness of the deception took hold of his stomach, like a fist squeezing it. Nothing made sense anymore, nothing was real. His saliva glands began to tingle either side of his mouth and the knots in his stomach had spread to his chest. Then, he took a breath all at once he burped and coughed, he couldn't stop his freshly drunk coffee from coming up, and he leaned over to his right as the vomit, he wanted so badly to stop, burst from his mouth in a simple, single explosion.

The silence around the table was broken as a mixture of cheering and laughing erupted, Desta handed the breathless Theo a napkin. Theo dabbed at his mouth as he sat there looking at Desta. He felt immediately better after throwing up and as he wiped the slimy spit from his face, he looked at the team, and smiled. It went quiet in the room as they waited for him to speak.

"So, I'm the Sacrifice?" he said with a little trepidation in his voice.

"Yes, Theo, I am afraid so." Desta replied, it felt like the whole room held their breath at once.

Theo paused, thinking for a second, before he slowly raised his arms to the sky, looking at his new team and said:

"Ok I'm in, what do you need me to do?"

Chapter 20

Sleepy Joe

White house - Oval Office
02/03/2022
5 :28pm

Kamala tilted her head sideways with a sympathetic lip pursing as she sat in the comfortable chair directory opposite Joe Biden in the Oval office of the white house. She nodded along as he stumbled through something to do with Jen Saki, the Press Officer managing the public announcements, about his vacation, keeping focus on the fact we will have the first ever female, Acting President while he is away. He blinked repeatedly as he struggled to get out his son's name. B,b,b, Beau. She absentmindedly brought her hands together in her lap, praying to herself. 'How could she be this close to sitting in that chair?'

Her respect and love for the President was waning as she grew impatient and obstinate. Since they won the election, she had been much further behind the scenes than she expected and, on many occasions, she had disagreed with where her time was best spent. Knowing she already had the job but had to suffer this 'dementia ridden joke of a President', as she had described him to her husband, was wearing her down and her fragile ego would bruise every time she heard about herself through the lens of Fox News or another conservative publication.

She wanted to be loved and adored once she finally had the reins of the country in her hand. She felt confident would be the Presidents last trip away. The episodes were becoming far more frequent, and harder to hide from the non-partisan press. Even the social giants were pushing back, unable to censor half as much as they could before. The election was won, the hard work was done. She was expecting a medical episode and a tap on the shoulder to ask her to stay at the white house a little longer than the two weeks he was scheduled to be away for.

"Joe," she started in her best soft, southern version of herself. "You have already done so much, go enjoy a well-earned break. You know I'll keep the seat warm for you until you get back." she grinned her big white smile and laughed the way she always did when she was lying.

"Jane must be thrilled that Hunter and the grandkids are coming along."

"Hahaha oh yeah," he began to reminisce in the broken voice of an old man on the edge.

"Caroline and Charlotte are coming in with Beau's mother Jane." He smiled through a vacant grin past Kamala's right shoulder.

"You remember Jane?" he asked

"Stunning woman"

"Of Course Joe." Her head tilted again, as she exhaled, this time through sadness. Despite what she felt, it was a shame to watch a once great man fall apart like this.

"Amazing woman." she assured him.

Joe's eyes focused on the Vice President and after a second to gather his thoughts, he smiled at Kamala, once again back in the room.

"Take care of the place for me while I'm gone Madame President.' He said while standing from his chair.

"Oh Joe," she feigned as she stood up, understanding this was her cue to leave.

He was struggling to keep it together, she could see that and as he brought his hand up to his head to salute her, a genuine tear formed in her eye as she had a moment of true respect for him. Even with his mind going he was able to unite the democratic party to get rid of Trump and Trumpism, and even now, when his mind is only half his, he is noble enough to walk out of here with his pride and integrity.

"Do me proud Kamala." he said while bringing it down.

"Yes Sir," she replied. Sniffing back genuine emotion.

"Now get out of here kid, you know I'm not great with goodbyes." His face was lit up with a beaming grin that shot Kamala back to her role.

Her stomach and chest were dancing inside as she turned and began her walk out the room, to her new reality, as the President of The United States of America. As she reached the door, she turned to look at him again, he had turned and was looking out over the rose garden, his hands clasped behind his lower back.

"Thank you Joe." She whispered before grabbing the handle and leaving.

As her door on the East side of the room closed, the opposite one on the West wall opened, and in walked Hunter Biden in a suit almost identical to his father's.

"Fuck, I didn't think she was ever going to leave," he announced as he walked the floor to sit in the same chair she had just come from.

"Oh man, seriously Son, that is one ignorant son of a bitch if ever I saw one." Joe quipped back as he sat back down at his desk, tieless and with a much more alert look in his eyes. He reached to his right and opened his bottom draw and pulled out 2 glasses, followed by a decanted, dark brown liquid.

"I am still blown away by the size of her ego, to believe that we would ever let a Spik, Nigger like her ever lead this country." Joe Continued. He was shaking his head in disbelief while he poured two small glasses and slid one across to Hunter.

"Thank fuck for Socials, CNN and her sycophantic husband. Ha, and of course BLM." Hunter finished.

"Fucking BLM." Joe said, nodding along and snickering as he raised his glass and drank a sip. Hunter downed his and proudly placed it back on the desk in front of him.

"So, when are we getting out of here?" He asked.

Joe fiddled with his glass in front of him as he replied.

"Marine one is taking off in thirty minutes and taking us to Andrews. We should be at the bunker by ten. Mum and the girls are meeting us there. They should already be in the living quarters and unpacked by the time we get there."

"The list I gave you, did you get it to Klain?"

"All taken care of, all of them will get the alert when I send it out." he said reassuringly.

"Just remember son, we have over a million people coming underground with us and we have to leave the alert until as late as possible to protect its integrity. There will be some collateral damage along the way."

"Hey, I get a first-class ride to the end of the world, what happens outside of that, stays outside of that." He flicked his glass in triumph as he finished his poignant statement.

"You really are in a good mood today aren't you son?" He flicked the end of his own nose and looked at Hunter. Looked at him hard and straight into his eyes. Searching.

"No." he protested, raising his hands.

"Just high on life, I'm not kidding around. We get a first-class seat to the end of the world as we know it and I get to come out the other side. I'm excited, for the first time in a long time, I am actually excited, without my usual assistance."

Joe sat for a second and assessed, before finally standing and saying

"I'm proud of you boy, now let's get ready for our first-class seats then."

With that he downed what was left of his drink and then left the Oval Office for the last time.

Chapter 21

The Bringers of Light

Lugano Switzerland – Zeta Mansion
3/03/2022
10 :10pm

Theo had been with the group now and through breakfast, feeling immediately relaxed and welcomed amongst, 'like-minded souls,' as Deena called them. While wolfing down stacks of pancakes, fresh orange juice and thick, smoked bacon, Desta had gone around the table and introduced the whole team to Theo.

The young, boyish, and very pale face at the end of the table belonged to Edmund Robbins. His Southern London accent cut through all the voices at the table when he spoke. Theo loved it, Edmund oozed enthusiasm, for the group, for Desta, and most importantly for their purpose. Apparently, Desta had found him sitting on the 110 South Circular bus one afternoon. His mother had recently died, she was your typical white English girl from South

London and through the grief and process, he had discovered his unknown father was of Arabic decent and a devout member of a Jihadist sleeper cell in the UK. He explored far deeper than he had originally intended, and in the end something inside him felt pulled away from the mainstream. When he finally met some of his father's colleagues and friends, he too began to see a clear purpose for himself. Unfortunately, like so many other Bringers of Light, this need to find purpose had been poisoned by the lies of man and religion and when sitting on that bus, Edmund found himself surrounded by innocent, beautiful life, whilst strapped to 3kg's of plastic explosives. Ready to wipe it all out, in the name of a false idol.

Luckily, Desta was on that bus too, though it wasn't an accident. Edmund's father had been a lost member of a strong BOL bloodline, and Desta's team had been watching him his whole life. Fully aware that this boy may be pure enough to start Soteria. It turned out, his mother's genes were dominant in him and even though Edmund was blessed with the ability to slightly slow time, and had never been sick in his entire life, he was only in the twentieth-percentile range, based on the genetic sequencing. He was not pure enough to start the machine. Even though, he was still one of the best stealth men in the business and a key part of the team, the search continued.

Alongside Edmund, was the dark, smooth, Arabic complexion of Mark 'Mina' Yakoub. Self-proclaimed, then loudly validated by the group, demolitions expert and with a voice, "smooth as Chocolate", as Edmund would joke. He, like Edmund, was in his mid-twenties and had come to the group through a similar path to his best mate, and Call of Duty partner.

Mark had been a young, aspiring musician living deep in the West Bank region of Palestine. He was just 13 the day his life changed forever. He loved to sing, and chant and though people couldn't understand the words, they it found hypnotic. He would fight with his father constantly about his 'gift' as he called it.

He would bury his head when his father and older brothers would frequently spew hate about the Israelis to the East. He wanted nothing to do with any of it, it seemed like a never-ending cycle that was perpetuated on both sides by intolerance and ignorance. Then, one evening, during the Seven Day war of 2011, bombs fell from the sky and destroyed his home. Mark was minutes away when he heard the explosion, and he knew instantly that something was wrong.

Inside, his mother and father were killed on impact, along with two of his sisters. One survived for several weeks after, long enough to fight for her life in the hospital. She suffered agonising pain and was horribly burned, Mark sat by her side and refused to leave. His tolerance for the Israeli aggressors lessened each day, and by the time the monitor by the side of her bed rang out a single, monotone, and unrelenting beep, he no longer wanted to bury his head.

The feeling in the pit of his stomach turned to rage, rage became revenge, and revenge led him to the Ashdod Market Square in Tel Aviv with almost a kilo of bearing filled pipe bombs strapped to himself. He was lost in the face of a child when a hand squeezed his shoulder and told him it was ok. He turned and that was when he had met Desta for the first time. Like Edmund, Desta and the BOL had been monitoring his bloodline and were hopeful he could start the machine. Unfortunately, he was not pure enough, and yet under the wing of Desta, he too became a vital part of the BOL.

Raquel was the women he had met when first waking up. She apologised again to him for playing with him earlier, then with her tough Aussie accent and masculine exterior, she gave the 'short version' of her path to the BOL. It turned out her Grandmother had, 'got knocked up,' by some Muslim bloke during a Kubutz in Israel back in the 60's' and had given birth to Raquel's mother 9 months later, back home in Sydney. This "Muslim bloke" was from a line well known to the BOL, though some sort of mutation had seen Raquel's mother with exceptionally high levels of BOL DNA markers. It meant that her eyes had a permanent light glow, and since finishing puberty in her teen years, she could move things with her mind and see the future, though she never admitted this to anyone. Raquel had never known her mother, she had unfortunately died during childbirth, and a lifetime in the foster system in Australia had seen her grow up into a tough, tomboy Aussie, with a fancy for shiny things.

Her first meeting with Desta was very different to the boys. Raquel had inherited some of her mother's power and was walking back into her Suite at the Vatican Hamilton hotel when she found a dark-skinned man sitting in the chair behind the desk. She was dressed in all black, in a sleek, skin-tight suit and she had on her back a black rucksack. Immediately she saw the figure in the chair, her right arm shot out and a knife flew. It slammed into the back of the chair, yet the figure was already gone, now sitting on the sofa to her right.

"Who the fuck are you?" Were her first words to Desta. She could be forgiven for being heightened. She was returning to the room just after stealing the nine bones of St Peter, from deep within the Vatican, on a contract from some "German Dick Head".

She loved adventure and was immediately down for joining a kick ass team to stop the end of the world. She didn't even need convincing. Desta had hoped with her mother's highly elevated levels that Raquel would be able to start the machine, but she too was not pure enough.

Nadev Imahn was the slightly older, more deliberate, chef, pilot and general Ops manager of the team. He made sure things worked and fitted together. He knew machines like no one else on earth, and by the stack of pancakes, knew pancakes like no one Theo had met. He managed the maintenance of the planes, choppers, weapons, and was also the unofficial counsellor to the other members of the group. He had a wise head on his shoulders, and when he wasn't working, his head was buried in another book. Part of his BOL abilities included his photographic memory, he was a walking Google as Raquel would joke and a vital part of the team's response.

His accent was hard to place, as it had come from a childhood in Russia, followed by his teen years and a life in the army in Israel. His English was flawless, though when he spoke, it was like a mix of Eastern European, French, and American sounds all fighting for dominance.

During his time in the military, he had become a deadly member of the elite Mossad, super intelligent and with unmatched reflexes, he was one of the best and was destined for a long career in the army before an incident involving his unit on an incursion deep into the West Bank. An assassination had gone wrong, and his team was ordered to 'remove' any witnesses. They were torn on the ethics yet, they were ready to execute the women and children as ordered, and then something in Nadev snapped. In the blink of an eye, he had killed half his unit and in the second blink, the other half were either killed or maimed.

The Palestinians he saved had survived, only to disappear a few weeks later. In the West Bank, Nadev had to live in secret, living above a sparsely stocked chemist with an old dog, sick on the pavement out in front. He wrestled with his conscience for weeks until Desta knocked on his door. Nadev was a strong BOL candidate on his Grandfather's side dating back to the first world war and in the thirtieth-percentile, yet it was still not enough.

The dark hair and flawless skin belong to the alluring Deena Abu Hamed, her accent had a hint of English, a sprinkle of American, yet certainly came from the middle east. She was shy, reserved, though very curious about the world and the people in it. She was from a very well-known family in the UAE and was chosen for marriage to the Saudi King's third son Alhambra Jehardi, to keep the blood pure. She was gifted far too young and what she had endured as a 10-year-old, she would never speak of.

Something had happened during one sexual assault and Jehardi had some sort of seizure, he started foaming at the mouth before swallowing his tongue and dropping dead at Deena's feet. It had come at a moment when she had her hands scratching at his face, trying to get him to stop while trying to yell. He had her mouth covered with his hands though, so in her head, she screamed at him "Choke on your tongue you pig" and he did.

It haunted her for days after, and she was accused of poisoning him by his guards and the Royal family. As she was praying in her prison cell, almost certainly going to be stoned for his murder, she whispered to a small cockroach to get her out of here. She held it in her hands, its small antenna searching either side of her face, she looked at it and pleaded as she realised her fate was sealed. It jumped down and scurried away, under her door, and into the hallway.

As Deena was sobbing in her room, a scratching sound appeared on one of the walls, and within seconds a hole had appeared. Thousands of cockroaches were devouring the plasterboard walls, creating a hole for Deena to walk through. One roach flew up and landed on her hand, she looked at him and it was the same roach. A warmth went through her as she realised what was happening and with a smile and her new friend on her shoulder, she ducked through the hole and made her escape.

Roaches came from everywhere and within a minute, hundreds of thousands of swarming insects surrounded Deena as she walked free from her captors, many tried to stop her along the way, yet she still she managed to reach a distant relative in the city, where she was able to hide. She planned to stay a few days before trying to make it to the US where she had a trusted Uncle. On her first night there, Desta knocked on the door and she followed a much more meaningful path.

Desta and the team had never seen the BOL gene manifest itself in such a way to provide its owner with the power of simple persuasion, though it seemed Deena could command pretty much any human or creature to do her will. During breakfast she had commanded Theo to blow a kiss at Simeon, while laughing in protest something took over and blow, he did.

Simeon was Desta's' shadow, and no one in the team knew anything about him, besides Desta. He liked it that way, he spoke rarely, and when he did the resonance his voice and choice of words, made everyone listen. His size would shock most normal people and he had gotten used to being stared at. Eight feet tall and with a neck the size of most men's waists, he was the muscle when needed. Blessed with supernatural strength, he could bench press close to 1000kgs, and yet, it was his ability to heal which was his most helpful ability to the team.

His eyes would glow so white one couldn't bare to look at them, yet when touching someone who was sick or injured, he could heal them almost instantly. Twice, Edmund had been pulled back from the edge of death by Simeon, and each time Simeon used his gifts it would drain him hard. So much so that the last time, pulling three bullets out of Edmunds torso, he had slept for close to three days while recovering, Edmund, however, was up jumping around that afternoon.

Kira was the only member of the group that Theo didn't feel a welcome from, being Desta's number two, she was as smart as they come. She was also, as Desta would remind her, not healed from her past, explaining why she didn't trust Theo, or practically anyone outside of the group. She was able to see 'what was to come,' as Desta phrased it. Unfortunately, like Deena, her gift hadn't started until puberty. She didn't foresee the men coming to take her Grandparents land and lives in the cold tundra of Novosibirsk, on the Easter boarder of Russia. At only 7 years old, she hid, terrified as they killed her grandfather, and frequently used her grandmother like a doll until they were done then, tossed her onto the fire to join her already ashen husband.

She had seen each of their faces, and something inside her died that day, though from death, comes new life and a hunger and hatred that kept her alive, scavenging in the desolate countryside for years. She trained her body and her mind, knowing one day she would see those faces again, and her determination paid off.

She was working the pumps at a petrol station when a Jeep appeared and, inside it, were three familiar faces, instructing her to fill the tank. The owners that had taken her in, were at a safe distance when all three of the men in the jeep died, screaming on the inside, though silent and in agonising pain as they burned together slowly, unable to move. The mivacurium she had sharply injected them all with, had kept them awake to hear who she was and why this was about to happen, but left them paralysed and unable to escape.

Desta had found her many years later, working for the Russian mob. Her gift had made her very accomplished at making people disappear. She had seen Desta coming into her life, though at that stage had very little control and no insight into who he was or why he was coming. The truth about the world shocked her, and yet she wanted in; her gift had made so much of where they were now possible.

"She will warm up when she gets to know you." Desta assured Theo.

All members of the team, including Theo, were now gathered on the sofas on the other side of the fireplace. Full stomachs and introductions out of the way, Desta had them gathered to get down to business, to finalise the plans, and to bring Theo up to speed with what was about to transpire.

A giant screen slid down from the wall above the fireplace and dropped to completely cover the flames behind it. Desta, with a clap of his hands, the lights dimmed. First up was a picture of the Vatican from the sky. The tell-tale shape of St Peter's Square and red roof tops got closer as the image zoomed in and Desta explained what they needed.

"First thing we are going to require is the cross of Christ, which as you can probably tell from this bird's eye view is held at the Vatican. This is basically the key Theo, to turning on the machine. They keep the cross deep within its own room, in a tunnel off of the forbidden library."

"Forbidden library?" Theo's face lit up at the prospect

"Exactly what you think it is Theo. Everything the Church and the Anunnaki deem important enough, ends up down there. Fifty thousand years' worth of history, but we are there for the key." He looked at Raquel when he delivered his last line and both Edmund and Mark threw little rolled up pieces of paper at her causing the whole team to laugh.

"We are going to be splitting into two teams upon arrival at this point." A laser pointer indicated the entrance to St Peters.

"Deena, Kira and I will be going in through the front door. Kira has seen they have bought the Ducaz and are laying some sort of trap. They are set up in the main hall of the forbidden library and after taking a few down we will use Deena to get them to bring us and hold us there. Our sources tell us orders are to bring us in alive if possible, so we will make it possible."

"So, you're going to get captured?" Theo asked.

"Precisely, and while we are waking them up through the main Basilica entrance, you, Simeon, Edmund, Mark and Raquel will be heading in through this entrance."

The screen zoomed in again and swung to show the front of the buildings and a 3d image of the main Papal residence, just to the North of the main Basilica.

"You four will enter through this balcony and use the old escape tunnels to navigate to what is a wall adjacent to the main hall. There Mark is going to work his magic and you will burn through the wall and enter the hall without being seen."

"We are going to burn through a solid brick wall?" Theo asked and turned his head to look at Desta

Mark piped up excitedly.

"Leave that to me, Chosen One. As Desta said it's magic." He ended with a smile and a puff of flame leapt from the palm of his hand. Theo couldn't tell if it was a trick or not.

"If the intel we have is still correct, then you will be entering the hall here?"

The original image was replaced by a CGI image of tunnels, and the main hall appeared. A red pointer indicated where the tunnels from the Papal residence ran alongside the main hall and, where they would enter. Based on the visions Kira had, had, this would be on the opposite side to where they would be held and should allow them to enter the hall unnoticed. She had seen a circular desk near the main entrance at the opposite end to the tunnel entrances, and a long road between tall wooden bookshelves.

"We expect to be held near the main admin desk at the front, and once in, you will split again. Mark will stay in the hall and prime it for our exit and contingency, whilst you, Raquel, Edmund and Simeon will head through this exit, and run along these two corridors until you enter this room. This is where the cross is being held." He paused for a second.

"We don't expect it to be easy down there. We understand as many as four pure Ducaz are on site and half of the Elite Ducaz human hybrid unit too." Desta stopped when he saw Theo put up his hand. Pre-empting his question, he continued.

"Sorry Theo. The Ducaz are an ancient, alien soldier, built by the Reptilians hundreds of thousands of years ago. We believe there are 5 of them left here on Earth, leftovers from the early wars and settlements. They look like a crocodile, but they walk mostly on their hind legs. They were their elite soldiers, built in labs they regenerate using a similar hormone to an Earth lizard losing their tails.

In a Ducaz soldier though, it never turns off. They live forever and will regenerate a lost limb or organ within an hour. They can be killed with trauma to the heart or through a small hole in their skull on the top of their heads.

They work with the humans, but are a very closely kept secret and know nothing other than obedience to their Nephilim, or Reptilian Master."

"Pretty much the most badass thing you could ever meet in a dark alleyway" Raquel's Australian vernacular joined the briefing.

"The Ducaz, Human hybrid unit is exactly as that sounds too Theo. They have built a unit of 40 soldiers, all enhanced with Reptilian and Ducaz DNA adjustments. They are faster, stronger and don't feel pain."

"Super soldiers?" Theo nodded along.

"Of course we have walking crocodiles and Super soldiers. Please, carry on." he said smiling and looking back to the screen.

Back on the screen, the red dot reappeared, and Desta continued with the plan.

"So, you guys enter through these tunnels and bring back the cross which will be in here, we expect you to meet resistance, but Raquel and Simeon are there to handle any of that. You and Edmund focus on getting the cross and getting back to the main Hall. Once you engage down near the Cross room, it will all light up in the hall and we will take that as our cue to take care of the guards and be ready to leave through the same hole you all came in through."

"Don't be surprised if you hear a small bang when you get back in the tunnels, once we engage, I'll be blowing the main entrance." Mark added.

"When Mark blows the entrance that will block the main way in and out, but we will be making for the tunnels," Desta continued.

The screen changed again and, the bird's eye view of St Peter's square appeared once more, this time with the route of the historic escape tunnels transposed over the top.

"The main Papal tunnels come up here, here and here." Destas' pointer circled the three spots in question.

"We however will be blowing through another section here and disappearing into the sewers." The bird's eye view zoomed out until the Tiber River could be seen to the West of the main Vatican hub.

"We will pop out here where Nadev will be waiting with a boat to take us up the Tiber, back to the airstrip we came in on. We will have allies guarding the strip and it's all aboard to our next destination. Any questions at this point Theo?"

"About a thousand, but nothing important at this stage, where is the next destination?" he asked without looking away from the screen.

The picture changed, Theo was looking at a bird's eye view of a dusty looking compound, small buildings nestled between large warehouse style structures and a large, solid wall encircling the whole thing.

"The American Embassy in Baghdad." Desta announced

"One of the toughest places on the planet to break into, but the home of Soteria, and where we need to take the key if we are going to prevent Nibiru's passing from ending it all."

Theo exhaled a single "Ha" as the enormity of the task began to dawn on him. Desta could again sense, and feel Theo's mind begin to tell him this was impossible and stepped forward until he was directly behind him. He placed his hand on his shoulder and reassured him.

"Theo, I know this looks impossible, but we have trained our bodies, and our minds to ensure we are prepared. This plan has been growing for the last 15 years."

"Yeah, don't worry about us mate, we have been through much worse and survived. American Embassy, piece of cake." Edmund assured him, the rest of the group nodded in agreement and without blinking Desta continued.

"Here to the South East, Um Al-Khanzeer Island is where Nadev is going to bring us in in the Jet. We have friendlies in control of a strip of land we will use to get down on the ground."

"Won't they see the jet on the way in?" Theo asked

Nadev answered as if he knew the question was due.

"Abigail does not show up on conventional radar, without no lights, they will not see us."

"We also have a large friendly group that will be creating diversions at these two points." The screen zoomed in on the compound on the right of the screen.

Some of the buildings had labels, showing the barracks, warehouses etc in more detail. Desta circled two areas, One, the main street entrance to the north, and the other, the goods and services entrance just over the 14th July Bridge to the East.

"What sort of diversion are we talking?" Theo asked and looked over his shoulder at Desta.

"A couple of thousand pissed off Muslims are showing up to fuck shit up." Raquel recanted as Desta was just opening his mouth to reply.

"Pretty much what she said." he said looking at Raquel, gently asking her to tone it down with his eyes and gifts.
"They will keep the main security from the compound busy while we come in through here."

Desta's pointer outlined where the south portion of the compound met with the Tigris River inlet that circled the Island they were landing on. The map zoomed in around this area and there was a rock wall that went directly down, deep into the water. On the other side of this wall was the main road circling the American Embassy compound.
"Twenty feet under this point is an old tunnel entrance dating back thousands of years, but it was flooded in 1914 by the creation of Al-Kahnzeer. It leads to this point under the embassy compound."

The pointer had stopped on the roof of a building. Theo could identify nothing special about it, like almost every other building on the map, it had a white roof. The screen again zoomed into the point circled by Desta, a stunning building surrounded by thick sandstone pillars appeared and came into focus.

"In the South West corner of the compound this old piece of the original Baghdad architecture sits about one hundred feet above Soteria. Once we scuba up through the tunnels underneath we will appear in an old bath house that was built around the key to Soteria in around 200AD. We don't know what for sure will be waiting for us in there but we are trusting in Kira's visions and Universal Karma to help us once we get in. Once we fight our way to the machine, we need to stand the cross directly in the hole at the centre of the platform to engage it, and that's where your blood is required. No one knows for sure what happens but we."

"I have a pretty good idea," Theo interrupted.

"I had a dream about how this last part goes down and I'm ready for it. I think there will be some sort of...

"Holy Fuck!!!" Edmund exclaimed loudly.

"Sorry to interrupt but we need to put on the news. Something big has just happened in Baghdad," he said, gesturing to a message he had received on his phone.

Desta signalled with his right hand, causing the screen to switch to a live feed of CNN World Edition and the room was silent as each of them read the headline scrolling across the bottom of the screen. *NUCLEAR BOMB EXPLODES IN BAGHDAD - MUSHROOM CLOUD SEEN FROM NEIGHBOURING IRAN.....*

Chapter 22

Mushrooms and Books

Baghdad Book Market
03/03/2022
12 :18pm

Malakai stood at the feet of his mother as the hum of Baghdad's famous book market buzzed around him. He had never seen so many colours in his entire life. Walls of books were piled in every direction he looked, built by thousands of multi-coloured bricks. Some stretched into the shops, while others were just laid on the dusty, sandy ground on blankets, or sheets, other piles were stacked on wooden pallets. The unmistakable smell of old books collided with the desert air, mixing with his mother's familiar perfume as he tugged on her Burka, while looking up at her.

In her hands, she held a small red book with gold writing almost piped along the front and the spine. She felt the gentle tug of her adoring son, and she looked down at him with her kind brown eyes pressing the book to her chest as she did.

Malakai tilted his head back to look at his mother, his protector, and saw the same beautiful eyes that his father had fallen in love with. Her eyes were perfectly framed within the black ring of her Burka. Just a tiny tuft of healthy dark hair fell harmlessly onto her forehead. She had lush, though subtle, lilac eye makeup and flawless glowing skin; Malakai thought of her as the most beautiful woman he had ever seen. The fact that he'd only seen about ten women didn't matter to him, his mother was his angel.

At four years old Malakai was already ahead of his grade, able to read both the English and Arabic alphabet, and able to form words from the letters on the page of both languages. Books excited him, as his father and mother had worked very hard to read to him every night since he was old enough to listen, and for the past week, his mother had been teasing him with the promise of a trip to his favourite book market.

Just inside the covered area in front of them, he had seen a table of what looked like hard backed Marvel Comic books. With a big giant grin on his tiny face, he pointed to the table asking his mother permission to go and look. She glanced over to the table and then back to see the shopkeeper sitting shoeless on a cushion with a cigarette between his pursed, dry, sun kissed lips. The sun reflected off the bald spot he was so desperately trying to hide as the smoke from his little cigarette gently snaked up his face, yet he wasn't paying attention at all; he had his head bent forward as he dove deep into a mysterious novel positioned on his lap.

"Go my baby." she said as she used her right hand to guide him in the direction of the shop opening. His light leather sandals slapped the floor as he excitedly skipped over to see what he could find. The noise caused the shopkeeper to glance up from his book though, only for a second and only to take another puff of his cigarette. His mother closed the red book in her left hand, and once again, began to look through the books in front of her, on the table, in the street.

"Mama, Spider man!!" he yelled, just as he reached his table. It was a statement without a need for follow up as he hungrily grabbed the first book of the pile and began to dig deeper to see what else he could find.

His crisp white shirt contrasted against his light brown skin though, matched his bright white teeth when he smiled. It was tucked neatly into his cream shorts, revealing his two thin legs, and on his feet were his favourite leather sandals. Although to most he was the spitting image of his father, he had been fortunate enough to inherit his mother's full lips. With his neat dark hair, at only four he looked like a perfect little man. He was going to be a 'heartbreaker,' his father would always boast.

His mother shuffled a couple of books to the side and pouted as if disappointed; she hadn't found anything that she was looking for. She looked over at Malakai and he was now sitting on the floor with his legs crossed, shoulders hunched, and a very colourful book open in his lap. A warm gust of air flicked the pages of his book, and with resolve, he used his hands to hold them and stop them from turning.

"Malakai my love what did you find?" He looked up from his book and his big brown eyes lit up with excitement.

"It is the Batman mother, like the man from the cartoon." he said barely able to contain his joy; yet his mother didn't hear him.

In the distance, at the main market, a text message arrived on the phone of the man in the white van on the corner. It read 'The new bed was just right.' Then there was a loud explosion. Loud enough to completely drown out Malakai's words, loud enough to feel it in her chest, in her ears, through her whole body. It shot past them like a mass wave of sound, enough to disrupt everything that it swept through, enough so that almost everyone instinctively dropped to their knees and covered their heads. Malakai's ears rang so loud he couldn't even hear his own voice as he screamed for his mother. She instinctively ran to him unable to hear anything herself, barely able to see due to the pain in her ears.

She fell to the floor next to him and cradled him in her arms, pulling his head into her chest and wrapping as much of herself around him as she could. She held him tightly as her ears rang. Although she couldn't hear him, she could feel his chest heaving as he cried.

The shopkeeper and the rest of the people at the market had all recovered to their feet, unable to hear yet could see a huge mushroom shaped cloud forming in the sky, no more than half a mile from where they were. The thick blanket of black smoke convulsed as lightning strikes exploded within, giving it power and energy as it grew, spilling over itself, climbing higher, wider, thicker. On the ground, on their knees in the shop they couldn't see it, yet they could feel the rumble beneath their feet.

From the sky, and the high-rise buildings, a wave of destruction, could be seen, circling out from the centre the explosion rippled through the city. Like a tsunami of invisible water washing everything away, the city of Baghdad began to crumble. Behind it, a storm of fire and lightning rode on its tail, incinerating those in its immediate path.

The table next to them fell to the floor and Malakai's mother gasped, showing her fear for the first time in front of her terrified son. Unable to hear, they felt the ground convulsed harder, causing the books surrounding them to fall like random apples shaken from a tree. He screamed, silently protected by his mother as the wave of terror tore through the meagre setting of the book market. Dust picked up, and carried by the huge explosion nearby, blanketed the area, robbing them both of their hearing, and now see. Malakai's mother grabbed her son tight and held his head in her hands.

The white sandstone buildings around them took the brunt of the impact and cracked under the pressure, books shredded and anyone out in the open practically imploded under the sheer pressure of the shockwave. Like a Tornado of debris, noise, and death tore through and ripped everything it could find to pieces. It raged around Malakai and his mother as they both prayed.

Malakai's mother began to whisper the words and ask Allah to bless her son. She held him like it was the last time she ever would, and he buried himself in her embrace. Tears filled her eyes,

"Allah!!! My son!!" she begged

Malakai too was praying to Allah, he believed in that moment, Allah could send Spider-Man to him, that when he opened his eyes Spiderman or Batman would be there to rescue him and his mother.

Unfortunately, all that came was a wall of heat and flames as their earthly bodies combusted, burning together in their final embrace.

Lugano Switzerland – Zeta Mansion
03/03/2022
12 :45pm

The footage on the TV repeated over and over. The pundits were as shocked and stunned as they were excited by the prospect of the biggest news story of the year. A huge mushroom cloud growing over the city of eight million people stunned the world, as it stunned each member of the BOL team. It was Desta who broke the silence.

"This, changes nothing," he said.

"Make sure your affairs are in order, and get some rest, because tonight we leave to do what we are destined to do. Kira, wrap up here and give Theo some weapons training. The rest of you, see you at 1am"

With that, Desta left for his office to get everything ready. Theo was still a little stunned by what he had just seen, but in the context of everything he had learned in the last twenty-four hours, it seemed trivial.

Chapter 23

Up and Away

White House Lawn — Marine One
02/03/2022
7 :28pm

The engine, atop Marine one, clicked to life and the long drooping blades began to move. The staff were all retreating to the White House to escape the persistent drizzle in the air. The noise level began to rise sharply, as it built momentum, and before long it was spinning above them at full speed and ready to leave the White House lawn.

"We are at take-off speed Mr President, Marine one is good to go." The voice of Captain Benjamin James Pritchard came through the overhead speakers of the lush new interior of the President's personal helicopter. It had, had a serious upgrade under the previous administration and now resembled the interior of a New York Limousine, all kitted out with a grey leather finish.

Two thick leather recliner chairs sat facing each other along one side of the customised VH-92 helicopter; whilst two more were on the other wall facing inwards. All the chairs were of the same design, and each had the unmistakable seal of the President of the United States embroidered into the headrests.

Joe Biden was seated in the direction of the cockpit; he reached and pushed the button built into the right arm of the leather chair. The cabin had been reinforced to protect those onboard from the sounds of the rotors, even at maximum yield it was barely louder than sitting on Air Force one, so President Biden didn't have to excerpt himself much when he said.

"Take us up Ben."

He looked at Hunter, sitting opposite from him.
'Was he clean?'
'Was he telling the truth?'
'Would this never end?'
He wanted to believe what he had told him earlier, but he had heard it so many times before.

The rest of the chopper was empty, even the Marine One guards that usually sat up front had remained at the White House. The two of them sat deep in their chairs and Joe joined Hunter in casually looking out of the windows as the world below them got smaller and smaller as they began their vertical climb.

"It's going to look a lot different when we get back," Hunter said with a subtle smile

"If only they knew," Joe replied, hinting at some regret in not warning some of the people left behind. It was enough to get

Hunter's attention. He looked at his dad, sharp eyes in a tired face looking down at the world they were leaving.

"What do you mean?" he asked, a little confused, he had never seen his father show any signs of doubt in the Anunnaki goals, and certainly any mercy in their pursuit.

"Ah," he asked, looking at Hunter, then as if snapping out of a thought he answered with a chuckle.

"Oh no, I'm just thinking of Kamala sitting behind that desk right now thinking that she has it all. I just wish I could be there when it all goes to hell in a petticoat!"

Hunter cracked a smile as Joe continued.

"If that piece of crap looked at me with that tilted head, and condescending smile one more time I swear son, I was gonna rip it clean off." He held his hands in front of him, miming a strangulation as he spoke but smiling while he did.

Her fate would be far sweeter for him. To see her drown in the blood of every American left on the surface. For the world to end, practically on her watch, to know that she would need to look at herself in those last moments and surely see the truth. Not about the Reptilians, Anunnaki, Nibiru, or the giant underground Arks they had built, though, specifically, that she hadn't, actually, earned any of it. She was merely a puppet, out of her league and played for the racial trump card that she was. She didn't earn her job, she just happened to be the right sex, colour, and background, and was egotistical enough to believe she belonged.

"I'll drink to that. To the last lame duck!." Hunter replied, miming a glass in his hand, and tilting it to his father.

243

At that moment, the chopper dropped about ten feet, causing Joe to sprawl in his chair. Like a cat startled, his arms and legs all flung out to wedge himself in his seat. His knuckles went white as he was gripping the arms of the chair. When it all evened out, the cabin filled with Hunter's laughter and Joe was not impressed. Hunter was trying to speak as Joe gathered himself and resettled while shooting his boy an angry glance, though, it didn't take.

"Oh. Oh." Hunter managed as he got his breathing and laughter under control.

"Did you piss yourself there Dad?" He was barely able to finish the sentence as just by saying it he set himself off again.

Embarrassed, Joe snapped back.

"For fuck sakes boy, it's just some fucking turbulence, get your fucking shit together."

Hunter wasn't fazed, his dad always swore when he was angry, yet he also knew that was the point to stop pushing and his loud laughter turned into a suppressed chuckle as the captain sounded over the speakers again.

"Sorry about that Sir, air pocket dropped us there. Should be pretty smooth from here on out." The announcement was far more casual than the first one and was enough of a diversion to switch the tension to humour and Joe smiled at Hunter as he finally gained control.

"Fucking turbulence eh?" Joe said in his softer, southern, fatherly way. He looked down at his watch, worn on his left wrist, as they soared into the sky and the White House became lost in the sea of lights below.

"Well, this is as good a time as any." he said, again looking at his son across from him. Hunter leaned forward in his chair, but instinctively also checked his own watch.

He watched as Joe held his right thumb on his watch face until the LCD screen turned into a red circle on a black background. It beeped twice, shrilled above the hum of the mechanical noises outside them. Joe held out his right index finger, nodded at Hunter, then placed the tip of his finger on the red circle. It read his fingerprint, beeped twice more and then nothing. He looked at it, Hunter soon followed, waiting for the next part of the process. Joe looked up at Hunter and Hunter looked back.

"Is that it?" The younger of the two started.

"I don't know." Came the reply

"I expected..." He tapped his watch again, drifting off mid-sentence, still trying to figure it out. At that second an alert sounded on Hunter's phone causing both men to divert their attention from the watch. Hunter grabbed it from his back pocket. It was a message from Uncle Joe - *The new bed is just right*, was all it read. He smiled as he finished the sentence. He turned his phone to show his father the screen.

"It's done." he confirmed.

"Ok. Good." Joe said, again turning to his watch.

There was a pause while Hunter checked his emails on his phone and Joe swiped his finger over his watch trying to get back to the alert app.

"What a piece of shit" He finally said and reached over with his right hand to take it off.

Chapter 24

Shooting Stars

Zeta Mansion – Gun Range
03/03/2022
2 :20pm

Kira stood at the table positioned near the front of a long, garage-like room that stretched back over fifty feet. Before her and Theo, was a thick wooden table topped with an array of weapons they had gathered on their way down from the armoury. The warehouse itself was bigger than Theo's apartment; he was beginning to see just how big this BOL complex was. They had used a little battery powered golf buggy and travelled through a series of underground tunnels and rooms to get around. Kira had been kind enough to submit when Theo asked to drive after they had filled the rear compartment with pistols and assault rifles.

They had only gathered a few guns, mostly what Theo would be using and the ones the rest of the team would have so he could familiarise himself, he only had a couple of hours so it was a need-to-know lesson that Kira had put together for him. On the way from building-to-building, Theo was able to ask Kira more about the Reptilians, The Anunnaki, Nephilim, and Nibiru. Theo had so many questions in fact, at times she could barely keep up.

It was shocking for him to hear that although the Human hierarchy in both China and India were fully aware of the threats, they worked mostly alongside the Reptilian counterparts in the West. The Royal houses all throughout Europe, the secret societies all over the world, it was beyond anything he could have imagined, he still couldn't believe the scale of the lie and cover up.

The whole Middle East lie, the way the Zeta's had been practically forgotten by having all their history erased. The Muslim suppression, the whole Muslim history, a lie. Nothing Theo knew to be true seemed to be any more. Hearing Hitler was Humankind's last roll of the dice to try and free the planet from the Reptilians all seemed too much for him to handle. However, the more lies Kira unravelled, the more he could no longer deny the truth. The concentration camps were a deranged man's way of saving humankind, at the worst possible cost, yet would have worked had the Chinese humans sided with the Europeans, rather than banking on the Reptilians.

Despite the grim new perspective on the world, this was proving to be a lot more exciting and fun than Theo had expected. Despite starting off cold, and very distrusting of their new companion, Kira was beginning to warm to him as she started her lesson on 'how not to die before they get to the machine.' She had already told him that she was confident he would make it to Soteria, she had seen it many times. She also warned him, that in many of her visions, 'something' happens in Baghdad. Although, her vision was cloudy and vague, she was able to see the world after the destruction caused by the passing of Nibiru. The mission hung in the balance.

"So pay attention because what you learn here will be the difference between us saving the world, or killing us all. Are you ready?"

Theo's eyes lit up, he had never fired a gun before, he was too proud to admit it and when they were talking on the way over, he had lied about some clay pigeon shooting in college, he didn't know why. Now, looking at the different types of guns he was like a kid in a candy store and wanted to try them all.

"Oh! I am so ready," he said with a giant smile on his face. His enthusiasm was endearing, and it forced a smile from the stoic Kira as well.

She stepped over to the table. On it, there were five different guns, each with spare magazines, neatly lined up. Beyond the table, the room disappeared to a series of targets that hung from the ceiling, along several thin, metal runners that the targets moved along electronically, like a standard gun range, just without the lanes, and most of the safest measures. It was like an indoor, open-air range, with white ballistic, and noise absorbing materials lining the walls all along to the cushioned end wall. It was a huge space, although only about the height of a tall room, and it was the perfect place for Theo to understand the inner workings of each of the guns the team would be using during their mission.

"This one," Her Russian accent cut into Theo's thoughts as he was looking down the room for his first target. She picked up the small black handgun on the far left of the table.

"Will be your main weapon, it is simple and will keep you safe."
She tossed it to Theo and picked up the second one for herself.

"Beretta 92 handgun, see this here?" she gestured and showed
him the side of the gun.

"You click here to release the clip."

Just behind the trigger on the left side was a small plastic lever
that Theo pushed. His clip fell from the bottom of the gun, yet he
wasn't prepared, and it clattered to the floor. Kira sighed as he
sheepishly bent down to pick it up.

"So, when you say this mission is still in the balance, what do you
mean, I thought you could see the future." He finished and slapped
his bullet clip back into the gun, proudly and with a look of triumph.

"It is not as simple as seeing an outcome, as I told you before.
The future isn't certain, free will still exists. I just get to see glimpses
of the paths we can encounter." As she finished, she held the pistol
clearly in front of her for Theo to see and then used her left hand to
pull back on the back half of the gun to load it.

"Now it is live, you have 19 in the cartridge, and now 1 in the
barrel. Understand?" Theo pulled back on the top of his pistol too,
and it clicked back into place.

"One in the barrel and 19 left in the clip, got it!"

"Laser guided, barrel mounted sight, means the bullet will go
where the red dot points, and this is your safety. On, off." She
continued.

Theo inspected his gun, he clicked on the sight and his red laser extended from the end of his barrel. He smiled again, the guys at the call centre would never believe this.

'Laser guided Beretta pistols.' He thought, playfully to himself

The targets that Kira had already sent down were at varying distances and she brought up her gun and aimed at the one at the far end of the range. It was a silhouette of a man on a white background. Theo looked at her, then followed her arm down the range to see her target.

"Aim, squeeze, Kill." On 'kill,' she sent six bullets searing through air, straight through the chest of the black silhouette before slapping into the gel wall at the end. The gun exploded loudly in the tight confines of the room, but the high-tech pyramid ceramics in the walls made it sound no louder than a balloon popping.

"Pick one and take a shot." she finished.

Theo looked down the room, over the table in front of him and decided to start with something a bit easier, so he brought up his pistol, clicked the safety to off and aimed at the target silhouette about twenty feet away and slightly to their right. The red dot sat on or around the target yet danced erratically as he tried to hold the gun steady. He jumped between closing one eye and trying to follow the barrel of the gun, to opening both eyes and trying to target by using the red dot. He tried his left eye closed, looking down the red line, that seemed to be the best, though he wanted to try his right eye shut again to see if it was better. Kira smiled at his youthful innocence; it had been a while since she had seen a man unfamiliar with a gun. She stepped over to him and put her right arm on his shoulder as he stood prone, and ready to fire.

"Your grip is good," she started.

"Both hands like this will keep you steady and accurate." Keeping her hand on his shoulder she stepped in behind him, to look over his right and down the gun at the targets.

"The pistol is not like the clay pigeons you have shot before, you need to think that it is part of your arm, part of your body. Where you point it shoots, and where you look you point." Her chin was practically resting on his shoulder as Theo stood doing the manliest thing he could ever remember. His legs were slightly apart, he had two hands on the gun and a bad guy in his sights.

"Look at your target, see your target." She paused for effect.

"Take a breath in and then on the slow exhale of that breath, point at where you're looking and squeeze the trigger."

Three loud shots exploded from the end of the gun in quick succession as Theo squeezed the trigger one, two, three. It was a little louder than he expected, though the recoil seemed like nothing in the movies. The shells popping out of the top as they were discarded, did surprise him a little though all up, he was proud of his first effort and stared intently at the target trying to see where he had hit.

"Very good." he heard in his left ear.

"Now lower your gun, and on three I want you to do the same again." Theo followed his instructions and lowered his Baretta. He felt so much like a cop right now, ten-year-old Theo would be so jealous.

"One, two," came softly in his ear again, and then she shouted the "Three." Theo wasn't fazed, he already had tunnel vision on his silhouette, waiting for the three. This was a quick draw shot out and he was ready. On three, he sprung his arms up and three bullets sounded off as they flew down the range at their target. He knew those ones hit, he could feel it as they flew away from him.

"Ow." he said as the sound of the shots subsided, rubbing his left ear with his shoulder.

"I wanted to see how you did with a distraction." Came the dry response, with a curled lip to suggest a smile

"How did I do?" Theo asked still looking down the range, and now very aware of the pretty blonde standing very close to him and breathing on his neck.

"Good enough," she replied, and stepped away and back to the table in front of them.

"You have no experience, so this Beretta will be what you use, anything bigger and you could hurt yourself or the BOL. Let the rest of the team take point, you follow at the rear and stay alive ok." She finished her sentence and picked up a gun a lot bigger than the Baretta still in Theo's hand. Holding it in her right hand she turned to look at Theo with a grin on her face.

Tight black pants and top, blonde hair, pretty face, and a gun half the size of her body held firmly in one hand Schwarzenegger style. Theo was beginning to run out of people that would be jealous of him right now, though he was sure the list was growing.

"That said, it would be silly for you not to know the other guns we will be using, who knows what will happen in Baghdad?"

"Umm, you!" Theo shot a sarcastic but friendly jibe at his teacher.

"Oh, comedian eh?" she asked before spinning on the spot, whilst bringing the giant gun up tightly to her shoulder and unleashing what was both terrifying and exciting volley of fully automatic rounds into the same target Theo had been shooting at.

Within a second, the target broke in half along the middle, and fell with a clatter to the floor. Kira turned back around and assumed her previous position, although this time smoke spilled casually from the end of the MP51K fully Automatic rifle in Matte black. It just made Theo smile more.

"This is what the team will be going in with, so it's not a bad idea for you to fire it and know it. Here" She extended her arms to hand him the gun. Theo reached and took it, like he was studying a new toy; he looked it over and turned it through his grip. She reached over and pointed at specific parts as he went.

"Clip release, safety, sights, round count." Theo had stopped listening though, as he bought his gaze up to her face…

"Why me Kira?" he asked, taking a moment to reflect on the overall goal and success criteria of their mission.
"I'm just a geek without a father and you guys really think I'm supposed to help save the world with this?" he gestured to the gun

.

"No Theo, you are here to save the world because of what is in your veins, and what is in here." she prodded his forehead with her finger as she finished her sentence.
"I have seen our success Theo, but it only comes when we all believe. I know this is a lot, I wish we had more time, but we do not.

For now, you just need to trust what you know is true and have always known. Ok?" Theo nodded in response.

"Good, now shoot that bad man to the left." and she jumped to their right.

Sensing the game and the challenge in the way she commanded and jumped out of the way, Theo swung the gun up to his shoulder perfectly and exploded about eight rounds clean from the end in a single squeeze. He felt the power this time, his whole-body shook, his forearms, and shoulders took the brunt, yet he was instinctively prepared and shot with the control and accuracy of someone a lot more experienced. His eyes shone bright white, and adrenaline surged through his whole body as all eight bullets found the silhouette and tore into it.

Kira began to giggle to his side. She saw his eyes glowing and could see how much Theo was enjoying his introduction to firearms. She was also pleased that despite his scrawny frame, he could handle the automatics, and seemed to be a natural. She was confident he would be an asset, not a liability out there, causing her to physical relax as she began to enjoy herself.

"This is awesome." he conceded.

"Yes, it is." she replied.
"Now let's kill some more bad guys." With that, she picked up her own MP51K, flicked the safety and stood next to Theo with her gun up, and trained to her shoulder. Theo knew what to do and had his in the same position, his finger lightly brushed his trigger.

"Far right rear." she commanded and in perfect unison they swung a few degrees to their right and short bursts of white-hot metal flew down the room, tearing onto the targets before slamming into the wall. Theo was in heaven.

Chapter 25

United Colours of Benneton

White House - Presidential Bunker
03/03/2022
7 :15am

Kamala sat in the thick chair at the head of the table in the Presidential bunker beneath the White House and looked at the room full of people in front of her. It had been almost twelve hours since the devastating news about Baghdad had seen the secret service rush the sitting President and her staff down to the more secure 'Bunker,' deep underground; safe from anything domestic and unforeseen. Every screen in the White House showed the news; updates live from CNN, Fox and even Aljazera and they all showed the same thing, a billowing black cloud of smoke, growing into the shape of a mushroom above a city of over seven million people. Upon seeing this footage, the pit of each person's stomach would tie into a knot, this wasn't just about Baghdad, this was going to change the world.

In this room though, something more was being discussed. The biggest disaster to occur since, well, 911 had just taken place; thousands of phone calls were going to voicemail. Calls to key staff and important officials were going unanswered, dozens of staff that were supposed to be on duty right now, had mysteriously gone, were on break, or had needed to go home, just before the strike.

There was a cacophony of noise as the men and women of the US National Security Council stood and sat around the table throwing ideas and blame around with half a dozen conversations all happening at once. Eventually, Kamala decided she needed to do something, she was the President after all, though right now she was terrified, she could barely comprehend what was happening with the attack in Baghdad, and all the theories and accusations were leading to places that just kept making no sense.

"The head of homeland security and one hour ago walks out of the Pentagon without a trace"

She made out from the Director of National Drug Control to her right.

Standing at the other end of the table, closer to the wall surrounding the room, Secretary of State Anthony Blinken was on the phone shouting something about finding Marine One right now, or tomorrow, packing up your desk.

"Then find the real fucking manifest and find the fucking president." He exploded down the phone, it was so loud it caused everyone in the room to simultaneously stop, look, and take a second. It gave Kamala the window she needed to bring some order.

"Ok, everyone, eyes this way, we need to stop all talking at the same time if anyone is going to be heard." She tried to sound stern and strong in her voice.

She had no idea what was going on or even where to begin trying to fix it, but these were just people, scared people looking for answers and she knew how to lead people. Half the table hadn't slept since yesterday and the other half were standing in for their bosses, who were missing. She needed to own this room, this was her time and moment. The room of men and women were silent for the first time in hours, even Blinken had hung up and was looking her way.

Her Navy-Blue suit was neat, pressed and she didn't look like she had been hiding under the White House all night since practically taking the chair. She looked fresh; she knew how to stay cool when others were losing their heads. She climbed to her feet to stand and placed both hands on the table in front of her as she began to speak. She was soft and deliberate in her tone.

"I know a lot of you are very confused and scared right now, but I tell you all, we are not going to get out of this by throwing wild theories around, we need to stay focused on the facts that we have, as we have them."

"The facts are that everyone that matters has fucked off." Blinken shouted down the room with a hint of degradation and a ton of sarcasm. It had the immediate effect of releasing the pressure and again it became a free for all.

The US National Security Council was created in 1947 by the National Security Act of the same year and was a way to ensure coordination and concurrence among the Army, Marine Corps,

Navy, Air Force and other instruments of national security policy such as the Central Intelligence Agency.

In the Hundreds of occasions that they have had to meet, never once had any of the statutory attendees not been in the room. Today both the Secretary of Treasury and Energy were missing, along with the Chairman of the Joint Chiefs, the Director of National Intelligence, the Attorney General, the Director of the CIA and of course, a missing President.

The noise within the tight room kept growing until Kamala chose her path. She picked up her coffee mug from the table, spun around, and threw it hard against the wall behind her. The white mug with the presidential seal printed proudly on it shattered when it hit the wall; the noise and action stunned everyone back to attention.

"We are it! There is no-one else coming to help." She started strong, her southern accent came out as she let them have it, it always did when she got angry. She paused for effect to make sure she had all eyes on her.

"We are it," she stated again, and looked directly at Blinken
"And Fuck anyone that's not here with us." she said, trying to reassure him, then turning to the rest of the US NSC, she held a fist in front of her chest and looked them in the eye as she spoke.

"I don't think it would be an exaggeration to say we have never been here before, but we are a nation built on doing the unknown and impossible and we will persevere, but for us to do so, we need to work together and focus on what we know not what we think. Right now, we don't know much, and that has to change." There was quiet as her words rested in the room for a second, everyone agreed, all except Blinken who felt something was off, his eyes were tired and puffy in his sharp white face as he dialled frantically on his phone to try and get to the bottom of it.

"Alejandro," she said, addressing the bald-headed Secretary of Homeland Security to her left. He sat proudly in his chair, seated next to the huge Secretary of Defence to his right, and like Kamala, looked fresh and alert. His mind was as sharp as his jawline and right now, he was looking around the room at 'diversity city' when he heard his name.

"I need you to coordinate with Colonel Ramon and General Raymond," she directed, indicating to the two men in uniform, sitting at the opposite end of the table.

Colonel Ramon Colon Lopez was the Chairman of the Joint Chief of Staff and could coordinate responses from all the armed forces, he had only been in the role a short time but had been a very popular addition to the cabinet. He was still finding his feet and was thankful to have General Raymond to his immediate right to work with. General Raymond wore the uniform of an Army General, even though he was the acting Head of the US Space Force and had taken the cushy role on the back of many years of hard work and relationship building within the establishment and other armed services divisions. He didn't like this at all, he had been around long enough to know that when it, "Looks like, smells like and quacks like a duck, then it is a duck. And right now, it looks and smells like anyone who's smart was going into hiding."

"Between the three of you we need a list of everyone that is missing," she continued.

"And we need the link between them all. Find me someone on that list and maybe we will start to find our answers."

"I've been pushing all my UN contacts for the last few hours, but it's like a ghost town down there. Since the blast, I can barely get anyone to actually come to the phone or answer. A Japanese Ambassador mentioned something about a mass evacuation in parts of China." Alejandro offered.

"We also have the same reports coming out of Eastern Europe, but none of it has been verified so it's useless." snapped Elizabeth Randal, the Homeland Security Advisor sitting opposite from Linda Greenfield. She hadn't slept at all well and despite her calm reputation did not operate well when tired.

"We have unverified reports from all over the world but none of them are leading to anything." she shrugged

"General!" Kamala commanded, looking directly down the room and at General John Raymond.

"Find us someone on that list." she said tapping her hand on the table.

He nodded his appreciation for the task and immediately began to write something on his iPad as Kamala turned to her immediate left and to her Secretary of Defence Lloyd Austin.

"Lloyd, I need you to work with Tina and Ron to prepare the public response to all of this. When I get up on stage to answer questions, I need you beside me and ready, we can't hold them off much longer, and Tina," She now turned to her right to her own Chief of Staff.

"You know how important the message is, understand." she confirmed as if cementing an idea.

Ron Atkins, Joe Biden's newly appointed press manager wrote something down and nodded. He was too green to know any better and he too was just finding his feet, when all this hit. He had no idea where Biden had gone, and half of his contacts were on the missing personnel lists. He had just tethered himself to the Vice President and Her Chief of Staff for now, this was where he thought he could have the biggest impact.

Her Attorney General, Merrick Garland was missing and, in his place, at the far end on the left of the table was Lisa Monaco, the Deputy AG.

"Lisa, I need you and Dana to get me constitutional approval for the shut downs and curfews, they will be challenged all across the Country as this continues." The two women, White House Council (WHC), and Acting Attorney General, looked across at each other and nodded.

Dana Ramus, WHC was on the right of the table and took another sip of her water, she was beginning to feel the walls closing in around her as she got more, and more flustered. She had only been in the role a few weeks and was incredibly thankful to have Lisa to work with.

"I've already pulled dozens of Covid related cases that provide us precedent under The National Security Act. Florida can challenge us, but they will lose." she said confidently to both Kamala, and the rest of the table.

"And when they do, the National Guard will be there to clean them up." Lloyd Austin's deep voice reassured them all.

"The Benga boys, or Golden Boys or whatever they call themselves will be put back in place pretty quickly. We already have forty-thousand boots on the ground, we are just working with

Homeland on their redeployment from the border." That seemed to settle the nerves of most of the people around the table.

Gentle chatter started between the small groups within the room that were now tasked to work together to bring the pieces of this puzzle to the surface. Kamala only had to raise her voice slightly to talk over to the far-right corner and grab the attention of Katherine Tai, the US Trade Representative. She was also quite new to her role, and despite some experience at the State Department, she had never been involved in National Security and couldn't really understand her place here at this table.

"Katherine." Kamala repeated, causing her to look up, she found a kind smile hiding an impatience.

"In 30 minutes, I want a briefing on any chatter you are hearing from any of your trade contacts. Go digging for me, ok?" She nodded to reassure her trade rep that she could do it, that she had some use, yet in truth, there were only two to three people in this room that had any real experience with anything like this before.

She was just gathering the strength to try and engage with Anthony again. Blinken had been on edge far more than usual and he was the one leading the search for Marine One, the presidential chopper. Trying to get an answer from him was like putting your hand into a lion's mouth.

"That's it, that's the plan?" Blinken bellowed down the room, stepping away from the wall with his phone off and by his side.
"Ring your mates, ask a few questions." he sneered, pointing at Katherine Tai just in front of him.

"You two, let's make sure we won't get out butts smacked in court." This time, he pulled his arms into his chest and waved them like jazz hands mocking and pointing at the same time.

"You three, find me someone on the list," This time he tilted his wrist and did his best impression of a southern belle accent.

Lloyd Austin's protective nature kicked in and he stood to defend the sitting President.

"That's enough Anthony." he said, trying to sound tough.

"That's enough?" Blinken questioned loudly.

"That's enough?" he asked again, but this time he was pleading with the room to see what he saw.

"Don't you see it Lloyd, Kamala, Dana, Alejandro, Rahul." As he said their names, he exaggerated the syllables and foreignness of the sounds.

"You're the fucking Diversity Picks, The United Colours of Fucking Benneton. You're what's left behind. All the powerful White Men that are normally in this room, they are somewhere else and we, dumb fucks that we are, are still sitting in here thinking we have a chance of getting out of this. This is checkmate, don't you get it."

Kamala tried again to bring him back, though before she could even open her mouth, he kept going, and this time he delivered his warning very clearly to them all.

"Whatever is happening, is going exactly to plan, and none of us are a part of it, there is nothing we can do to stop it." He smiled at that thought, it kind of liberated him, he had just spent almost twelve hours straight pulling out his hair trying to find answers to a question that was going to be irrelevant anyway.

He was out of here, he had put together enough to know this wasn't ending well for the people in this room. He clapped his hands, pointed at Kamala with one hand and Lloyd Austin with the other and said:

"And their called the fucking Harvey Boys Lloyd, and I bet they probably know more about what is going on that you do, you useless fat wanker."

With that, Anthony Blinken left the White House Bunker, to try to find out where his boss and friend Joe Biden had gone without telling him, leaving Kamala Harris and the rest of the room a little shocked, yet still determined to find their way through this; with or without Anthony Blinken.

Chapter 26

Papal Games

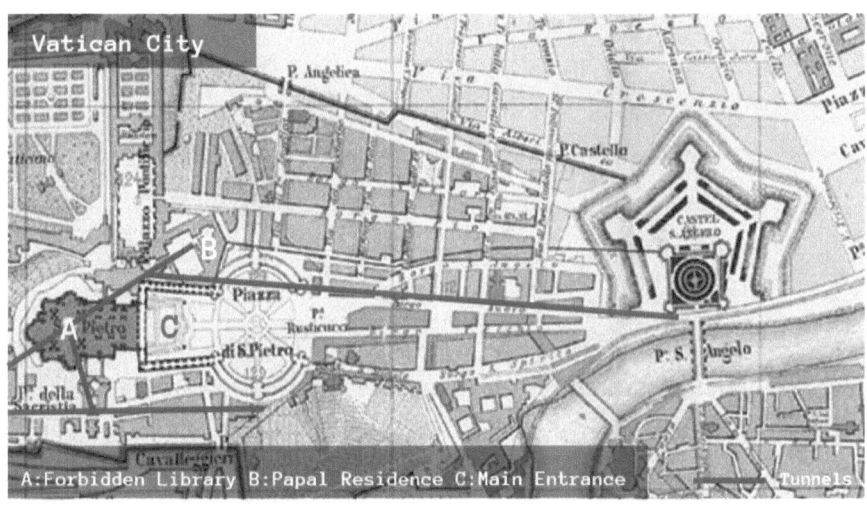

A:Forbidden Library B:Papal Residence C:Main Entrance Tunnels

Vatican City - St Peters Square
04/03/2022
4 :15am

The sun's first rays hadn't quite climbed high enough to light the architectural masterpieces of one of the most holy sites in the world. Silently, the shadows from the streetlights sat cool in the fresh breeze blowing in from the Alps to the North. Even though the sky was still black in the West, a thin, bright line in the

East showed the sun was not far away. It was the eerie silence, just before the birds and the world around them awoke. Walking proudly, up through the centre of St Peters Square were the black clad figures of Desta, Kira, and Deena.

Each of the women wore black pants with numerous belts and straps wrapped around their legs, each containing a holster for another weapon. They also had on black tops, covered by thin looking Kevlar vests, as they carried small little black rucksacks on each of their backs. Their boots made very little noise as they stepped on the concrete, the rubber soles keeping them light and quiet, in contrast, Desta's footsteps echoed off the circular columns surrounding them. Whilst the other two members of his advanced team had gone for the cat burglar look, Desta wanted to make an impression with his Reptilian hosts, especially the Ducaz. He had worn his favourite suit under his knee length Wood & Wood wool lined overcoat.

He had even gone with the matching waistcoat and had a 1200-year-old pocket watch slotted in there for good measure. His expensive leather soled shoes were clomping loudly on the ground as he stepped forward with his companions. His rhythmic two steps were cut through with a third tap, coming from a sleek black cane he held in his right hand. He was certainly not trying to sneak in through the back door.

Kira's eyes were already glowing white, she felt as though they were being watched from the windows all around the circular 'Square,' causing her heart rate to increase. She looked up to her right at the Apostolic Palace where the rest of the team were getting ready to enter. They had no communication method, Desta had decided that the plan required, him and the girls needing to look like they are alone, to at least try to sow some seeds of doubt so they were not mic'd up.

Kira protested strongly at the time, and even now looking over at the still, cold building under the fluorescent spotlights, she didn't like not knowing what was going on. She had an intuitive link to the others, though under these circumstances, she was more focused on the obvious trap they were walking right into and couldn't centre herself to feel them.

Deena had her hair pulled tight into half a dozen braids that swirled on her head, her black jacket was zipped all the way to her chin and as she strode forward next to Desta a cockroach noisily appeared, his wings loud in the empty silence around them. He clumsily crash-landed against Deena's arm and clung on, spinning in place until his antennas were pointing at her face and he paused, just looking at her.

She was pleasantly surprised and gently reached over with her right hand to provide him with a platform and he stepped on. Desta looked over and saw Deena's companion. She bought her right hand up to her face as they walked and whispered something to the cockroach before lifting her hand into the air to give him a head start. He opened his wings and took to the air. Deena looked at Desta with a look of determination he hadn't seen before, and she nodded. He had a good feeling about this, he checked his right as they reached the top of the stairs and saw Kira looking up at the Papal Residence. They were now at the Basilica entrance and could see the doors.

"They'll be fine Kira." he reassured her.

"Stay focu.." He couldn't get the last S out before something soft, black and round slammed into his chest.

All the air in his lungs burst out of him and as Kira and Deena slipped into their Zeta defensive state, Desta's jacket and arms shot forward in slow motion as his torso jumped back due to the force of the small black ball that bounced off him, morphing its shape back to round as it fell to the floor.

Kira was like lightning and already behind Desta to manage his fall before the ball had hit the ground, she stabilized him, helping him stay on his feet. Deena reacted by jumping into a defensive position, feet wide apart, knees bent, head steady and level as she scanned the building in front of them for the aggressors. She had jumped between the Basilica before them and Desta to stop any more shots, and while her eyes shone, she instinctively had drawn her thin Katana sword, hissing as she spotted movement ahead.

Behind her, Desta was bent over catching his breath, coughing lightly as he too looked over at the building where the shot had come from. He held his hand to his chest, and his whole palm lit up, his face grimaced for a second before, like a defibrillator delivering a shock. His entire torso took a hit of light from his hand and sent it to his eyes. He looked up and now saw the same thing Deena was hissing at, and that Kira was aiming her gun at.

Before them, was one of the Vatican's most treasured buildings and one of the most holy sites in Catholicism. They were close enough now that the building loomed over them, and the orange glow of the artificial lights were broken by a much brighter, white light that burst out when the huge main doors opened. The shot was a large-scale rubber bullet and had come from one of the first-floor windows. Kira had her assault rifle up and aimed on the person the shot had come from, though was now more concerned about the flood of men approaching.

Desta reached his right hand out and put it on her barrel, lowering it as he counted fifteen men, all clad in black trotting out of the door, all with fully automatic Maglev weapons, locked to their shoulders and locked on the three BOL before them.

Standing in the doorway, was a figure. The light behind it was too bright compared to the dull artificial light from outside so, all Desta could see was a silhouette, though given the height and shape he could tell who it was, and when it spoke, he was certain.

"Bring them inside," it hissed and boomed in a victorious way. The sound echoed with a fullness that bounced all around the square, startling the few birds that were already there to catch the worm.

About five hundred meters to the North, the rest of the team had reached the building behind the Apostolic Palace, the Papal residence, and had already climbed the clad building to reach the roof. From their vantage point, they could see the city surrounding the square, lit up with sporadic streetlights, or occasional light from the windows, glowing like small stars in a black sky. The city was still in slumber, the small amount of Vatican City wildlife was still in their nests, or burrows, and were just beginning to smell the start of a new day.

Atop the roof, Raquel was leading Edmund, Mina, Simeon, and Theo in their part of the mission. Each of them wore a snug pair of glasses that brightened the night sky around them. They were not quite night vision, yet when Theo looked over to the adjacent roof, they were about to zipline to, he could see almost as clearly as when it was daytime. It was like a greyscale scene, as if the brightness has been turned up, but all the colour washed away. He flicked them up to see the scene with his own eyes just as Raquel began to speak.

She was adjusting her zoom on the frame of her glasses and now had a clear view on the Pope's balcony.

"Ok Sim, Mina, send them over." She declared and instantly two pressurised gas canisters hissed loudly shooting 2 titanium alloy hooks past her head.

Thin black nylon rope spooled out behind them, flapping in the air and Theo dropped his glasses over his eyes to see them slam into the solid wooden eaves above the ornate balcony that the Pope often enjoyed having his breakfast on. Fortunately for him, he was deep underground in the Southern European Ark, as it had been christened, so wasn't in residence. Half of the Swiss Guard were on leave and those that remained were on minimal duties. The Apostolic Palace was on level one security while the Pope was away, meaning the alarm was on, motion sensors were activated, yet security was only stationed at the main reception on the ground floor.

The whole group held their breath for a few seconds, while they waited to see if the sound of the metal biting into the wood had attracted any unwanted attention. Edmund and Mina scanned the windows around them and the other balconies across the way, whilst Raquel stared intently at their target, the balcony.

Theo looked behind him at the giant figure of Simeon, dressed in the same black fatigues he was wearing, yet he somehow still didn't look threatening as he beamed a reassuring smile back at Theo. Simeon, the mountain of a man, stood there with a giant backpack pinned to his shoulders, his black rimmed glasses and in his giant right hand he held a large black bag. The thought of Simeon as some IT computer geek flashed through his mind and Theo's smile grew

"A Geek?" Simeon asked.

Theo didn't get time to register that he hadn't said it out loud, because Raquel's voice cut in and all eyes snapped to her and what was next.

"Alright boys,"

"Ah, Men," Edmund cut in whilst finalising his ropes anchor point and getting a reassuring nod from Mina. Raquel let out a long breath.

"Ok, Men!" she said, looking at Edmund when she did, he looked pleased with himself, though it was all just a way for them to ignore the nerves. This was it. Failure meant the end of everything that mattered.

"Hook on and secure the landing site."

Quick as a flash, both Mina and Edmund had their legs hanging over the edge of the roof as they sat and connected the motorised clip that clung to the rope and propelled them across. They were at roughly the same level as the balcony. The boys had tied the other end of the ropes to two large ringlets dug into the concrete rooftop. They both swung out from the edge and under the rope, immediately the motor in the clip kicked in and grabbed a hold, pulling them both across to the empty balcony on the other side. Around them, the city and world continued as if nothing was happening, Theo's heart was racing, though he wasn't sure if it was due to fear or excitement. This whole thing kept getting cooler and cooler, and now, here he was, about to break into the Pope's bedroom.

"C'mon Sweet cheeks." Raquel said, looking at Theo and extending her hand to pull him up onto the roof edge.
"You and me next."

Theo instinctively adjusted his glasses and grabbed Raquel's hand whilst stepping up onto the ledge she was already on. Once up there he sat with his legs hanging over the edge, he looked down past his feet which was a mistake, he instantly felt dizzy as the dark buildings disappeared below him into a courtyard devoid of light. He blinked hard and grabbed for his clip, using his left hand he connected it to the rope with a click.

Mina and Edmund had already landed on the balcony and had swept past the basic door locks to take up holding positions, securing the room. Although, it was pitch black, through their glasses, they could see everything clearly in a bright colourless shimmer. Edmund took the door to the hallway whilst Mina made for the fireplace built into the far wall and under the giant picture of Michelangelo's Vita.

Mina ducked down and stepped into the fireplace, obviously looking for something, he reached in behind the flume at the top, where the chimney began, slapping his hand around working his way along.

"Anything?" Edmund whispered from across the room while he held a prone position by the door. It was complete overkill, but he lived like he played his video games, always ready, there might not be zombies popping out from behind walls and doors, but he knew to always be prepared.

Mina held his breath as he fumbled for the latch, he looked to his right as Raquel and Theo's boots slapped onto the balcony. He let out a breath and smiled.

"Got it." he confirmed.

"Sweet," Edmund whispered back under his breath, still refusing to look over at the mechanical whirring, or to the balcony, when Raquel had just stepped through. Instead, he just kept looking at the door, instinctively knowing what was on the other side if he stayed focussed.

In front of Mina, the dusty brick wall that formed the back of the fireplace, had rotated on a central column, with half the wall receding away and the other half coming forward, disturbing the ash on the floor. It was crude, and very dated, yet allowed for simple passage into the brick lined tunnel behind, it could only be activated if you knew where to look. The lever moved a pulley that dropped a large weight turning the heavy stone and as it opened, Mina immediately went prone and swung his pistol up in two hands, keeping it aimed on the darkness that receded away from him.

As he adjusted the focus on his glasses, the tunnel became clear; colourless, and Mina was able to see deep into its recesses, there was no sign of anyone or anything. He heard Raquel step into the fireplace just behind him.

"It's all clear." he said quietly, whilst holstering his gun and stepping forward to the gap on the left side, where he grabbed a piece of burnt wood from an old fire and jammed it under the wall like a door stop. As he gently kicked it with the end of his boots to get it firmly in place, he heard Simeon landing on the balcony. The whole room shook slightly, and a small sprinkling of dust fell from above, coating both Mina and Raquel as they prepared to enter the next phase of their mission.

Out in the room, Theo was sliding on the black rucksack Raquel had just handed him. He was standing next to the fireplace, and while he wiggled his shoulders to try and get the bag to slide down, he was looking at Edmund. Six feet away from the door to the room, on one knee, with his rifle stuck to his shoulder like glue, and not once had he looked back at the team. He got the bag into position between his shoulder blades, then looked at Mina, wedging something under the wall that had now turned inward like something from a Scooby Doo episode, when his stomach turned for the first time.

Nerves were beginning to take a toll on Theo. Through the greyscale glasses, he was looking at the Pope's bedroom, the bed, carpets, paintings on the walls. All of this was where the Pope slept. Even before, when landing on the balcony, the reality of the situation hadn't yet set in; though now, seeing Edmund so focussed on that door, he knew the danger was here and now.

He felt as though he was going to be sick, until Simeon's strong, massive hand, landed on his shoulder, squeezing gently to reassure him. The effect was instant and physically Theo felt amazing, despite his worries. He turned his head to see another smile from Sim and together they looked at Raquel, and Mina as they both checked the entrances for any alarms or traps that hadn't been in the original plans.

Mina had stepped a good thirty feet into the tunnel when he waved Raquel forward. She then turned to the team in the room, looking back at Simeon standing with his hand on Theo's shoulder. She smiled at Theo's glowing eyes as he looked eagerly towards her and Mina. He was nervous, this was good, it might keep him alive, she thought.

"Edmund, Gents. Let's do this." she said.

With that, Edmund broke off from the door and as Theo and Simeon disappeared down into the tunnel after Raquel and Mina, he kicked the wooden stake out from under the rotated wall and joined them. After a few seconds, the mechanism moved again and the weights on the other side dropped causing the wall to return to its original position. As it clicked shut, the room, once again, became silent. No trace of its previous guests remained, except for a footprint in the dusty floor of the fireplace.

While Theo and co. headed into the tunnels, Desta and his team were staring down a semi-circle of black clad special force soldiers all with weapons focussed on him, Kira, and Deena. The Ducaz, at the lead, had begun his slow and deliberate walk down the steps, getting closer to his prey. The soldiers hadn't yet approached, they were aware of some of the Zeta powers and were giving Desta and his team a wide berth until ordered in.

"I take it that's you, Kahn." Desta shouted past the soldiers at the huge creature descending towards them.

"Give us the cross and you can live for another thousand years." Destas voice rose in volume as it echoed off the solid floors and walls that surrounded them, in the shadow of the entrance to the great Basilica.

A low rumbling laugh rolled out from deep within Kahn's stomach as he continued his descent down the stairs towards them.

"I and my brother will dine on you and your friends tonight Human." he bellowed, before tilting his head back and laughing menacingly.

This was the moment Desta had hoped for, The Ducaz were notorious for their over confidence and uncanny ability to underestimate humans. He was banking on some showboating from them when they first captured him and the girls. All he needed was a three second window, and this seemed like as good a time as any.

As Kahn's head tilted back to get his last laugh out, Desta slapped the pocket watch in his waistcoat. Instantly, a blinding white light tore outwards in a giant sphere so fast, it was over in a blink. Though in that moment, everything in the sphere slowed down, including time. This affected everyone and everything within half a mile of the team, though not Desta, Deena, and Kira. Their BOL abilities shielded them from the time phenomenon that Desta had created, it was their window to strike. 'Three seconds,' they figured, for the Ducaz to react. So about fifteen seconds in their time, though even in a stasis state, the Ducaz's reactions could probably keep up, so they had to work together as a team.

Kira acted first and quick as a flash had her gun up to her shoulder, and half a clip searing towards the soldiers directly in front of them, the ones at the foot of the steps, between them and Kahn. Time was slow for the three Zeta, they could even see the bullets spiralling away from them, followed closely by a faint wave of blurred light. Kira continued her part of the plan and swung hard to her right and unleashed another spray at the soldiers that were beginning to flank them before immediately coming back to her left and finishing the job.

None of her bullets had hit yet, in real time it was all happening so quickly that in less than a second each of the fifteen men surrounding them had a small gift on its way. A sea of pain was unleashed and behind it were Desta, and Deena.

The second Desta had smashed his hand down on his wrist, Kira was already unleashing hell; yet, Desta and Deena hadn't fired a shot. They both had a far more important target, the small patch of soft skin directly on the top of Kahn's head.

You see, the unfortunate thing about fighting a Ducaz is that not only are they incredibly strong, their scaly, reptilian skin gets harder and thicker as they age. By the time a Ducaz reaches the age of Kahn, it is practically impenetrable; no number of bullets, arrows, or even explosives could break through. Kahn was basically impossible to kill, aside from the small soft flap of skin that all Reptilians possess. Similar to a fontanelle on human babies, although in Reptilians, this small gap in the skull doesn't close over as they grow.

Deena was silent and moved like a blur, chasing the bullets in front of her with her sword drawn in her right hand, and a small gold dagger in her left. To her right, Desta was at full speed, having launched forward just as Deena did. His long coat billowed behind him as he ran, opening to reveal his waistcoat and shirt. He only had his cane in his hand, though as he picked up speed, he pushed a small button in the middle transforming it into a long, metal spear head. They both ran fast, unaffected by the time lapse, they were almost fast enough to keep up with the bullets ahead of them. When Desta was just a few feet from the soldiers between him and Kahn, the first of Kira's shots began to hit home with devastating results.

The two of them were only looking past the soldiers at Kahn, as his head rolled forward in slow motion to look towards his prey. It had only taken a second for his laughter to stop and for him to realise what Desta had done while he was celebrating. He had no chance of keeping up with the time lapse, he hadn't even managed a muffled warning to his soldiers, or if he did, it was too late, their fates were already sealed. However, Kahn at tens of thousands of years old, had the reflexes of a cobra, and was almost as intuitive as Kira.

'Stupid humans,' he thought to himself before the men in front of him began to fall.

Whilst Kira shot at each of the men surrounding them, they were not all perfect head shots that were expected of her, it was now clear that she had sacrificed accuracy in favour of speed. Although, the first one to hit home, was an epic shot.

As Desta, and Deena charged forward, they were close enough to the line of soldiers to see in graphic detail when the one directly in front of Deena, had a bullet enter through his right eye, to then explode out of the fist sized hole in the back of his skull. In the slow motion they were experiencing, the spray of blood appeared and created an aerosol of red particles through the air, and then carnage as the rest of the bullets began to slam into each of the helpless soldiers.

It was strange to watch, a soldier's head exploding and none of his comrades reacting. They were all frozen, as one by one, bullets slammed into shoulders, breast plates, legs, and arms. Red mist filled the air as blood exploded from impact after impact. Yet Desta and Deena still only had eyes for Kahn.

Kira had now aimed her gun on the huge Ducaz and had sent what was left off her clip his way. She hoped that this would cause a distraction, as Desta and Deena drew closer.

Desta and Deena both leapt from the ground at the same time. The line of soldiers was now incapacitated, though most of them were still semi standing, with limbs flinging out as they were reacting to the bullets. The team moved together, Desta, jumping off his left leg, leapt towards and over the falling soldiers, using his right leg to step on one, launching himself even higher, getting closer to Kahn. Deena leapt from her right foot, soaring as her blade rode above her head.

All around them, time was slow, yet as Desta climbed through the air it seemed gravity was also wavering. He was looming over Kahn, eight to ten feet in the air, long jacket billowing and a determined glare in his glowing eyes. He held the spear prone over his shoulder, ready to slam it down and with a loud yell announced to Kahn this was it. Deena was still silently matching her leader, and whilst not as high in the air, she was diving headfirst, sword in front of her, aimed at the mighty Ducaz,

Desta's body tensed, and coiled, ready for the one strike he was going to get. As he instructed his muscles to contract and slam the spear down, he was almost directly over Kahn's giant body, and Deena was within reach with her razor-sharp blades. At that point Kira's last bullets caught up with the action and whipped past both airborne warriors, exploding one after another as they collided with the stone like skin.

As the first of the bullets pinged off Kahn's thick breast plate, the time lapse ended. Like a switch had been hit, everything around Desta, and Deena had fully caught up with them. Luckily, Kira's bullets were the first thing Kahn dealt with once he was moving at full speed again, allowing Deena to continue her momentum, she slammed into his right leg. Her sharp blade hit as hard as she could punch, and yet, simply sparked and skipped off. Her shoulder followed through, causing dislocation as her sword connected with the beast. Fortunately, it knocked him off balance for a second, allowing Desta, from his height, to come down hard and fast, directly on target for the top of Kahn's head.

The spear came down with Desta, he could see the Ducaz stumble, he swung fast and true, instantly causing a loud roar to erupt, as the giant stone beast reacted faster than Desta could. Then, he stepped back, and grabbed hold of Desta in mid-air. One hand was engulfing Desta's neck, the other held his spear arm. Kahn squeezed, crushing the wrist he was holding, forcing Desta's hand to open and for the spear to drop loudly to the hard stone floor.

Deena was still where she had landed after bouncing off Kahn, and was just getting herself up when Kira, who had been running towards Kahn as well, had been surrounded and prone against at least six remaining soldiers that had survived her first wave of bullets. At least five of the men were still on the ground, having taken a lethal shot, though the rest had either taken the shots to their vests, or simply taken a flesh wound and were already up and ready to round up what was left.

From her position at Kahn's feet, Deena looked up to see Desta's legs hanging limply as he was trapped, like a rag doll in the arms of a child. Khan was lowering Desta's face to his, unperturbed with Deena in his space, in this moment, he only had eyes for Desta. The recovering soldiers had already surrounded Kira, as others were coming back to grab Deena from the floor.

Even though her shoulder was dislocated, and in so much pain, causing her much distraction, she wasn't done just yet. Using the strength, she had left, and leaving her damaged shoulder to hang limp from her side, she jumped up and used her good arm to wrap it around Kahn's neck as she tried to cling to his back. Kahn flinched his massive shoulders and as she was whispering something to him, Deena lost her grip and fell towards the soldiers coming to get her. Landing in a heap she was immediately set upon and restrained.

Kahn looked down, dismissively at Deena, and over at Kira who was now bound, being brought to him.

"I need them alive, bring them to the library." Kahn commanded, and with that he tossed Desta towards his men as if throwing meat to his dogs and turned to walk inside. As Desta flew, he braced for impact, yet also had a small smile in the corner of his lips. The Ducaz were not immune to Deena's persuasion.

Back in the tunnels behind the Pope's fireplace, the team had been progressing well until they arrived at something that had not been anticipated.

"Fuck, Fucketty, fuck fuck bollox." Came Edmund's final assessment.

He was studying the locking mechanism and basic biometric scanner that was linked to the heavy metal door they found, as they turned into what was supposed to be the tunnel leading East, under the Fontana Del Sacremento.

"Even if we can open it, everyone in Italy is gonna know we are here," he confirmed, looking at Raquel, and the team.

Mina stepped forward and began running his hands around the edges of the door, into where it joined with the old, though solid brick linings. Raquel looked down at her watch, Time was running out, Desta and the others should be in the library by now. She looked at Simeon.

"Sim?" she asked, seeking ideas on how to get around this new obstacle.

"If we cannot blast through an obstacle, maybe we can go around it?" he said to her, calmly, whilst touching his hand on the brick wall next to him.

"Mark?" she said, turning to Mina who was still studying the edges of the door. He turned to look back down the tunnel.

"Out and in, let's go round?" she instructed, pointing at the wall near the door.

"What do you think?"

Mina immediately understood, despite having no idea what was on the other side of the wall, he could certainly get them through it to find out. If they were lucky, there would be some sort of cavity alongside the original tunnel, if not, it would just be packed dirt which may cause the tunnel to collapse.

"No time to think." he responded energetically.

"Throw me my bag Ed, let's take a look on the other side of that wall."

"Simeon, Theo, drop back thirty and cover our six." Raquel commanded gently, adapting with the new plan. She turned to look at them as she spoke, and took a moment to connect with Theo.

"You still with us saviour?" she asked with a smile and a wink, in her trademark Aussie twang.

"Oh yeah," Theo replied energetically.

"Just get us through that door boss." he said tapping the pistol on his left hip, whilst turning along with Simeon to drop back into the tunnel to cover the entrance behind them, as the rest of the team worked out a way round if not through. Raquel couldn't contain her joy as she smiled, Theo's enthusiasm, and the way he had thrown himself into this crazy adventure was giving her hope that this was going to end their way.

"Titty fuck." She heard Mina exclaim back by the door. She turned and he was standing with a single brick in his hand and in the grey light of her specs, small black particles were sprinkling through the hole he had created. Edmund stood next to him as, in unison, they looked back at Raquel.

"Dirt." they both said as one.
"Keep trying." she instructed. Edmund immediately tossed something to his mate, and Mina turned bringing his small laser torch up to the wall, on the other side of the door. She looked back down the tunnel, taking a second to think about Desta and the others.

Desta's part of the plan had gone quite poorly yet wasn't a complete disaster. Even though Kahn was still alive and very much in control, getting into the library as his prisoner had been the expectation, just not the hope. The initial, and very much ideal plan would have saved Desta and the girls a lot of pain and suffering whilst they waited for Raquel and the others to get to the library. As Desta found himself held tightly by two juiced up gene soldiers, he swung his gaze over to see the unconscious Deena.

She had struggled when the first of the soldiers set upon her, her shoulder was fully dislocated and despite dodging their first attempt to grab her, a strong fist flashed past her. She was unable to block it. Desta had closed his eyes when he saw her head snap violently backwards, taking the full force of the blow from one of the strongest soldiers in the world. In that moment, her front teeth shattered and with a sickening crack, so too had her nose and jaw. Blood sprayed out in all directions and in an instant, she was out cold.

In the darkness and artificial lights, Desta had watched her silhouette crumble to the floor, to be instantly grabbed like a sack of rubbish then slung over the shoulder of the soldier that had knocked her out. She hadn't moved since, and all Desta could hear from her was a laboured, gargled breath becoming fainter with time.

Kira hadn't fared much better and despite being on her feet as they were taken further inside, the severe swelling of her right eye, impaired her vision, and it was as if she suffered at least three broken ribs as she tried to breathe. Like Desta, she had a soldier either side of her as she was dragged, strong hands held her in place. Truthfully in that instance, even though her head was swimming with a major concussion, she was thankful for the moment, giving her the chance to clear her mind.

At the head of the party, Kahn boomed forward, step by step until he reached a large wooden door which he impatiently kicked open and continued through without missing a beat. The group had been travelling through doors, and tunnels for a couple of minutes, and as best as Desta could tell, they had certainly been going down. He figured they were deep under the Basilica. Then, he was pulled through a set of double doors which opened dramatically to reveal the Forbidden Library. Although it wasn't under the circumstances they had hoped for, they had at least made it there in one piece.

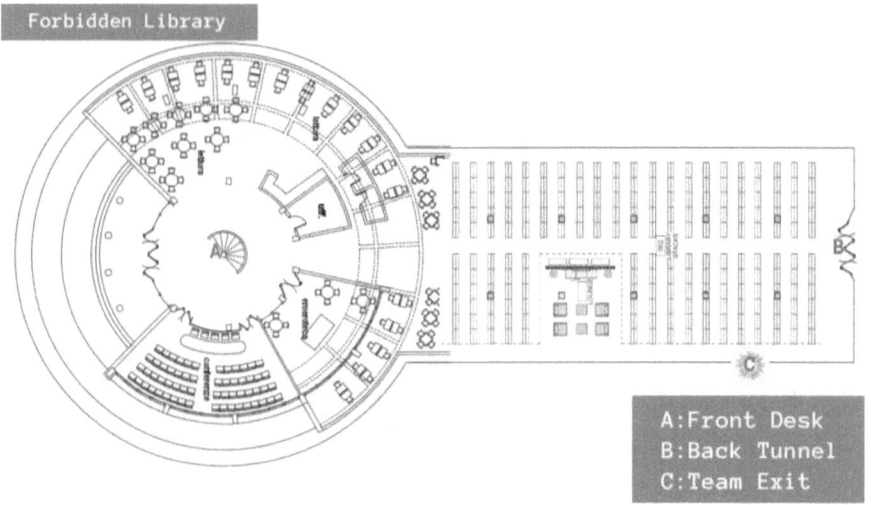

A:Front Desk
B:Back Tunnel
C:Team Exit

Deena was still limp and lifeless over the shoulder of the soldier that broke her teeth and knocked her out. They entered the library, making their way to a circular counter in the middle, then he dumped her on the floor. Desta and Kira were taken over to the same counter that usually housed the Vatican Curator, though was now just a central point for Kahn and the team to work from.

The counter sat like a tiny island in the vastness of the library and seemed to disappear in the waves of books that lined the miles of shelving. The library was easily the size of an aircraft hangar and the entrance to the tunnels were towards the back. The shelves were arranged in such a way that from the circle counter, one could walk directly towards the back of the library. It was like walking down a thin road and for hundreds of meters, it was isle after isle of wooden shelves and books that you could only find here.

Globes of light hung on long chains from the ceiling and provided a glowing light, emulating the daytime. The lights only glowed in the presence of life and as such, most of the library was bathed in darkness. In the distance, it looked like the library had disappeared into black.

Desta was thrown to the floor where he landed next to Deena. They had taken his watch, his cane, and his weapons, yet right now, he wasn't thinking about fighting. Deena still hadn't moved and the second he landed, he reached for her.

Sitting up, he pulled her head onto his lap, using his hands to push back the matted hair covering her face. His heart felt like it had stopped for a second, as he saw the power of the punch on her beautiful face. Her lips had both split, and blood oozed from the inch long gashes. Behind this, were her front teeth, or rather, what was left of them. Broken or missing, as she breathed small bubbles through the blood. Desta stroked her head and looked over to Kira. She was nearby now, though had made the mistake of pushing the soldier near her when they let her go.

The side of Kira's head cracked with a vicious headbutt, blindsided, she stumbled then lost her footing, landing at the base of the circle counter, making no attempt to get up.

Behind him, within the large circle desk, Kahn was speaking with someone. Desta hadn't seen anyone when he came in, he was preoccupied with his team. It wasn't Vol, the Ducaz he travelled with, Desta would have recognised that voice. Instead, it was a Southern accent, deep, educated, and hard in its tone.

"There must be others here." He overheard Kahn saying, "Have your men in the tunnels, conduct another sweep."

"Our men in the tunnels and your brother started sweeping the tunnels and the Basilica the second these three showed up on the steps. What's of more concern, Khan, is why the fuck you bought them into the library? Kill on sight, you're orders, not mine"

"We need them alive; they will tell us where the rest of them are."

"You know they never talk." There was a slight pause before the second voice continued.

"Did you let the Arab girl speak?" Another pause and then the Southern accent had a small chuckle.

"You didn't read the dossier, did you?"

"What about the Arab girl?" Khan asked in return, Desta could hear Kahn's agitation, Ducaz are very proud, so much so, that it was a certainty he hadn't read the dossier. To a Ducaz there is nothing they can't handle, so reading about the humans they face will just be a waste of time.

"She is a whisperer, Kahn. A strong one too if she got to you."

Desta heard what sounded like a shove and a growl from Kahn all at the same time, and the next thing he knew, Kahn's huge form and body was sailing over the desk towards Desta and Deena, to land with a resounding boom as almost a full tonne of stone hard alligator slammed himself and his tail down violently. He spun and quickly, like a snake, and had his huge mouth and jaws in front of Desta's face as he cradled Deena.

"Is this your whisperer Fool?" He hissed, allowing his hot rancid breath to fester over Desta's face.

Before he allowed him to answer, he snatched her from his arms like a bully grabbing the small kids' teddy from him. Desta instinctively protested though before he even got to his knees, he took a fist to the head from one side and was stomped hard in his ribs from the other.

Kahn didn't give Desta's words a second thought, or any of the humans for that matter. He held up his new trophy in his strong claw-like hands, holding her upright with her arms pinned by her side. Her head hung limply forward and rocked gently as Kahn studied her battered face. A steady stream of blood dribbled from her mouth and fell to the floor at Kahn's feet. Kira watched from where she was, barely able to move, she felt helpless, she too tried to get to her knees, to shout something, to get Kahn's attention. She had barely moved before a large size twelve foot stamped down hard on her knee, then the butt of someone's gun got rammed into her ribs again.

Both Kira and Desta were defending blows from above when she left. Though they both heard the guttural sound of Kahn's voice, neither of them could comprehend what he said. Desta thought he had heard the word 'witch.' They didn't see it, and yet in an instant, they both felt Deena leave. Desta could only see Kahn's legs from where he was, prone on the ground. He had his left hand up, covering the side of his head when he felt it rip through his whole body.

Starting in his stomach like a violent nausea, his whole body convulsed with pure sorrow. Instantly his eyes filled with tears, he felt it, and then, blood. It poured onto the floor in front of Kahn's feet, lapping over his claws and into his robe. Desta hadn't seen exactly what caused it, though Kira had. He wrapped his giant hand around her head, placing his palm over her face and lacing his giant fingers in behind, he squeezed like he was destroying a piece of paper. Her skull crumbled, fragments of bone crunching and cracking through the soft tissue of her brain.

"Fucking Witch!" Boomed through the library before Deena's practically headless body dropped to the ground right in front of Desta. She landed in a thick puddle of her own blood which was growing and inching closer to him. From his left, he heard Kira's screams of anguish, mixing with the menacing laughter coming from behind the desk.

Commander Isaac Frost, the only member of the Ducaz Elite unit to have not undergone the genetic enhancements, was enjoying the show. A sick, sadistic member of Black Watch in Iraq for over a decade, he had been recommended as the commander of the Ducaz unit after an impressive run at the head of the Control Risk 'Special Ops' team. He had shown an incredible disdain for human life, and a willingness to always 'do what it takes.' Including drowning the French Ambassador's seven-year-old daughter, whilst he was made to watch.

The scar that ran through his right eye was the result of a bar brawl, he was the perfect soldier until he drank, then everyone was a target, and one night, one of those targets pulled a blade and sliced him across the face. Frost then used that same blade to disembowel the guy in the middle of the bar, and in front of dozens of stunned witnesses. Twenty years of service, not a single nick, yet a drunken bar brawl almost costs him his sight.

Frost continued laughing, he loved a bit of gratuitous violence, it satisfied the malevolent streak that ran through him. Khan wasn't laughing though. Having felt the skull cracking in his fingers, feeling the life of Deena leaving, the blood that sprayed all over him, had put him into an intense frenzy.

The witch had been able to poison his mind, and both Desta and Kira were still alive right now, only for that fact. A fact he intended to change immediately. His moved like a lizard as he slinked forward to grab Desta from the floor, his intense speed belied his size and weight. Before Desta had finished processing Deena's fate as it had unfolded, the soldiers looming over him backed away and he too was held in Kahn's unforgiving claw like hands.

"You thought your Witch could help you." he hissed, closing his strong hand around Desta's throat a little tighter.

He held him with one arm, dangling and twitching in front of him. He closed in so the end of his snout-like jawline was right in front of Desta's face. When he spoke, Desta could see into the back of his mouth and throat, smelling the foul stench of death breezing through his multiple rows of teeth.

"Where is she now human?" he whispered whilst staring dead into Desta's blood shot eyes.

He tightened his grip slightly and Desta felt like his head was going to pop off. He couldn't breathe and the blood was trapped in his head, whiteness was beginning to appear in his vision and was spreading from the edges. His blood shot eyes became even redder, as a panicked look began to show. His weak arms were feebly grabbing at Kahn's robes, Khan felt that panic and fed from it.

Kira couldn't look away, she had seen this moment in her dreams, right now she was just a bystander, unable to shake the two men standing over her, the second she flinched they rained further blows upon her. Her eyes filled with tears as she prepared herself for Desta to leave, all hope left her body as she realised the others were not going to get here in time to save them. Something must have happened in the tunnels.

Desta's last thought was very peaceful, the whiteness had completely consumed his vision, and a high-pitched ringing made him deaf to anything around him. Like all soldiers, he fought to the very last second, desperate to not leave the battle while the war raged on. As peace washed over him, there was a very different scene unfolding in the library.

The central desk that Frost sat behind was at the front of the vast library and disappearing into the darkness were hundreds of giant book shelves that stretched up to the ceiling. Deep in the darkness, at the other end of the library a small explosion had started a chain of events that was causing the giant shelves to tumble, like dominoes, one after the other, colliding into each other. Frost, Khan, and the soldiers with them, stopped and looked towards the sound. It was too dark down there to see what was happening, but the crack of wood on wood, the sounds of the books falling, were all announcing what was coming.

Frost was the first to speak, as Kahn kept his focus on the look in Desta's eyes, he loved the second just before a person died and he wasn't going to miss this.

"The rest are here." Frost half announced to his men around the counter, also picked up by the neck mic he was wearing, connecting him to Vol and the rest of the men down at the artefact room. He then turned directly to his men and Kahn.

"Weapons hot and prepare for anything," he said, not taking his eyes off the source of the sound.

"And Kahn, stop fucking around and, kill him already." he finished, turning back to the stone giant playing with his rag doll.

Just in time to see something out of the corner of his eye. Like a shadow flickering through light, something was flying towards Kahn and Desta. He didn't get time to warn him, for the second he noticed, Mina was already within striking distance and about to come down on the top of Kahn's head.

It had been perfect, except for only one thing. Kahn had seen Mina in the reflection of Desta's dying eyes, and despite Mina's enhanced speed, he was able to react like a cobra. Mina brought his blade down to puncture the soft patch on his head, though, the monster flung up his arm, catching his wrist with a slap. Mina wasn't done however and immediately released his grip on the blade, causing it to fall. Before Kahn could react, the blade was falling into Mina's other hand, his free hand, which he caught perfectly. Then, in one swift move, it arched through the air and disappeared through the soft patch of skin atop the giant croc skull, where Mina twisted it hard for good measure.

Mina's momentum carried him forward and he bounced from Kahn's huge shoulders landing on the floor in a roll which immediately became a jump, then up onto the counter of the desk in front of him, and another leap high into the air and over the head of Frost. It was like he had springs for feet and with his enhanced speed, he wasn't easy to follow. Suddenly every soldier within eyeshot was cocked and loaded. Kahn had still not moved; it had all happened so fast no one had noticed the handle of the six-inch blade sticking directly up from the centre of his head.

Desta fell to the ground first; practically unconscious he fell hard and didn't move when he landed. Then, Khan buckled at the knees and landed with a giant thud as he rolled backwards and landed, dead weight, loudly on the library floor.

Boom! Boom! Boom!

As Kahn fell, the sounds of the falling bookshelves were getting louder, faster, and closer and in the chaos of Mina's attack. Kira took a chance and used what little energy she had left to get to her feet. She used her foot to kick hard at the knee of the soldier beside her which caused him to buckle a little, though not enough. He'd had enough and swung his prone gun in her direction, pointing the barrel directly at her head, then unleashed. Kira closed her eyes; luckily, he never quite got to the trigger, and instead just fell backwards, landing flat on his back with a fist size whole in the back of his head.

Desta began to wake next to her and all around them both it was bedlam. The soldiers holding them were firing at what they thought was Mina, as he disappeared behind a column to the left of the counter, whilst Edmund delivered shots from the darkness of his high-powered sniper rifle. The booming thuds from the falling bookshelves was growing relentlessly louder and more dominant yet, over it all, Frost was shouting through his throat mic to the other half of the unit.

"Full assault, library breached." he yelled over the burts of automatic weapon fire.

"Kahn eliminated, I repeat Kahn is down." He popped his head up to see what was going on, and the back of the chair, just inches from his head exploded in a cloud of dust.

Edmund had them pinned down, whilst Mina took up a better position. During it all, Kira was able to make her way to Desta and drag him across the floor, away from the counter in the middle. She herself couldn't get to her feet so they both inched, moving out of the firing line. All the soldiers were too busy trying to keep their heads, whilst tracking Mina, to notice them slipping away. Edmund sparked to life in Mina's ear.

"They're clear Marky. Light em up."

Poised behind the now decimated pillar, Mina had been waiting for the green light to do what he loved to do most.

Frost was keeping his head down, so didn't see a thin, black clad arm poke out from behind the column and flick a series of small explosives his way. Hockey puck shaped discs soared through the air, and began to land amongst the soldiers, with the one aimed for the counter bouncing off the light wooden top, landing on the floor next to the remaining leader of the group. He looked at it questioningly, then instinctively reached for it to throw it back. It was too late though and within a two second window Frost and three of his men disappeared from existence, heated instantly to one thousand degrees, and then nothing.

There were still half a dozen hybrids taking shots at Mina, searching the darkness for Edmund, and looking now for Desta and Kira, yet between Mina and Edmund, they were pinned down and losing ground. The crashing of the bookshelves was at its loudest and at that second, the last row of shelves before the large opening that housed the circular admin desk, finally collapsed, falling forward into their space, and spilling thousands of books onto the hard stone floor and for one brief second, there was silence.

The light all around the library swayed, as the long balls of light on the chains swung in time with the shifts in energy and explosions. The silence was broken by a piercing shot from Edmund, causing another Soldier's chest to explode out of his back. Immediately, their guns spat back, and the noise continued.

Down at the back of the library, where Mina had originally set the charge to domino the bookshelves, there was the main tunnel entrance to the archives section where they held the cross of Christ. Theo, Simeon, and Raquel had raced down there once Mina had broken them into the library, through the side wall as planned. They expected to run into some soldiers, though the few they did meet, had already been killed by an infestation of determined cockroaches. They were pouring out of their dead mouths, ears, and noses. The three of them got deeper into the tunnels, passing more dead soldiers that appeared to be running towards the tunnel to escape, only to fail.

Unfortunately, the bugs were ineffective against the Giant Ducaz stationed with the Cross. Vol had heard about his brother's demise and was eager to meet the people responsible, even as he watched the soldiers being attacked by the insects, he simply grew more elated at the prospect of a worthy foe and a chance of revenge.

Vol always wore a skull cap that was impenetrable to most conventional weapons. Three of the BOL stepped into his trap, in the Cross Room, and he launched. Raquel was quick enough to strike first, if it wasn't for his helmet, he would have joined his brother without landing a blow.

Raquel was hands down the fastest of the BOL and used that speed to tackle the Ducaz whilst Simeon, and Theo grabbed the cross and managed to drag it into the tunnel. Simeon's massive frame made this possible, the two of them followed Raquel's orders and took the Cross to the rest of the team in the main library while she kept the Ducaz busy.

Vol didn't care about the Cross, the mission, and nor this fucking planet. What he did care about, was his brother Kahn, and these people had killed him. She wasn't leaving alive, and he had no reason to rush, he was going to enjoy this.

"I'm going to climb inside you and fucking kill you from the inside, you little cunt." he whispered to her. The small stone room was still lit with the artificial lights that kept the cross illuminated, though the space where the cross had sat for over two thousand years was now empty.

"Is that your idea of foreplay?" Raquel sneered back at him,
"cos you got catch me first fuck head."

Then it began.

Like a cat fighting a snake, Raquel pounced and dodged a snap of Vol's jaws. She unleashed three quick blows as she passed him, fast enough, they could barely be seen, though he felt her sharp blade jab into his jaw line, into a tooth, then ricochet off his stone snout.

He flicked up his tail, anticipating where she would land, yet Raquel wasn't done with this pass, and as she fell away from him, she flipped backwards and slammed her steel toed boot under his chin, sending his head flying backwards, knocking Vol back a couple of steps. He adjusted his tail to stop himself from falling, and Raquel landed, poised, steady on her feet. She formed her stance and hissed at Vol, with her eyes glowing white enough that the room looked like it was bathed in daylight.

All in black, silver blades shone in each of her hands, two steps to her left, she then leapt off her left foot to launch at Vol off the wall. She moved so fast it was practically a blur, though Vol was equal to the task and his lizard like eyes followed her trajectory. He swung his strong right arm and stepped forward, hitting home, yet not fully. Raquel managed to compose herself, at the last minute, as she saw his arm coming, it bounced of her shoulder. Hard enough to knock her off her balance, yet not before she was able to jam one of her blades into his left eye.

She clattered to the floor as Vol took a couple of steps back and roared loudly as he reached up and pulled her knife from his face. Petulantly, he threw the knife at her, and after a half second to adjust to now only having sight in one eye, he went on the attack.

Vol came hard and fast with each punch, at Raquel. Every flick of his tail, or his snout was not enough, as Raquel ducked, dodged and kept ahead of his blows. As he relentlessly advanced, his attack got faster and more varied, bit by bit the power behind them was pushing Raquel backwards, step by step, until she had her back to the wall. Vol swung firm from his right shoulder and Raquel was ahead of it. His tail shot over his right shoulder, like a lightning bolt, straight for Raquel's face. It slammed point first into the wall, catching a clump of her hair as it did.

She dropped to her haunches, leaving her hair up with Vol and jumped at his feet, herself doing the splits and kicking his legs out from within. She kept her momentum moving and went through his legs to appear behind him just as he was beginning to fall. She was already on her feet and sprung up again, jumping past Vol's head, high into the room's recessive ceiling yet on her way she was able to jam another blade under Vol's skull cap as she tried to remove his protection. It was all in vain though, as the tail didn't miss on the second attempt.

As Raquel was congratulating herself for cracking the seal in his skull cap, his tail was already snapping like a whip and on its way above him. As she reached her highest point, she didn't see the long snake-like weapon rushing up towards her. When it hit however, she certainly felt it.

Jabbing hard into her thin Kevlar vest, Raquel tried to shift her shoulders to deflect some of its force across her chest. It still hit hard enough to break a rib and rip the Kevlar down the middle, though at least it didn't impale her. Vol was already spinning his upper body and swung his elbow hard into Raquel's legs whilst she was still in the air, beginning to fall. She spun like a windmill and even with her lightning reflexes she couldn't correct for any kind of landing and smashed hard into the stone floor. No time for a breath, Vol was already on her back as she was now flat on the floor, crushed under his massive frame. He locked one of his strong arms around her neck, almost popping her head off.

Raquel was pinned and tried a last flick of her head back into Vol's snout, though with the speed of a cobra launching at a mouse, he managed to lock his big jaws either side of her head and bit, just hard enough for his teeth to crack her skin and grip her skull, yet not too deep as to break through to the grey matter.

With his jaws locked on her head, he now had both hands free, and with his massive, long body holding her down he reached under himself and ripped at Raquel's cargo pants, pulling them off and exposing her underneath him.

"From the inside." he whispered from the back of his throat as his claw lined hands grabbed her thighs and pulled them apart.

The smell and heat of his breath flooded every sense Raquel had left, her whole head was pinned and bathed in his smell and if she didn't do something this was about to be worse than that time she went to that R-Kelly concert when she was fourteen. Nothing would move. Everything was stuck, he was too heavy.

She felt something very hard and wet, slapping against her back.

"Fuck No!" she screamed into the concrete floor and gave another attempt to shrug him off, it was useless, with her head in his mouth and almost a tonne of muscle, all she was able to do was jam her right arm under her stomach, trapping her even more.

"Fuck you Cunt!" she screamed again, in her dirtiest Australian accent.

She could hear him laughing from the back of his throat as 'it' slid down her back and between the skin of her buttocks. He lifted his hips just a fraction to allow the angle he needed to assault her. Raquel braced herself, there was nothing between him and her soft insides. She held her breath, and then felt a bulge by her trapped hand. Grenade? Ring? Fuck yes!

She flicked her finger, it was the only part of her body that she was able to move, and prayed it was enough. The head of Vol's other snake had found its target and was pressed against her tense opening, he jabbed down in triumph, though not before the M97 Grenade ripped through Raquel like she didn't exist and slammed its full force into Vol and his filthy, slimy cock.

It ripped into his stone skin, which caused some lasting damage, yet nothing he wouldn't survive. His soft organ though, was exposed and was torn to pieces by thousands of fragments of metal and explosive heat. This he would not survive, there would be no way to stem the bleeding.

He roared as he rolled around on the hard floor in complete darkness. All the lights had been blown and the bright white light from Raquel's eyes was gone, as was she. His skin was torn in a thousand places, his cock was gone and blood was pouring from him, his brother was dead and his lonely roars continued with no one to hear, and no one to come and help.

Theo, and Simeon emerged into the library from the tunnels, and could hear the sporadic shots and muzzle flashes coming from the far end. They were looking down a dark aisle, approximately 5 meters wide, with hundreds of meters of fallen bookshelves all laying silent. The path to the action near the circular admin desk, was littered with thousands of books and as planned, Simeon and Theo headed for the same point they came in through, by heading down the aisle about fifty feet then turning to the far-left wall. Simeon took off yet, Theo's thoughts were set on going back to help Raquel. It was at that point; he heard the explosion echoing off the tight walls of the tunnel he had come from. He spun to look at Simeon. Simeon had stopped the second he heard it too.

He held the giant cross over one shoulder like he was carrying nothing and as he spun, the base of it dragged along the floor, kicking up old books as it did. Theo looked into his eyes, asking the question without verbally asking. Simeon took a deep breath and looked past Theo into the darkness they had come from. He waited, searching for what felt like an eternity to Theo, before bringing his eyes back to his. Simeon shook his head and gave Theo a reassuring smile, before turning and continuing with what had to be done.

Theo didn't know what to do, something in him still wanted to head down into the tunnel, he still hoped he would find her and be the one to save the day. He looked back, deciding what was right. Then a giant explosion from the other end of the library reminded him of his mission. Mina and Edmund were causing havoc as they rescued Desta and Kira, and Theo needed to be at the exit when they were ready to leave.

The explosion had come from a little gift Mina had laid, whilst Edmund picked off targets randomly. Homemade, plastic explosive, stick on pucks, Mina called them. Microchip controlled detonation, powered with his smart phone app, and stuck on a wall with double sided tape. Its blast capacity equal to a claymore, just fewer metal debris, and more heat and concussion burns.

Behind the desk, Frost was stuck, unable to pop his head up so crawled over to the side, where the circular desk opened to the library. He was hoping to get out from his little prison and as he looked out, he saw Kira, still on the floor, pulling Desta with her, headed away from the battle. It was as if she was rescuing him in the water, the way they were both dragging backwards, but she was making good progress and had them both out of the line of fire. Above him, one of his men popped up and fired a volley of shots towards Edmund, he looked up and saw the end of the gun light up above the light wooden desk. He noticed an unusual little thing stuck to the side, he didn't give it a second thought as he pulled out his pistol and centred himself on Kira's head.

'Nice try' he thought to himself as he squeezed the trigger to snuff out her light.

At that second, the small black disc, did what it was there for and with the help of the dozen or so others, it incinerated the desk at the centre of the Vatican's Forbidden library as well as the five remaining soldiers that were the Churches last line of defence.

Silence followed, as the remaining members of the BOL all took a second to assess. The explosion was so vast it was unclear if all targets had gone down, so to be sure Edmund's high zoom scope patrolled over the burning embers of blasted wood and body parts.

"Clear." he announced to the room, and from nowhere Mina appeared next to Kira and Desta.

"We got it." he told them.

Desta didn't look as happy as Mina did, he looked back at the explosive mess they were leaving behind.

"Deena?" he asked, shifting his gaze up to Mina, who then closed his eyes and bowed his head.

"And Racquel." Mina stated. Desta sighed at the news, and took a moment to think, and compose himself.

"Let's finish this," he finally declared and held his hand up to Mina who clasped it hard and pulled his leader to his feet. Desta winced in pain, and Kira looked battered, yet they were still alive, and now they had the Cross.

Chapter 27

Radioactive Plague

Baghdad – American Embassy
05/03/2022
4 :44am

The American Embassy in Baghdad is not just a single building, it is a vast area housing upwards of eight thousand staff at any one time across over sixty buildings. On the north side of the giant compound was the main entrance to the Embassy area and either side of this there was over half a mile of solid concrete wall topped with rotating razor wire. Giant concrete blocks and erect metal pillars were strategically placed to stop any would-be truck or car bombs from getting too close to the protective outer shell.

The gate itself was eight inches of reinforced steel that slid out of one wall, across the gap and into the other and above the gate there was a thick walkway that led to two glass walled towers that sat proudly just either side. It housed the gate team, and just in front, on the street level and about fifty feet from the actual gate, there was a small boom that lifted to allow deliveries and other vehicles through. Here there was a small hut, ringed by concrete barriers, this was where the road team checked the vehicles and credentials of those wishing to enter.

Right now, in the early threat of morning, there were no Americans anywhere to be seen. Both the gate and road teams were gone, in fact, since the explosion, the entire compound had been deserted. All that was left were the Ducaz, and their teams buried deep within the Eisenhower Mansion, directly above Soteria.

There was one set of eyes looking over the cameras from all areas, and on the full bank of screens in front of him, almost everything was in the green light of 'night vision'. For the last three hours he hadn't seen a single moving object, so when something moved in the top right corner, he spotted it right away. It was the main gate camera, which immediately changed from green night vision to a colour picture. It was lit up by a dozen giant spotlights that were triggered by the movement, he looked closer. A couple of locals had walked into frame.

He leant forward in his chair and reached out to grab his mouse which he clicked, and the image appeared on the screen directly in front of him. He clicked again and zoomed in on a small group of men walking slowly towards the embassy. His eyebrows creased as he looked at them, something was not right here, each of them looked like walking corpses, and half of them had lost giant clumps of hair. They all had what appeared to be chemical burns across their faces, and any exposed skin was red, or covered in what looked like boils. The clothes on one of them was melted to his legs, then it clicked.

"Holy shit!" he exhaled and brought his hand up to his mouth in shock.

'Radiation and heat blasts, this was from the bomb.'

He and his team had arrived before it had hit, and with their reptilian DNA upgrades they were immune to the radiation that was raging through the city. They hadn't even considered it, yet here it was in all its glory. The small huddle of men was joined by a few more, they stepped into shot. They were more animated than the first group, and a quick look up to the screens, at the long-range cameras covering the Qadisiya Express Way, showed a sea of people, filling the streets and moving as one around the expressway ramp. Slowly they ambled down onto the street running alongside the Embassy borders. They weren't at the front gate yet, though it was quite clear that they were coming this way. He pressed the black circle on his throat.

"Sir, we have company arriving at the front gate." While he spoke, he clicked and moved around the images, taking in at least a hundred people. Men and women, even children amongst them. Some had energy to move, others appeared to be right on death's door. Then, another wave of people rounded and grew. Now, thousands of dying Iraqis, desperate, lost and forgotten were coming to see the Americans.

"Looks like locals Sir, survivors from the blast looking for help." The voice in his earpiece spoke again when he finished.

"Few hundred, maybe a thousand." It crackled again, providing his instructions.

"Affirmative sir," and with that, he adjusted his mouse and clicked again. Immediately the lights at the main gates went dead.

"Sorry guys, nobody's home." He said to the screen showing the main gate as it once again changed, from bright light and colour to the eerie glow of night-vision green.

He bought the Expressway Camera up on the main screen and clicked again. The wave wasn't stopping, it was still coming round the large concrete bend and the main street leading alongside the embassy towards the gate was filling from one side to the other with people, and for each step they took forward, another line stepped round the expressway, it just kept growing.

He couldn't hear what was happening on the streets, though, the group was animated, waving their arms in the air as they walked as one, and a gentle, rhythmic roar of:

"A-lah Ak-bar!' Filled the morning air and bounced off the buildings around them.

Baghdad was dead, no electricity, no vehicles, barely food or water. Nothing in the City stirred, except here. It was the last hope of a desperate city that were watching their children die slowly in front of them.

Chapter 28

Last Prayers

Baghdad – Al Hurajabi Island
05/03/2022
5 :12am

Nadev had landed with the remaining members of the team on Al Hurajabi Island, on a small airstrip that had been cut into the large, flat field of grass on the side facing the river. The Island sat in the heart of Baghdad and dominated the Northern side of the Tigris as it meandered through the now baron and burning metropolis.

The bomb's epicentre was about a mile to the Northeast and during his descent, Nadev looked down at it, he couldn't think of anything else in his life that had seemed so hopeless. The entire city, North of the river was still burning, fires raging out of control and from the sky, the full extent of the misery almost brought a tear to his eye, yet in the end, strengthened his resolve to make the Reptilians pay.

After the final explosion in the library, they had made it out very easily, it seemed the only plan the Nephalim had, was the Ducaz and their soldiers, and the team had taken care of the first unit. The flight had been a sombre one for everyone on board, the loss of Deena and the way it happened weighed heavy on all their minds and Raquel's sacrifice in the tunnels wouldn't leave Theo's mind. He could've gotten back down there in time. He knew it.

They had all had plenty of time to digest the first half of the mission, the failures, the successes. Conversation was scarce and while they had cruised through the skies, Simeon had used his gifts to practically heal Kira and Desta. Kira had barely said a word, she had seen Deena's head crack like an egg, and it had shaken and angered her. All that was on her mind now was avenging Deena by destroying the remaining Ducaz at the Embassy.

As they departed the plane, they were met by a small group of locals. Radiation poisoning was evident, although they were not as far gone as the group heading for the Embassy's front gates. Each of them wore clean white Thobes with matching head pieces, bowing their heads when their guests emerged. One dropped to the floor and began to pray to them, desperation and awe flooded through, as they welcomed the BOL.

The team walked down the steps of the plane, Simeon emerged last, with a giant object over his shoulder, wrapped in a black cloth. As the cool night-time air began to warm with the impending sun, the team and their new guest made their way on foot to the boats awaiting their arrival, and equipment they had prepared.

Theo's first thought as he stepped into the cool, pre-dawn air was the smell, it was unlike anything he had ever been exposed to. It sat at the top of his nose, and he could practically taste it, a combination of burning plastic and hair, making him instantly want to convulse and be sick. Seeing the burns on the face of Jihad Amir Farah, as he introduced himself in English, reminded him very quickly what the smell was, as if the images he had seen from the plane window when flying over the city were not enough.

As they walked across the dark, empty fields to the Tigris inlet where the boats were waiting, the sun's first orange glow was just beginning to show on the Eastern horizon. Theo looked at the stunning Jadira Bridge as it climbed over them, and swung to the right over the Tigris, to the University sector and the South side of the river. It sat dark and still, its silhouette beginning to darken and brighten all at once as the sun's rays started to form its shape. The same orange glow that was building in the East hung ominously over the entire city to the North as it burned and heavy smoke drifted in thick plumes gently to the West.

One of their guides was speaking with Desta when he coughed into his hand, he looked at it with fear and damnation when he saw thick blood clots sitting in his palm. Theo couldn't believe that this had all been done with the malicious intent to stop them.

They reached a small pontoon that had an inflatable, hard bottom rescue style boat with an electric engine mounted at the rear tied to it. Mina and Edmund immediately began to load up the gear as both of them stayed focused. Both had barely said a word since the Vatican, Deena was like their little sister, and Raquel was like their big brother, sister. They both were hurting, wishing that they could have done more, so were staying on task with a renewed determination to finish this, and finish it well.

Desta took a moment to heal some of the wounds on the men that had helped them, Simeon loaded up the cross and got comfy on board of the boat, causing it to rock as his shuffled. Nadev had started the electric engine and had it running at idle, Kira was already on board waiting so when Theo sat down, they were ready to go. Desta hopped on and untied the rope connecting them to the land as the four men in white pushed together and eased the BOL team into the calm waters of the Tigris Inlet.

Theo looked back to see all four men on their knees, on the riverbank, praying in their direction. As they got smaller and further away, their chants of 'Allah Akbar' got fainter and lost, as the sound of a burning city began to take over.

Chapter 29

Head In The Sand

Baghdad - Office of Control Risk
05/03/2022
6 :15am

B rad sat on the sofa in his suite like residence, eleven levels beneath the lobby of Control Risk. Built with multiple exits, through a network of underground tunnels, he and his team could access any of the seven locations throughout the city. Right now, though, it was the Ark for him, his men and a few select members of Baghdad's elite and powerful that hadn't made it to the main shelter further South in Kuwait.

He was confident he would ride out whatever Nibiru's Passing would bring from this secure bunker and it also enabled him to stay connected and comfortable right up until the end. In this moment, however, he wasn't feeling so comfortable. The sun was already up in the city above him, and he was yet to fall asleep. He hadn't slept for what felt like weeks, and for the last twelve hours he had been working with the American and European air forces trying to locate Desta's plane so that it could be destroyed.

He had been informed immediately when the Vatican was breached and since he had heard that the cross was gone, his phone had been ringing off the hook. He had dealt with all the logistics, and exhausted every avenue possible, and still, nothing came of it.

The phone on the coffee table in front of him rang again, USO appeared on the screen. Brad looked at the phone, then at the note pads, and ripped out pages, covered in his scribbled writing. He had been working here for hours and was beginning to feel as though it was all in vain, there was nothing he could do from down here. He continued to look at the phone, deciding if he would answer it this time. Then it stopped. He took a deep breath, almost a sigh of relief. Then there was a sharp knock on his door.

Without waiting for a cue to enter, the head of the Control Risk field security team, barged in holding his mobile phone in his hand.

"Sir, I have the USO on the phone, I was told to hand it to you." he said, regretfully.

Brad's look said it all, he shot him a glance to cut him down, resentful that this was being brought to his attention.

"Of course, I was just about to call him back." Brad said loudly, trying to smile in his voice, hoping the person on the other end of the phone would hear him.

"Hello Sir?" Brad started to talk and charm, though was cut off.

"Update Sir?" Brad tried to sound in control, though it was obvious he didn't have good news. He paused for a second as the voice on the other end loudly shouted a stream of obscenities, he even pulled it away from his ear, while he waited for them to calm.

'Fuck this.' Brad thought.

"You know what Joe, IF we all survive this, you can do your fucking worst, but for now, it's all down to the Ducaz at the Embassy. We have played all our cards, and now it's up to them. There's nothing any of us can do now, so stop fucking calling me."

With that, he pressed the screen to hang up and looked up at his field team manager.

"I'm done taking calls now, are we clear? You and the team contact the embassy and get updates on the quarter hour." He threw the mobile through the air and his staff member caught it, then turned to leave.

"Get Mary to send me an Alaha and a bottle of whiskey too." he demanded, then stood up to walk slowly to the bathroom.

Chapter 30

Cat And Mouse

Baghdad – American Embassy
05/03/2022
6 :19am

"Allah Akbar, Allah Akbar, Allah Akbar."

Ten thousand desperate, sick, burning and dying Iraqis had come together in one last effort to save themselves and their City. Since the bomb had gone off, no help had come, either from the Iraqi government or from overseas, they had been completely abandoned.

They stood together, men, women, and children, covered in a myriad of burns, boils, scabs and sickness, as the numbers grew, the soldier watching the screens was getting more and more concerned. They filled the main screen now, the camera on the hut at the front gate was now a sea of desperate faces and angry gestures. They bashed on the gates, threw things at the walls and as their numbers grew, the sun made its appearance, climbing into the sky. It was like the light woke them further and they began to surge, trying to climb into the compound.

"Sir, we have an escalating situation here." He paused and waited for the response through his earpiece.

"But sir, they are beginning to try and breach the walls." He protested

"No sir, no sign of them yet?" Further instructions were being barked through his ear piece.

"Yes Sir, I'll let you know at once." and with a heavy exhale, he looked up at the other monitors in front of him to focus on his main task, report any sign of the BOL.

A quick scan of the monitors. There was no movement anywhere except for at the front gate. No motion detection reports, everything was happening in the North and down the main street along the compound walls which was still filling with more desperate Iraqis.

The main monitor was still on the main group at the front and as the natural light of the sun grew, it filled with colour and on the screens, the extent of the burns and damage from the nuke was becoming clearer. He used the small joystick in front of him to zoom in and move amongst the crowd and even as a soldier in the Ducaz Unit, the look of horror on his face showed his humanity. Blood oozed from people's ears, noses, even eyes. Skin had been sizzled by either heat or radiation and most clothing was charred or melted away. He saw makeshift weapons of all kinds, and large blades in the hands of those that could carry them, yet no guns.

He continued to pan over the crowd and was looking closely at a mother holding what appeared to be a dead baby in her arms, he got lost in her anguish and thoughts. It was a small notification on the screen that snapped him out of it.

Movement - Camera 6 - Riverfront.

He clicked on the notification in the bottom right corner and the scene in front of him switched from the crowd at the front gate, to the inlet on the Southern side. The second he did his entire camera feed, and all his monitors went blue.

No IP. Error 430111x

Flashed up as a warning in red across the top of the screen. He immediately reached for his throat mic, a concerned look in his face.

"Sir, we have movement on the main riverfront cameras," he paused, listening to the reply

"Unknown sir, the camera feed died immediately after they were detected," he paused again.

"Yes sir, I'll do what I can." With this last statement he jumped up and began checking the cables on the back of the machines in front of him. The basic computer connections were all good. He pushed back his chair to go check the modem quickly when a loud explosion rocked the room and shook the ground. It was far away yet close enough to knock him off his feet.

Chapter 31

Perfect Entry

Baghdad – American Embassy Riverfront
05/03/2022
6 :19am

O k, Cameras are down, we should be good to go," said Mina confidently. He was seated at the head of the small boat, skimming through the water towards the large outlet pipe built into the riverbank as the sun rose into the Baghdad sky.

Unfortunately, Desta and the team had run into some delays; a head wind when getting out of Europe, as well as having to refuel in Syria. And now, they were forced to gain control of the Embassy in the early morning light, rather than in the darkness they had hoped for. As predicted, Mina was able to hack into the Embassy cameras, shutting them down before they had come into frame. In an instant, they shut done in unison, which ordinarily would arise suspicion, luckily, they only needed to be down for a few minutes to hide the team's entry point. Besides, there was another distraction due any second.

As Theo sat next to Nadev at the stern, they rocked up and down as they hit small ripples within the river's inlet, as the wind tousled their hair. It was gently blowing down from the North, bringing with it extra smoke and the bitter, burning smell of radiation. As they silently cruised along, he could hear what seemed to be a soccer crowd chanting in the breeze. The from nowhere, as he stared directly ahead of them, a giant explosion shot up into the sky, at the side entrance of the Embassy compound.

Desta smiled, he didn't know what to expect, though judging by the size and scale of the explosion, it looked like the distraction was a car or truck at the main staff entrance near the bridge that loomed over them and over the river up ahead.

That was all the team needed. Nadev took the boat right up to the end of the inlet and beached it on the dirty sand. Within seconds, they were unloading. Nadev jumped out and dragged the boat up the bank, placing it against the wall directly under the camera Mina had shut down. Thus, preventing the boat from being seen once the cameras returned.

Simeon had the large cross, wrapped in black cloth over his shoulder. Edmund grabbed two rucksacks from the ground and tossed one over to Mina, before slinging the other over his back. He pulled the lever of his matte black rifle, looking with one eye inside the chamber. Satisfied, he rocked back the lever again, and bought up a small plastic mask which he placed over his face. He pushed the button on the top, and with a gust of air, it sucked into place creating a seal. Without hesitation, he jumped into the warm water of the Tigris River inlet and disappeared below the surface.

Kira was right behind him, now, purely here for fire power. She never believed she would see tomorrow and judging by the grenades and thermo charges on her belt, she intended to go out with a bang. Carrying the same automatic rifle as Edmund, and a pistol on either hip in a leather holster she had forged together. Although still in pain; with a slightly swollen face and aching ribs, Simeon's therapy on the plane had restored her ability to carry out the game plan: to kill the Ducaz. Once her mask was pulled into place, she too then disappeared.

Mina strapped his rucksack on, just like his best mate, then grabbed his rifle off the ground and flicked the lever to the side to check the chamber. Satisfied, he put his mask on, already jumping in on his way down to the tunnel entrance. Theo took a final look over the South to see the picturesque half of Baghdad, bathed in the early morning sunlight, immaculate, untouched, and silent.

The river radiated an orange glow and as he looked upstream, he could see the silhouette of the Al-Mualack suspension bridge in black against it, it was like a postcard. Theo took the mental image, and put his mask on, turning as he did to jump into the water to disappear into the dark pipe running under the American Embassy in Baghdad. It was complete silence as he descended towards the lights of his teammates. Still no fear, which surprised him, just fear that they might fail maybe? He smiled.

'What a way to live' he thought.

Nadev was next followed by Simeon, and as Desta disappeared into the warm water, the cameras throughout the whole compound came back to life. The first part of the plan had seemed to go perfectly, they had made it in undetected and the distractions above ground greatly exceeded Desta's expectations.

'We might just have a chance,' Desta thought as he saw his team below him make it into the pipe entrance.

Up in the camera room, the lights had turned back on, and safe to say, since the explosion, he had been working frantically to get a pair of eyes on the situation. He mumbled to himself and occasionally grunted…

"Not Yet Sir." He had tried everything to reboot the modem and allow for the IP port to be reset, yet the computer kept delivering a data limits error that was frustrating him so much. He had been shouting at the monitor when it had all started to reboot for no reason, then as one, all the monitors were showing in full. He didn't care how.

"Sir we have eyes again." he immediately reported and began to scour for the information he was being hounded for. It didn't take long, one of his monitors was zoned in on an apocalyptic scene of fire, twisted metals, as well as the burning shells of cars and buildings. He clicked and immediately this camera's footage took over the main screen in front of him.

"South West compound entrance sir." he reported again, and zoomed in a little, concentrating on the images.

"Looks to me like a car bomb at the staff entrance sir." He looked up at the camera covering the main entrance.

"Major damage to building fronts, vehicles, no sign of movement." He waited for a question.

"Negative sir, there is still a large crowd but no sign of an explosion." He paused, listening to the questions coming in at him.

"Negative again sir, we had confirmed movement but the cameras died before I was able to verify it was them." Again, another pause, this time instructions.

"Yes sir, I agree," he finished.

"I'll let you know immediately."

Inside the Eisenhower riverfront mansion, Southwest of the compound, General Karl Vos ended the conversation by pressing the button on his left ear. In his comfortable leather director's chair, he sat behind his borrowed desk in the offices and rooms he and his men had taken over. He of course had the Ambassador's office and was pleased to find a fully stocked whiskey bar in the adjoining suite. His sharp, slightly sunken face showed age, wisdom and experience and his southern accent seemed to always be delivered with a hint of sarcasm. He had seen it all and bought the t-shirt as he would say, and today was no different.

He looked at the two giant figures in front of him. Ang and Set were the last remaining Ducaz on Earth. They stood proud in their traditional robes, both had heard about the Vatican and decided they wanted to end the BOL whilst honouring their fallen brothers. The Ducaz cared for very little, except their Nephilim, or Ducaz brothers.

They were excited for it all to begin and the explosion near the bridge entrance had been like a starting pistol going off, now they wanted to join the race. Head to toe in their dark robes, they were almost identical. Both their hoods were down as they tried to convince Vos they should head out to greet some of the locals at the main gate. They had giant snouts and rows and rows of small, sharp teeth, glistening as they spoke with their deep guttural tone, from the back of their throats.

Vos was swigging his whiskey, filling in time with a pointless story that would lead him where he wanted to go. His short, spiky hair cut was for a much younger man and against his older features gave him a very confusing facade, yet Vos didn't care. He ran his own race and it had gotten him this far.

"So you see Ang, if my Grandaddy had've pulled that watch out of his ass the first time he thought he needed it, well then it wouldn't be here right now around my wrist almost 50 years later, would it?" He finished politely and showed his wrist to the two monsters before him. They looked at each other, looking to see if the other had a clue what he was talking about, then back at him. Set was about to speak.

Vos stood up.

"It's about patience, elegant, simple, patience." He had a flair for the dramatic, which you either loved or hated about him.

Both the Ducaz stationed with him, were in the later camp, though Vos had a very close relationship with the last Nephilim so they both held their tongue, most of the time. Right now, there was a very uneasy silence in the room. These Muslim shits had killed their kin, they weren't ready to be as patient as Vos. They both stared at Vos, it was clear that his speeches and charm were wearing thin.

"Ok, Set, take six men out to sweep the perimeter, and go check out the front gate for me." Set snared at him, dissatisfied with Vos's plan.

"Where there is noise, there will be BOL, they are already here." Set heard this and looked to his brother Ang, then back to Vos, appeased.

"Well go find them." He instructed whilst taking a final sip on his glass and finishing the golden warm liquid.

"Ang, you, and the rest of the men, head down to the hot baths." Ang lifted his head to speak and interject.

"Trust me old boy, this is all smoke and mirrors, they will come straight to you."

Both the sharp headed creatures looked at each other, their yellow eyes flickered and closed in from the sides as they blinked. They didn't speak, though there seemed to be an agreement between them, Ang turned to Vos as Set marched like a soldier leaving a room, allowing his cloak to float behind him.

"Very well, but tonight we will dine on human flesh one way or the other." he grunted before he too left. Vos didn't care.

"What do you have for me Stefaniak?" he said after touching his ear and settling back into the soft chair and spinning it slowly, allowing himself to turn a complete 360.

Down in the tunnels under the Embassy the team advanced quickly, they had come up in the large sewage system that ran under Baghdad and were on their way to the drainage system under the Eisenhower Mansion. They each wore night vision goggles, so they could see clearly. Mina and Edmund lead the way, and were sweeping along the tunnels, covering each other, and aggressively checking every nook and cranny along the way. Their constant chatter played in the ears of the whole team and as Kira listened it reminded her of them playing video games in mansion.

The tunnel was about nine feet in diameter and every fifty feet or so, intersected with smaller tunnels, and run off pipes. It stank like rotten meat and occasionally they would have to step over a group of rats fighting over some scrap of food they had found.

Theo was walking alongside Kira, behind the boys, she was nervous and had her gun up on her shoulder, poised and ready to strike at the first sign. She felt this was going too smoothly, there were no cameras, no booby traps, and no sign of the Ducaz unit. She hoped Desta was right and they had taken the bait, that most of the unit was now out at the main gate dealing with the locals, or out at the bridge entrance sweeping for them, yet in her gut, she knew how cunning the Ducaz were, she couldn't believe they had overlooked the sewage system.

Desta shared her apprehension and was trying not to let it show. Behind him Simeon trudged on, carrying the large cross on his back, every third or fourth step, the base of it would tap into the floor, echoing off the close concrete structure. Nadev was at the rear walking backwards most of the time, keeping an eye out behind them. He had seen enough combat over the years to trust his instincts which were telling him this was a trap, yet Desta had told him…

"They had no choice now but to take the action with the right intent, and then trust in the Universal outcome."

Up at the main gate a handful of the protestors had used rugs and blankets to scale over the wall and razor wire to get into the compound. Set and his team had heard this and were heading there from the Mansion in a couple of yellow dust coloured, Army Jeeps. They arrived just as the group of insurgents was able to access the gate controls, allowing the dam to break and the sick, dying and desperate people of Baghdad to flood through, one step closer. The road leading from the main gate, Southwards towards the river and the Mansion, filled with people as they spilled through in all directions, looking to cause chaos.

Set's driver ploughed the Jeep heavily through those on the road, dozens of bodies were unable to get out of the way in time as the second jeep took its lead and swerved out to smash mercilessly into the men, women, and children around them. As they tore through the road, and then spun on the grass to get another pass, Set and the soldiers in the other jeep all began to open fire. The whole unit laughed and yelped liken drunken yahoo's shooting from the back of their pickups. All around them the people scattered, running in different directions. They fled trying to escape the screeching tyres, roaring engines and sizzling bullets crackling through the early morning air.

Set suddenly leapt from the side of his jeep, surprising the driver and the man in the back. He rolled like a ball across the ground, before unfurling and leaping into the air all in one movement. He soared a good ten feet high, unwrapping his strong tail and neck and flinging his arms out to his side as he roared loud enough to be heard from the Mansion. He landed and immediately got to work ripping apart anything that moved. With the speed of a striking snake and the strength of a rhino nothing and no one stood a chance.

The flood of people hadn't stopped, and as Set brought his heavy foot down on the chest of a young woman he had just floored, the sounds of her ribs splintering into her lungs was lost as dozens of bullets pinged off his stony back. He instinctively winced, ducked his head, and spun with malice in his eyes to find the shooter. As he stepped off the young girl, she tried desperately to gasp for a breath, though instead, she drowned right there in her own blood.

The ground next to him exploded as a grenade spewed dozens of white-hot metal shards into his skin, he brought his arm up to protect himself before taking hits from over a dozen automatic weapons. Amongst the crowd, were now hundreds of armed, young men, most wearing burnt or dirty Iraqi army uniforms and they were all firing on the jeeps and the 'abomination' attacking the people around them. None of them dared to believe the giant crocodile ripping into their people was real, though whatever it was, needed to be stopped.

Theo's heart was racing, he was walking in silence, death felt imminent, either at the hands of the Ducaz, or on the cross. It had all been easy earlier, when he was just the saviour, the chosen one, yet as he got more time to spend with his thoughts, his survival instinct was beginning to gnaw at his conscious mind.

'He didn't want to die.' Flashed through his mind.

"Don't worry Theo, none of us do." Kira squeezed his arm as she spoke and jolted him back to reality. He looked at her whimsically, as she looked back at him and smiled.

"We're here." Mina instructed the team as they rounded a corner, and the pipe opened into a larger space, though with a much lower ceiling.

Here it was, all tiled and low enough that the boys were required to crawl to the opening that spanned the entire width of the 15 feet wide space. Metal bars ran from top to bottom along it, allowing water through, though not intruders. It was the water run off for the ancient baths above them and was only a few feet high, yet wide enough for Simeon to drag the cross through.

The team all waited as Mina used a small mirror on a stick to look behind the bars, and around the edges. He shook his head and pulled a small torch from his belt. They were going through.

Upstairs, on the top floor of the Mansion and no longer sitting in his chair, now looking out of the window, Northwards towards the gate, Vos pressed the button on his left ear, swirling his whiskey with his right hand. Looking out over the city as the sun rose, becoming warmer, he got a little tingle of excitement. The destruction was magnificent. Smoke still climbed from dozens of raging fires, joining together to form a slow-moving fog that drifted past tower blocks and skyscrapers that were now just burning shells poking from rubble.

Though he couldn't see the main gate, he knew Set and his team were on a rampage, and he was looking for updates from Stefaniak in the camera room.

"That's it?" he asked into his earpiece.
"What about the backup system?" he quipped and took another sip of his whiskey.

He pursed his lips and winced like he saw his favourite boxer take a stiff as he saw another flash and large explosion over near the main gate, where Set was tussling with the locals.

"Ooooie." he whistled at the window.
"Should've just fucking listened." Then there was a voice in his ear again.

"No, not you dick head. God Damn it! I'm heading down to join Ang. Let me know if it comes back online." With that, he turned to walk back to the desk, tossing his whiskey glass against the wall as he did.

It shattered into a thousand pieces, yet he didn't care, he was buzzed enough. He grabbed his pistol off the desk, tucked his shirt in and went to make sure Ang and the remaining team didn't fuck this up.

Back underground, as Theo slid between the opening below, Kira's hand popped into view and he grabbed onto it, she pulled him hard and he slid out from the drainage system of the ancient Roman bath house into the shallow end of what was an empty swimming pool, stretching at least fifty feet away from him.

The pool was rectangular with giant marble pillars lined on either side, half of each pillar cutting into the sharp straight lines. At the end, opposite him was a strange stone structure, it stood at the head of the pool with a white marble bench arched around it in half a circle. It resembled a termite mound, such was the rough, rocky surface and shape.

Polished light blue square tiles reflected the light coming from the ceiling. Theo looked up to see the same glowing orbs he had seen at the Vatican's Forbidden Library and then forwards to see both Mina and Edmund sweeping their guns along the raised balcony above them. Kira was sweeping left to right focusing on their level and the giant wooden doors on both their three and nine o'clocks. Desta slipped out from under the water outlet shelf and reached behind him, helping Simeon pull the large cross into the empty pool. Simeon struggled to get his massive frame through the opening, though eventually managed to join the team, Nadev closely followed.

When Nadev popped out, he saw Desta staring towards the other end of the pool, lost in the unusual stone structure. Simeon had the cross on his shoulder again, Theo was aiming his pistol at the balcony and Kira flicked from one door to the other.

"Is that it?" Nadev asked Desta, placing his hand on his shoulder? Desta turned to look at him with a smile on his face, they were so close.

"Yes it is my.." Two shots boomed through the empty space and stopped Desta mid-sentence.

They both came at the same time, fired as one. The shots had not come from any of his team so Desta slammed his hand against his stomach, hitting the watch in his waistcoat pocket hard, causing it to activate.

Instantly, everything around the team slowed, even the sound of the shots echoing around them sounded like they were underwater. They all knew what was happening and all the team looked around them, first for the bullets, then for the source of the shots. Edmund spotted the first one before anyone else. Small, blurring circles dragged through the air behind the bullet, from the balcony over Mina's left shoulder, straight towards his best mate.

Instinctively, he leapt the few feet between them pushing Mina out of the way. Simeon spotted the second one, coming from the other balcony, headed straight for Kira. Thankfully, he had time to warn her, and she spun her head in time to see it coming. She flung her right shoulder forward, dipping her head and flowing into a roll, which was so fast it was barely visible to the naked eye, and the bullet slammed into the perfect tiles next to her

Although, the watch wasn't anywhere near full strength, it had enough charge to cause the first shots to miss their targets which, realistically, was all Desta could hope for. As time came back into alignment, Desta could hear the deep clapping of hands echoing around the giant roman pool house. It was coming from a single source and as he looked up to where the shots had come from, on the left side of the balcony, the giant figure of Ang stepped forward and looked down upon them. Slowly clapping his giant scaly hands together, a rather mocking applause. As he did, dozens of men appeared as one, along the sides of the balcony, equally split down either side, each one holding a fully automatic weapon on Desta and his team.

"You Mother fuckers!" Mina screamed up at the Ducaz and his unit.

He was on his knees, holding Edmund on his lap. None of the team had noticed though when Edmund had pushed Mina aside, he had fallen into the bullet's trajectory, he pulled Mina to the left and when they fell together the hot metal had caught him in his lower back and exploded out of his stomach, taking half of his insides with him.

Right now, Mina was using his free hand to try and stop his 'brothers' insides from spilling onto the tiled floor. It was a useless exercise, Edmund shivered and twitched as his best mate held him in his arms, he couldn't feel anything, all he could see was Mina looking at him, crying.

Edmund tried to speak yet only blood and bubbles came from his mouth. His eyes were filled with tears as he looked up at his soul mate one last time, he couldn't verbally tell him he loved him, though the desperate look in his eyes did.

Kira instinctively jumped from her position to go and help. Edmund had been like a little brother, she couldn't resist and yet, the second her foot left the ground, another three shots rang out, almost simultaneous in their execution. Theo stood stunned. Blood was already flooding under Mina and Edmund, the clapping and laughing was loud and overwhelming, echoing as it bounced around the solid empty walls. Suddenly, within arm's reach, Kira's head exploded, spraying blood, and brain all over him; the first bullet ripped through the side of her skull and the second two dug into her shoulder and chest.

It all happened too fast for Theo to react or move, Desta, Simeon and Nadev were also helpless, and each had three guns focused on them. The clapping had ceased, though the laughter continued, the deep baritone laugh of a Ducaz.

"Anyone else want to move?" he enquired, whilst leaning on the balcony edge and looking down at them.

Theo turned to look back at Desta, his eyes told him to stay calm. It was a shame Mina didn't get the memo. He held Edmund's head with his right hand and looked into his mates' eyes. He watched them searching at first, looking for what he didn't know, then they fell into acceptance. Tears ran from his eyes down his cheeks as he held Edmund one last time, then he watched the light disappear, when it did, he snapped. He had come here today to die, he knew this was likely a one-way trip, and now he was pissed. He laid Edmund on the floor in front of him and holding his hands in the air made to stand up. He did so slowly and deliberately, slow enough that the guns on him hadn't fired yet.

As he got to his feet, he twitched his back and quickly swung his rucksack around from behind him to be in his arms. He had just reached inside as the first bullet slammed into his back, luckily hitting the Kevlar plate he had in there. It just gave him enough time to spin and throw his bag far to the left side, out of the pool, under the balcony that the Ducaz was standing on. Three other shots came flying towards him, one crunched through his clavicle and bounced around on its way through, eventually bursting from his lower back.

He fell to the floor, hitting the ground hard, landing on his side just inches from Edmund. He couldn't move and felt nothing, and as his brain began to shut down, he looked down at the pool where he could see the balcony with the Ducaz looming over its edge. His vision began to fail and white was closing in from each side.

Then it happened.

The explosive Mina had prepared was way bigger than he had expected. Fifteen thermal grenades and three M97 grenades combined in his rucksack and blew through the left side of the pool with devastating force. Tiles from the pool flew, and the blast from below lifted the mezzanine, ripping through many of the thick columns that held it in place. Dust, debris and unimaginable heat seared the whole left side of the ancient baths, and as the remaining BOL members used the distraction to run for cover by way of the right-side balcony and column Unfortunately, the left side of the 2000-year-old structure began to crumble and fall.

Ang surged high into the air, jumping from the falling balcony, at least thirty feet. Massive marble sheets and concrete blocks fell, taking a group of men with them, and as the whole structure fell into the pool, Ang landed safely in the middle, cracking the tiles under his giant feet as he hissed at Theo and the rest of the team.

Nadev bought up his gun and unleashed a round at the balcony above to the right that was still in one piece, His bullets chewed into the concrete and tiles around his foes, forcing the soldiers to duck for cover, giving Simeon and Desta enough time to drag the cross up, out of the pool, under the right mezzanine, concealing them from the bullets above. Nadev's clip ran dry, though he was already moving to take cover with the two of them, when one of the soldiers from the fallen left balcony re-emerged and fired at the first thing he saw moving.

The first two bullets struck the walls behind Nadev, the third slammed into his left hip, shattering it and his chances. As he stumbled and fell, the soldiers from the right balcony were back in position and in the blink of an eye his light was gone under a hail of bullets from above.

The Ducaz loomed tall and only had eyes for Theo. As he stood smack bang in the middle of the action, he saw the crumbled mess of the left balcony, and Desta and Simeon were both covered on the right. Shots were beginning to come from the rubble on the left, bullets began to ping around Simeon and Desta as they searched for better shelter.

"Enough." roared Ang and he held his arm high in the air. All around him the guns fell silent.

The rubble had settled, yet the dust lingered. The globes above them swung forcefully, knocked around by the explosions and debris causing the shadows on Theo's face to dance from left to right. Ang towered over him from only five feet away and once he had his silence, he turned his attention to the rabbit in front of him. Ang had been one of the fiercest competitors in the Colosseum during the Roman Empire and right now, with the thick marble faced columns, tiled arena floors and spectators in the galleries, he smelled history.

He roared for his fans and without notice struck with the speed his kind was famous for, reaching with his right hand to grab Theo by the throat. Shocked, Theo was equal to the thrust and ducked under it, instinctively he jabbed his pistol up into Ang's ribs and pulled hard at the trigger.

Bam! Bam! Bam!
Three shots rang out, though had minimal effect, grazing off Ang's hard scales and before Theo could unload the fourth shot, his hand and his gun were engulfed as one in the giant palm and fingers of the eight-foot, pissed off crocodile. Theo couldn't drop the gun and as Ang squeezed, his fingers snapped and broke, he dropped to his knees, agonising pain running up his arm.

He looked tiny in the middle of this vast, open room with nowhere to scramble to. On his knees, almost paralysed, Ang gripped his hand tighter, squeezing the metal into his bones and flesh whilst leaning in for a better look. Theo wanted to be brave, yet right now, he was staring several rows of sharp teeth and the back of Ang's throat as the monster sniffed the air around Theo from above. Then like lightening, his free hand shot forward and with a closed fist, pounding into Theo's chest three times.

On the third strike he let go of the hand and Theo flew backwards, sliding across the tiles as he landed. The soldiers on the balcony cheered whilst others, that had dusted themselves off from the fall, were watching from ground level, from under the other mezzanine. Desta winced as did Simeon and without a thought, the two of them broke free from their cover, rushing to help Theo. If he was lost, then all was lost.

As they burst into the open, the thick wooden doors behind them that lead up to the mezzanine and to the main Mansion reception flew open, surprising Ang and the soldiers that could see it from the pool level.

Theo was still flat on his back on the cold tiles of the pool floor, since he had landed, he hadn't moved except for a couple of grunts and arm twitches. Ang had hit him hard, square in the chest, judging from the blood already pooling in his mouth it was likely a rib had gone through into his lungs. He didn't feel any pain, even his crushed right hand was fine.

He did feel a little cold, a shiver ran along his spine as he remembered the cold mornings as a young boy, the sound of a vacuum humming round the house. His eyes were open and he could see the ornate artwork in the architraves above the pool. He could hear his mother's vacuum getting closer, he loved to snooze to the sound of her vacuum as a little boy.

Motionless on the floor, bleeding out and struggling to breathe, Theo peacefully turned his head to see his mother. She was in her tight jeans, baggy t-shirt and was walking around with the big electric vacuum, pushing it back and forth through the thick shaggy carpet. Her hair was up in rollers, and she gazed over at him while her arm rhythmically, pushed then pulled. She flashed him a loving smile, before mouthing something to him. He didn't catch it, his eyes were growing heavy, it was ok to take a little nap

.

Whoa, now he was floating, it must have been a dream...

It wasn't a dream. While Theo drifted in and out of consciousness, the Mansion had been breached by the many thousands of Iraqis that had been storming the compound. As Desta and Simeon leapt forward to rescue Theo, the doors behind them had opened and hundreds of locals had come storming into the ancient baths. At the same time, they stormed the mezzanine above them, all hell had broken loose. Some of them carried guns, yet most of them had large blades and clubs. Initially, the soldiers, heavily armed and trained, mowed them down. Dozens fell before, panicking and trying to keep up, the soldiers eventually became overwhelmed and a brutal hand to hand slaughter began.

Simeon had made it over to Theo with Desta by his side and with the help of some locals, Theo was lifted into the air to lay flat on the hands of three men. It kept him still and out of the melee that was taking place around them. The locals kept coming through the door, most of the soldiers were down, drowned under a sea of fists, clubs and blades, naturally, Ang was still thrashing and thriving. He ripped into anything that moved and was already standing on a pile of dead bodies that was continuing to grow.

As Theo laid on the ground, next to where Desta and Simeon had left the Cross, he let out a feeble cough which sprayed further blood from his mouth and onto Desta. Desta placed his hands over Theo's rib cage and looked up to the sky, his eyes rolled into the back of his head and the familiar white glow appeared. The same bright white light appeared around the edges of his hands, it was growing in intensity, like Desta was channelling the energy from somewhere and storing it ready to use. Behind them, the noise and the chaos had stopped. All the elite Ducaz soldiers were dead, their bodies littered the floor amongst the hundreds of locals that were riddled with bullets or torn to pieces. There was barely a tile visible on the pool floor as it was now flooding with blood or bodies.

Ang stood tall at the top of a pile of dead Iraqis, the pile was at least five to six people deep. His cloak had been ripped off and he was naked in his full Reptilian glory, standing upright like a crocodile with huge, human-like arms and legs. He was surrounded, everywhere he looked there were more locals, all now just staring at him. Up on the balcony dozens of then aimed their newly acquired Mag-Fire weapons directly at Ang. He stared them all down from his mound of death and glory. He raised his strong arms in the air and beat hard against his chest while shouting.

"I am…" He didn't get to finish.

As soon as he opened his mouth everyone on the balcony with a gun opened fire. His strong stone skin deflected and saved him from a few of the shots, though under the barrage of direct fire from their own, high-powered rounds, one by one they began to rip off chunks of his flesh and skin. A final loud roar ripped through the chamber and rolled down the walls, his mouth was wide as he sneered with anger, and then one after another, three bullets snuck their way through the rows of sharp teeth, past the long snake-like tongue and into the back of his throat. They ripped through the soft tissue and slammed into the skin from the inside but were unable to pass through his stone skin, so ended up bouncing around inside him.

The gunfire stopped. The room fell silent again as Ang just stood silently. Like a statue atop a gruesome plinth, he dominated the room. Steady and ready to fire, the guns from the balcony stayed focused on him. Then, like every muscle in his body shut down at once, he crumbled, falling where he stood, landing with a splat on his victims.

The whole room erupted. Almost two hundred locals lay dead on the floor, yet over a thousand were still standing in the enclosed, ancient Roman pool area. The hard walls, ceilings and marble columns rang like bells as, as one they cheered.

"Allah Akbar, Allah Akbar"

Theo shocked Simeon when, from nowhere he took a quick sharp breath and immediately began to cough. Although, blood splattered from his mouth, he was instantly made to sit up and after clearing the blood from his mouth and throat took a long hard breath of air. He sat with his back to the hard wall, in front of him he could see the scene in the middle of the pool, he had missed it all and was waking up to an army dancing around, and an overwhelming chant in his head. The energy in the room was phenomenal.

As Desta helped him to his feet, he stared in awe at the crowd that had gathered to save them. Suddenly, as they cheered together, Theo could see a white glow projecting from the top of each of them, creating a small white cloud at the top of the room.

Desta was speaking to him, but he couldn't hear and he didn't really care, it was like he was in a trance now. Allah Akbah sang to him and filled him and his own eyes, which were glowing white and bright, and got lost staring at the light.

Theo had his arm draped around Desta's shoulder as he stumbled his way forward, walking along the poolside with Simeon behind them carrying the cross. The crowd was thick though parted instinctively, as Theo and Desta approached and now the Ducaz was dead the crowd turned their attention to the 'Saviour'

The chants continued and even grew louder as all eyes were on the small party working their way through the tightly packed crowd. Like a rock star trying to make it to the stage through a packed mosh pit, or the boxer entering through a packed stadium Theo stumbled forward. Supported by Desta, they eventually made it to the far end of the pool and to the small concrete like structure that looked like the giant ant hill. They were now standing above the rest of the room, looking back on a sea of faces as the chant got louder still

They knew there was no time to waste, the closer they got, the more anxious Desta became that it would all be taken away. Simeon unwrapped the large cross and the chants within the room stopped, when as one they gasped at the ancient artefact before them. Simeon ignored the murmurs and chats, and lifted the cross high into the air, placing its long end directly into the opening in the small concrete pile.

The murmurs stopped, the chat died as the entire room held their breath, waiting to see what was going to happen next. Desta and

Simeon were both looking at the Cross, waiting for something to activate, so they didn't see Theo stand up behind them. His eyes shone, a white light had appeared directly in the middle of each of his hands which he looked down at now, a wonderment and peace wrinkling in his smile. He stepped forward and placed his hand on Simeon's shoulder, he immediately felt something he had not before, he turned to see Theo in his light and was overwhelmed, fighting back tears.

Theo looked out over the crowd and smiled, the light shone from him, igniting the cloud above them and as one they cheered louder than ever, coming together with unbridled joy and happiness.

"Allah Akbar" Roared and repeated!

He looked at Desta, who looked back with pride in his eyes, it was too loud for last words, still, Theo reached out and touched his cheek, cupping it with his hand and saying goodbye with his touch.

He then turned and looked up at the Cross standing over them, dominating the room. Simeon stepped forward knowingly and offered his hand as a step for Theo to climb on. Theo had feared, that when it mattered, he wouldn't be able to follow through, he was worried his instinct to survive would kick in, though right now there was not an ounce of fear or doubt in his mind. Nothing about his past, or future mattered to him, in this present he felt complete peace as he stepped onto the small platform for his feet.

He was still wearing his black combat pants when he finally stood tall over the room with his chest bare and naked from where Desta had removed his shirt earlier. He had blood, mostly his own, smeared all over him and he leant back, pressing himself against the wooden structure. His eyes shone white, his ears rang with love and finally when it felt right, he lifted his arms and placed them out to his sides, along the Cross. As if sensing the occasion, the Cross then flicked out two small bands which wrapped around his wrist, locking Theo into position.

The crowd couldn't hear it over the noise of their chanting, yet could feel a gentle rumble in their feet as they stood. As the floor shook, the Cross came further to life and from it came dozens of black, metal, snake like worms. They moved around, as if sniffing the air around the cross and Theo..

Up on the balcony, everyone stared down at the wonder before them, no one noticed Vos, walking in the rear door, he stood and looked down at the spectacle before him in the pool He saw thousands of people, at the centre was a pile of dead bodies, easily one hundred deep. He could see the lifeless shape of Ang at the top. The noise and roar from the crowd was deafening as he brought up his arm and steadied himself.

Theo looked out to the crowd, burned faces, blood, pain, anguish all cheered at him with joy, with hope. Allah and the Universal truth filled them all with love. He closed his eyes and as one, the metallic snakes stood upright, there was a short pause, before they dived at Theo. They bit into him to take the blood they needed to start the machine.

At the very second they touched his skin, a single shot rang out in the enclosed stone room. Theo's head snapped back and exploded, immediately extinguishing the light in his eyes and causing him to go limp, held in place by only the wrist straps. Everyone gasped, and up on the balcony there was shouting and a scuffle before eventually, Commander Vos was tossed over to be caught by the crowd below. Hands and teeth ripped into him before he managed to get to his feet, even so, he grinned a bloody smile as the locals exacted their revenge. At least he had stopped them turning on Soteria.

Desta stared at Simeon, stunned. Both men were sprayed with Theo's precious blood and such was the shock that neither could speak or comprehend what had just happened. Vos lay on the floor, taking his last breaths, and just as he was congratulating himself, something happened, no one could quite explain. Every person in the room felt it. A giant wave of energy swept through them, in fact, it swept through every living thing in the world. It was like, when your stomach drops on a fast roller coaster, or when you drive over a small hill too fast.

Across the globe at 8:01am local time, seven billion people's stomachs all dropped as the machine sent a concentric wave of energy into the sky, powered by the core to provide a dome of electrical and magnetic energy, protecting the earth from the harmful effects of Nibiru's Passing.

Twitter would have gone crazy, so would Facebook and Tiktok, but with the wave of energy, came an electromagnetic pulse that fried every microchip on earth as the world plunged into a new Dark Age. The sky was lit up with all manner of electrical and magnetic reactions as the new force field protected us from the gravitational destruction going on in our Galaxy, but down on the surface, seven billion people's lives changed forever. A new dawn was coming, a dawn with no electricity and no technology, the fight for basic survival was about to go global.............

END OF PART 1

Interview With The Author

So, the first question and the one on most people's lips, why The Anonymous Author?

That's a great question and also a very easy one to answer. This idea for the novel has been brewing for a long time, since watching some fun conspiracy theory videos on YouTube. The content matter involving the Jewish people and Hitler was enough to ensure my publisher would touch it, but then the scene with the Pope, and the scenes with Joe Biden got the people around me genuinely concerned for my safety. For me, that doesn't mean the story shouldn't be told, in fact it made me more determined to write it. So, with the support of those same people, I have created The Anonymous Author_official, as a way to tell this story and others without having to look over my shoulder each day.

You mention the Conspiracy Theory Videos, so to be clear do you believe any of this could happen in the real world?

That's the million-dollar question, but comes in two parts I think. Do I believe it is happening? Versus do I believe it *could* happen? The great part about being a creator is that there is no limit to what we can imagine, and as a creator, practically everything I create *could* happen. I believe in everything and nothing all at the same time because we will never know the truth, it's a great place to exist, because everything is possible, no matter how unlikely. But to be clear, do I think Joe Biden is a sociopathic narcissistic Alien? No, I'm a believer in Occam's Razor, or at least in the bastardised version of it that states that the simplest explanation is usually the best one. This is just an elaborate story spawned from an overactive imagination.

This is Part one of the Nibiru Chronicles Trilogy, what made you decide to release this story in three parts?

Ever since my planning stage for this novel, I had in my mind three distinct stories all flowing in the one new universe. It was a lot of fun to work on and write an "End of the World" book, and all the videos and articles I followed down the rabbit hole kind of ended there. Just like when you go to the movies, the big Hollywood Blockbuster, World ending disasters, only a pocket of the population has survived aaaaaand "roll the credits." I'm always left wondering what next? How does everyone survive and rebuild?

So, with the Nibiru Chronicles, at the end of Part 1, we have averted destruction of the planet, but the Earth's power has been crippled and will take years to rebuild. That's 7 billion people about to go tribal. Now as mentioned before this is where most stories will end, but for me this is where the story begins, and this is where Part 2 - The Last President, will take over as Kamala tries to keep some kind of order whilst trying to find and punish those buried deep underground. Desta and Simeon go forth to recruit the new generation of BOL and the Religious institutions try to use this new technological plague to get a stranglehold on the survivors. Revolution takes hold all over the world and billions die.

The destruction of the Earth's social construct deserved a whole book, and also then left me plenty of space for the rebuilding of society in Part 3. There is also so much of the Earth's history that needs to be re-written. I have started that process with Part one, but as the Humans try to figure out what is happening, they begin to uncover even more specific and diabolical truths. I figure we need to unravel the great wars and some of the planet's most memorable moments, including 911.

What is your favourite part of the book?

That's a tough one, Theo's chase through New York was a highlight. When I started the chapter, he was supposed to just end up on the floor of the train, but as I typed away, it developed, starting with him losing his towel. When I finally wrote that last line, I actually jumped up out of my chair and punched the air. You see I do love a little bit of comedy, but mostly originality, and I couldn't remember a scene like it in anything else. Cue the hundreds of emails…

Outside of that, at the end, when the people of Baghdad come and save the day. I wasn't sure exactly how I was going to turn the tables inside the ancient pool at the end. I had the heroes dropping like flies, the bad guys holding all of the cards, and originally Deena had actually survived the Vatican and she was able to use her powers of persuasion and they are aided by insects again. It had already been done, and also turned out she was a bit too powerful with her abilities. "Why not just use the insects everywhere if they are that effective?" So I had to kill her early on. Now as I was saying it left a gap for a distraction or last-minute saviour. In the end, they had already swarmed the base and helped them enter, so to bring the desperate people of Baghdad in as the Heroes of the book actually gave me chills as it developed. I love it when the victim in any story stands up and refuses that label, this is exactly what the people of Baghdad do at the end and look at the results.

And do you have a favourite character?

Wow, another hard one. It's like each of them are a part of me, even the bad guys.

I think over all, Edmund and Mina are my favourite characters in this part of the story. All the way through I was considering a love interest, someone for Theo to fall for to add a dimension to the story. In the end I didn't like the cliche and decided to keep part one all about the action. However, inadvertently I think the love story was still there. The relationship between the two BOL lads, even though not physical, or sexual as we would say, developed deeper as I got further into the story and Mina's reaction when Edmund goes down brought a genuine tear to my eye when writing it. It was at this point I realised I already had my love story, it just wasn't your traditional hero meets girls story.

I also had a lot of fun writing Raquel, when planning Part one, she was a much smaller character, but her humour and enthusiasm kept coming out, so she got more and more involved. That was such a fun part of this writing experience, nothing was set in stone, everything was planned, but constantly fluid and as such it is probably the most fun I have ever had writing.

What one thing do you want readers to take away from Part 1 - Nibiru Rising?

There are so many answers I want to give to that one. I think overall, just like anything I write, I want it to be fun. I actually don't want you to have to think too much, just strap in and enjoy the ride. There are some undertones throughout the book that I will be exploring further in parts 2 and 3. The Universal Law that Desta mentions a few times being just one part and it would be nice to hear that readers are enjoying this. Finally, whilst writing this answer I am reminded of the fact that I am writing this under an Anonymous label because the content could honestly be enough for some people to physically harm me, but most of the "woke mob" will probably try to cancel everything I have ever done and ever will do if I released this under my true identity.

What I want people to take away from this book, is that in a free society there are creative rights of storytellers, journalists and comedians to take aim at any and all situations in the public eye. The freedom to tackle any subject from any perspective needs to be fought for, and this book is a way to fight for that. The cancel culture is fighting to close down freedom of speech and expression and it is working to divide the populous. The fact I have to hide my identity is like holding a mirror up to society and asking, why? So I guess, it would be nice if they took that from the book too.

What's coming up in the future for you?

Right now, I am busy also writing a screenplay for another novel I wrote a few years ago, but overall, my next couple of years involve relaxing poolside with my laptop as much as possible as I spend time with the family that has given up so much to help me get to where I am today. This new universe all stemmed from a crazy "What if", and above all other projects, I want to explore it further. Rewriting the entire history of the world is a fairly large task, but it also offers the largest opportunity, it is so much bigger than anything I have attempted before and there is so much room for me to really push the boundaries. I think it will depend on how the public receives Part 1 as to how dark we take it.

Any final words?

Yes. Don't be offended, it is just a story. Don't think too hard, it's not that kind of book bruv.

The Anonymous Author_Official

www.ingramcontent.com/pod-product-compliance
Lightning Source LLC
Chambersburg PA
CBHW030519120726
47904CB00005B/1528